THE SILENT VOICES

Undercover to catch a serial killer

ROBERT McCRACKEN

Published by The Book Folks

London, 2021

This book is a work of fiction. Names, characters, businesses, organizations, places and events are either the product of the author's imagination or are used fictitiously. Any resemblance to actual persons, living or dead, events or locales is entirely coincidental. The spelling is British English.

ISBN 978-1-913516-10-9

www.thebookfolks.com

The Silent Voices is the third standalone title in the DI Tara Grogan mystery series.

CHAPTER 1

She sucked the cold night air. Each breath was a struggle for survival. Her body rolled from side to side and jolted at every bump in the road. She had to keep breathing. To breathe, to pray for release and pray for an end to her fear. That was all she had left. Vibrations of the journey shuddered through her mummified body, the rattle of the metal floor, the rumbling of the engine. They had allowed her to breathe, so maybe they did not intend to kill her. She hoped. But where were they taking her? Why? What had she done? Who were these people?

The vehicle swerved; she rolled to the back. She heard voices shouting yet muffled because of her cocoon. They swerved again. It was reckless driving. The rear doors flew open. For a second, her body teetered at the edge. Another swerve and she rolled out. She hit the ground, tumbling and bouncing, the air shaken from her lungs. She thought her rolling would never end. Pain wracked every part of her body and she panicked for breath. At last, she came to rest. The only sounds were the rush of vehicles passing on the road and her sucking for air just to stay alive. No part of her could move freely. Someone must see her. Surely someone would help. She realised then that her captors had not stopped. They'd kept on going. She was lying by the side of a road. That was it. They had dumped her. No one was going to kill her. She could breathe and soon someone would find her, and she would be safe.

Maybe she could stand. She tried to bend her knees. Her body rolled. She was face down. She rolled again. Now she was on her back. Standing was impossible. In frustration, she rolled again. Traffic whizzed by. Where could she be? By the roadside – or in the middle of a highway? Disoriented, she tried to move away from the sounds of cars and trucks speeding by. But she'd rolled in the wrong direction.

The truck driver saw a package not far ahead, but not far enough for him to stop in time, or even to apply the brakes. Sixty miles an hour, he felt merely a bump at the front wheels, and nothing as the rear wheels of the trailer made the impact. He couldn't see what he'd hit, not in the darkness. But the parcel was swept to the centre lane. In seconds, a tanker mashed her body within its wrapping. A van, following behind the tanker, braked hard, collided with the body and slewed to the central reservation. Hazard lights flashed a warning. The traffic slowed. Another lorry stopped and added to the flashed warnings. Then another. Soon the late-night traffic on the carriageway had come to a standstill. Several drivers got out of their vehicles and approached the package. At first, no one was certain but, under torchlight, the blood oozing from the plastic film and legs severed from the torso told the story.

CHAPTER 2

Tara

Adele, clutching her teddy and snug in her onesie, pushed open the door of her Aunty Tara's bedroom. She padded to the bedside where Tara lay in a deep sleep. For a few moments, the child merely looked on as if waiting for something else to stir her aunty awake. Finally, she pushed her tiny hand into Tara's shoulder. With no response, she tried again before using teddy to snuggle into Tara's face.

At last, Tara opened her eyes, took in the scene before her, the smiling face of her god-daughter and her blonde locks dangling over her eyes.

'Hi, sweetheart, what's the matter? Can't you sleep?'

Adele shook her head.

'Are you feeling OK?'

The child nodded.

Tara pushed herself up, resting her head on one hand. Then she reached out and switched on the lamp. No more questions, she waited for Adele to speak. Usually, the child would head for Kate's room if she needed anything during the night. Tara glanced at the alarm clock on the bedside table. It wasn't yet one o'clock. Adele pointed towards the door.

'Oh. Let's go and see,' Tara said.

Slipping from her warm bed, she took Adele's hand and they padded into the lounge. Adele went to a mobile phone abandoned on the sofa. Tara usually kept her mobile beside her as she slept, but last night was one of those nights when thoughts of telephone communication hadn't registered as she collapsed into bed.

'Did it make a noise?'

Adele nodded.

'I'm sorry, darling. You go back to bed and I'll make sure it doesn't make any more noise.'

The child trotted away as Tara picked up the phone, hoping it wasn't the type of call she dreaded most. When she gazed at the three missed calls, all from Wilson, her shoulders sagged in dismay. It was at times like these that she regretted not going through with her resignation from the force. But what else could she have done? Qualified in law, with a degree from Oxford, and yet she had chosen a police career. She no longer felt inclined to change direction. She was more able to cope with the rigours of the job since her friend Kate and daughter Adele had moved in, albeit temporarily. Now she had company, someone to speak to and to help take her mind off unpleasant things when she got home to the flat. She gently closed the door to Adele's room, returned to the lounge, hit the call button and placed the phone to her ear.

'Hi, John, what's up?'

'Morning, ma'am. Sorry to wake you at this hour. We have a body on the M57, near Aintree.'

'Surely that's a problem for Traffic?'

'Not an RTA, ma'am. Seems like the body was dumped on the motorway. It's in a hell of a state.'

'I'm on my way.'

'Westbound carriageway, ma'am, Junction seven, close to the ASDA store. The motorway has been closed. Traffic is tailed back, but you can use the hard shoulder.'

Ending the call, she dressed quickly in jeans and sweatshirt. In the kitchen, she scribbled a brief note on the back of an envelope for Kate when she got up. It was Tara's turn to drive Adele to her grandparents, but Kate was well used to plans being altered at short notice.

By her door, she pulled on a pair of suede ankle boots, lifted her keys and bag from the hall stand and quietly closed the door behind her.

She made the journey in twenty-five minutes. It took another ten to negotiate the stalled traffic and to reach the hard shoulder of the westbound carriageway. Several police vehicles from motorway patrol were already present at the scene. She noticed also the distinctive van used by the forensic emergency response crew. She felt the chill on her face of early morning as she climbed from her car and walked towards the bustle of activity.

'Morning, John, so what do we have?'

Detective Constable John Wilson grimaced at what he was about to impart to his DI. He looked awkward and rather bulky in a blue protective coverall. They didn't have his size to hand, and he'd squeezed into an XL rather than his normal XXL.

'Female, indeterminate age, ma'am. Her face is badly smashed up. The entire body is wrapped in plastic film, as if it's been shrink-wrapped.'

Tara, as she listened to John Wilson, gazed at the hub of activity. A medical officer and some forensic personnel were standing over what Tara assumed to be the body of the victim. It was strewn between the centre and outside lane of a three-lane carriageway.

'What do you think, so far?' Tara asked.

'Not sure if the victim was dead before being run over by at least two vehicles, one of them was an oil tanker. The body was ripped in two.'

Tara sighed, already steeling herself for what she was about to see.

'Thanks, John. I'll have a word with the medical officer.'

She picked her way around groups of uniforms and forensic personnel and was heartened to see that the duty medical officer was Dr Brian Witney, the most experienced pathologist serving Merseyside Police.

'DI Grogan, I wondered if you were about to show up.' The doctor, in his late fifties, always had a smile for Tara no matter how macabre the circumstances. The sturdily built man saw no reason not to observe pleasantries.

'I couldn't stay away, Brian.' She managed a glance at the stricken body.

'Quite so,' Witney replied. 'Far from pleasant, I'm afraid. Severe crush injuries over the entire body. Right leg severed and left, partially severed. Smashed pelvis, several broken ribs, fractured skull and massive loss of blood. If she wasn't already dead before the traffic hit her then I think death was probably instantaneous. We might learn more from the post-mortem.'

Tara attempted a question, but the sight before her seemed to trap the words in her throat. And why did she always experience a shivering pain at the base of her spine when confronted by such carnage?

'Any ID?' she managed at last.

Witney shook his head.

'Nothing yet. She was lightly clothed, just a blouse and jeans.'

'Thanks, Brian. I'll speak to you later.'

'No doubt, Tara.'

She wasted no time in moving away from the scene. There was little she could think of to do right now. Unless they found witnesses, everything would hang on the post-mortem.

Tara didn't even reach the shoulders of John Wilson. She looked up to his face and spoke in her usual soft tone – soft, that is, when she wasn't in an argument with her DS, Alan Murray. So far, he was nowhere to be seen.

'We'll see if traffic cameras picked up anything,' said Tara. 'Put out a request for motorists who may have captured something on their dashcam. Check with all these bystanders. Find out what they saw. What do you think happened here, John?'

'Hard to say, ma'am. Nothing much to go on. Was she dumped intentionally, on a motorway? Bit weird. Had she fallen from a vehicle? And what's with all the plastic wrapping?'

CHAPTER 3

The choir

'Altos, I can't hear you above the basses. Let's try the chorus again. Remember! Cheerful voices! It's a happy song, people.'

Esther Dodds, a rather heavy touch on the piano keys, played a brief lead into the chorus of *Penny Lane*. Twenty-six voices in the room took their cue and began singing. Now on a roll, Esther played them through the entire song and by the end everyone knew it sounded good. They were good. They had a delicate blend; they were enthusiastic, and it shone through in the performance.

'Good,' said Esther. 'Now, once more through *Isn't Life Strange*, and we can call it a night.' She lifted her music for the song and set it on the piano then waited for everyone to get organised.

Esther was fifty-six, looked more a woman in her early forties and dressed like a carefree girl in her twenties. She was young at heart and dedicated to her music and her choir. As for her husband, he was long since history, shacked up with his floozy in Manchester, and Esther was the happier for it. Her two grown-up boys kept in touch from opposite ends of the country. Esther Dodds didn't have much by way of worries, until today.

The noise level rose in the room as the choir belted out the chorus. A great way to finish the evening practice. It could be said that two dozen people living on Treadwater Estate had found new horizons simply by singing in the community choir. Esther was proud of that fact. She was proud of what these people had achieved by working together as a team. There were alcoholics, single parents coping with kids and depression, low-income families, pensioners, jobless, addicts and former gang members. In some cases, there were multiple problems for the individuals in her choir family. But since they had been formed, a little over three years ago, anti-social behaviour had decreased on the estate. Gang warfare was a thing of the past, and residents were beginning to act like Treadwater was an old-fashioned community again, like it had been decades ago.

Most of the members filed out quietly from the community centre, while a few stayed behind to put away chairs and brush up. Esther packed away her electric piano. One or two of the stronger boys always hung around waiting for the chance to carry her instrument out to her car. The slightest encouragement from Esther, though none was ever forthcoming, and these lads would be offering to do much more for their alluring choir mistress.

When all the chairs had been stacked and moved to the side of the hall and Esther had pulled on her suede jacket, ready for home, she noticed some people lingering behind. She knew by their demeanour that they were holding an impromptu meeting. Whispered conversations were taking place.

It had been a long day. Esther was tired. Practice had gone well but precious little else had. She had a lot to think about and without a gin and tonic before bed, she doubted she was in for a good night's sleep.

CHAPTER 4

Esther

Esther kicked off her shoes in the hallway, but did not remove her jacket, and wasted no time in pouring her long-awaited gin and tonic. So exhausted, she couldn't be bothered to fetch a fresh lemon, or ice from the freezer. After closing the blinds at the lounge window that overlooked the playing fields on the estate, she settled into her sofa and switched on the TV to check the latest news.

Her home was comfortable and functional, one of the better kept houses on Treadwater. Everything in her sitting room had been carefully chosen over the years, from the velvet curtains to the coffee table made from the reclaimed wood of an old sailing ship her great-grandfather had owned a hundred years ago. The mahogany cabinet in one corner displayed her trophies and other mementos gathered from a history of her family life: wedding photos, christening gifts for her two boys Neil and Patrick, a gold medal for participation in the North-west Choir Festival when she was seventeen, photos of her time singing in a pop band, and a bent teaspoon fashioned and signed by Uri Geller. Esther attached meaning to everything she owned, to everything she did.

By the time she'd finished with the national and then local bulletin, she needed another drink. There was no further information on the finding of a woman's body on the M57 – no names or details on what might have happened to her. Rumours on the estate were that it was Mandy, their Mandy.

The second helping of gin eased her anxiety over what this might do to the choir. Everything she'd worked so hard for was now at risk all because of a silly girl who had refused to do as she was told. The idea of going to bed, despite her tiredness, was slipping from her mind. She retrieved her handbag from the hall. Before settling down on the sofa again, she poured herself another hefty gin, the proportion of gin increased, and the tonic decreased.

She pulled a folder from her bag and read the list of songs she had planned for the forthcoming concert in the leisure centre. They'd practised most of them, but a few hadn't gone as well as she'd hoped. The Beatles' songs *Penny Lane* and *Good Day Sunshine* were fine but there were definite tuning issues with *Take Me to the River* and *Lifted.* These were good problems to have, sorting out the music, working with her soloists and making plans for performances. It kept her going, gave her a sense of importance, that she was improving the lives of ordinary people. She should feel proud that she was making a difference. Instead, she was lolling about on her sofa, two o'clock in the morning, unable to sleep, getting drunk and wondering why everything was suddenly going wrong. And it was all because of her most talented soprano, Mandy.

She prayed that it wasn't Mandy who had been found on the M57, and yet there was a part of her that said if it was her, things might get back to normal.

CHAPTER 5

Tara

Despite the stark environment of the post-mortem suite, its blank décor of tiled walls, and disinfectant smell, Dr Witney maintained a modicum of pleasantness for the visit of Merseyside Police detectives. The corpse lay upon a stainless-steel bench and had been sliced open to facilitate the removal of organs for testing. Visible also, were the gruesome injuries which caused it to be there in the first place.

'Good morning, Tara and Alan,' said Witney. 'I trust you managed some sleep since we last met?'

Murray scoffed.

'Not much, Brian,' Tara replied, her eyes unable to look at the focus of the pathologist's attention.

Witney was removing the victim's liver. Tara, no stranger to seeing these processes, remained uncomfortable and questions she had planned to ask failed to come. Instead, she hoped that DS Murray would plough on with business. Brian Witney was not insensitive to the discomfort of witnesses present at a post-mortem, even if they were experienced police officers. Rather than continue with his practical activity, he removed and binned his protective gloves then led his visitors away from the corpse to a bench where there was a folder containing his early findings on the case. He leafed through several foolscap pages then began to read aloud.

'Female, obviously, estimated age at late teens to early twenties. Height is five feet five inches, and weight is ten stone, three pounds, give or take for blood loss.'

'How did she die?' Murray asked.

'I would say death resulted from the impact with several heavy vehicles.'

'You mean she wasn't already dead before being left on the motorway?' Tara sounded shocked. The thought that someone had dumped the woman alive on a motorway and this had resulted in her appalling death, added to her view that the world was becoming more callous by the day. Who would sink to this level of depravity? What kind of life did they lead that would drive them to commit such an act? Such thoughts were the reasons why she had considered resigning from Merseyside Police. And yet, here she was, at the opening of another disturbing case.

'It was difficult to reach that conclusion, given the multiple injuries,' said Witney, 'but I feel that all of them resulted from being run over. The entire body was wrapped in this stuff.' Witney stepped away and retrieved a strip of clear plastic film from the bench next to the victim.

'Looks like cling film,' said Murray.

'A bit stronger than that. More like the stuff they use to shrink-wrap parcels or to hold boxes in place on wooden pallets.'

'Wouldn't she have suffocated?' Tara asked.

'I didn't find any evidence of suffocation. The film around her head was in such a state I can't be certain that there were holes at the mouth and nose for her to breathe.'

'Did you find anything that might help identify her?' Murray asked.

Brian Witney shook his head, looking as disappointed with the fact as Tara and Murray.

'She wore jeans, a cotton blouse and a pair of trainers. There was nothing else found within that plastic material.'

'Thanks, Brian. We'll get on and let you finish up,' said Tara, relieved to be getting out of the depressing environment where the only subject ever discussed was death and how it occurred.

Murray drove them to St Anne Street station. On the journey, it was difficult to talk about anything other than the latest murder. Sights, sounds and smells were still fresh, and thoughts raced to possible motives, perpetrators and, in this case, the identity of the victim.

* * *

Alan Murray had worked alongside DI Tara Grogan for five years. He knew when to keep quiet. He was a well-built man, hefty rather than obese, his fitness regime in constant battle with his appetite. In his late thirties, he was settled into his status as a Detective Sergeant. If a promotion was on the horizon, then so be it. He no longer burned with an ambition to get to the top. This morning, in addition to concerns over the latest Liverpool killing and what it would mean for them, he wondered about Tara. She'd been through a hard time in the last two years, and she had mentioned writing her letter of resignation from the force. So far, she hadn't explained the reason for not going through with it. He was glad, of course. It was hard to picture his working life without Tara in it. Lately, she seemed happier. He was aware that she now shared her apartment with her friend, Kate. This morning, however, her silence unnerved him.

'What are you thinking, Tara?' He knew he'd boobed as soon as he said it. She looked sideways and raised an eyebrow. 'I mean, ma'am.'

'First thing we have to do is check the missing persons database to see if anyone matching the victim's description has been listed.'

'What about the MO, very weird don't you think?'

'Nothing surprises me, Alan – the reasons for people to commit murder and the way they go about it.'

'Me too, ma'am. Doesn't help when we're getting too long in the tooth.'

'Speak for yourself.' She smiled as Murray pulled into the station yard.

By lunchtime, they had begun a search of the missing persons database, had a meeting with Detective Superintendent Harold Tweedy over a course of action, and conducted interviews with the three drivers who had run over the victim on the M57. Tara's conclusion was that none of them could be blamed for what had happened. It was dark, and the traffic, although sparse, was moving quickly. And who would expect to find a body rolling into their path on the centre lane of a motorway? It had been the consensus from the drivers that the victim had rolled into the path, firstly, of an articulated lorry with a consignment of supermarket goods, next a tanker hauling petrol and then a white van that careered into the crash barrier of the central reservation.

The van driver was the most traumatised of all the drivers. The other two were not aware of what they'd hit nor had the impact altered the path of their vehicle. The white van, however, was splashed with the victim's blood and the driver had been the first person to inspect the crushed bundle on the road.

'Nothing suspicious on traffic cameras in the vicinity, ma'am,' said John Wilson.

Wilson stood by Tara's desk awaiting instruction. He was the detective on Tweedy's team who did a high proportion of the office donkey work, while Tara and Murray did most of the exterior leg work.

Tara, always cutting such a slight figure when both Wilson and Murray stood close by, gazed at her DC. Her large blue eyes could smile without accompanying movement from her lips. She was a beautiful woman who didn't look her age, although several years of homicide investigations were taking their toll.

'If we don't get a lead from missing persons,' she said, 'I really don't know where to go next.' She rose from her desk and meandered across the operations room to Murray.

'Anything?' Tara asked.

'Two possibilities,' said Murray. 'One of them is a long-term missing person, though, so I wouldn't be too hopeful.'

'And the other one?'

Murray turned his screen slightly to let Tara view the photograph.

'Mid-thirties, a housewife from Crosby. Been missing for three months.'

'Doesn't fit with the age Witney is suggesting. What about the long-term?'

'She was nineteen when she disappeared fourteen years ago. From Manchester.'

'Neither one fills me with any confidence. I suppose we should check them out. Let's see if we can get DNA from these missing women and cross-check with our victim. Keep looking.'

'Yes, ma'am.'

Already, Tara did not believe they were going to make swift progress with this case. Someone out there had deliberately placed a woman in mortal danger. God, she prayed this was not another nutjob taking on the entire world.

CHAPTER 6

Carrie and Ian

Carrie usually walked home from school. She lived at the furthest point on the Treadwater Estate from her academy secondary school, but it only took twenty minutes to cover the distance. Lately, though, Carrie could hardly wait for the final bell of the day, to rush outside and hurry down the avenue leading away from the estate. Her heart skipped a beat when she spied Ian's car, a silver Volvo, and her pace quickened.

No one else from school had made it this far by the time she tossed her books into the back seat then climbed into the front beside Ian, who was looking so happy to see her. They hugged and kissed briefly, both aware that their relationship should not be noticed by others. Ian could not afford to be seen with a fifteen-year-old girl. He was no seventeen-year-old lad but a forty-one-year-old divorced man with three children, all of them older than Carrie. He had a council job as an administrator in the parks and cemeteries department. Despite the gossip among fellow choir members that he was the man most likely to succeed romantically with Esther, Ian had struck up a friendship with Carrie. At first flirtatious, very quickly it had developed into something more serious.

'How was school?' he asked, although he realised that he sounded more like her father than her lover.

'Fine. Not much homework.'

She gazed at the side of his swarthy face as he drove them away. She couldn't resist touching him as if to reassure herself that she was going out with such a lovely bloke. Good-looking, kind, generous and good at sex. Her hand brushed the dark hair at the side of his head then slipped onto his neck and shoulder. Carrie was adventurous. She had a streak of devilment in her. She was of a large build for a fifteen-year-old, and easily passed for an adult. Tall, athletic, long fair hair, her full lips currently practised a seductive pout. Carrie oozed teenage sex appeal, and yet she had never shown the slightest interest in boys of her own age. Her aspiration in life was to find an older man who adored her and hopefully had plenty of money to spend on her. For now, that vision stretched as far as Ian Bankhead.

They bought a McDonald's drive-through. Carrie was famished and tucked into a Double Big Mac and fries. Ian settled for a plain cheeseburger.

'Where are we going?' she asked, eagerly.

'Crosby.'

'But we went there the last time.'

'I know, Carrie, but it's handy and it's private.'

'When can we go to your house?'

'I've told you before. We must be careful. Anyone sees you coming into my place and all hell would break loose. It's risky enough with you staring at me all through choir practice. People are bound to notice, Carrie.'

'Let them. I don't care anymore. I love you.' She lowered her window and tossed her burger box into the road as they sped along.

'Bloody hell, Carrie. Don't be doing that, will ya. The bizzies could stop us if they see you doing that. And then we'd have to explain what we're up to. Four months from now you'll be sixteen and it won't matter anymore. Right now, in the eyes of the law I'm classed as a bloody paedophile!'

She stroked her hand along his thigh, all the way to his crotch.

'Calm down,' she said with a giggle. 'No one is going to find out. Besides, they can't prove we've done anything. We could just as easily be friends from choir.'

CHAPTER 7

Raymond and Mary

Raymond and Mary sat by their kitchen window, eating a light lunch of sardines on brown toast accompanied by mugs of strong tea. Retired from thirty years as a bus driver, there was not much else for Raymond to do these days than potter in his garden, watch telly and, once a week, attend choir practice. He enjoyed gardening more than anything else and often boasted that he had the best-looking garden on Treadwater.

'Wouldn't be hard,' Mary often said, considering the number of people around them who used their gardens merely to dump those things they no longer used: rusty bicycles, toys, furniture, trampolines, paint pots and barbecues. Only yesterday, she noticed that someone had spilled a pack of cotton buds on the pavement and hadn't bothered to clear them away. With the rain they were getting trampled and scattered everywhere.

Raymond cared for his roses and took pride in his dahlias. Out the back, he had managed to squeeze in a greenhouse and potting shed, although it had limited his growing area for vegetables and potatoes.

Mary was content with her morning telly programmes of property renovations, relocations to the sun and *Loose Women*. Once a week she went to bingo, and on Wednesdays she went to choir practice with Raymond.

'I don't think I'll bother with the bingo tonight if this rain keeps up,' said Mary. 'I'll get drenched just walking to the bus stop.'

'I can drive you, if you want.'

'I thought there was a match on TV?'

'There is, but I don't mind missing a few minutes, if it gets you out.' Raymond smiled, playfully.

'Thanks, you're all heart, you are.'

'I aim to please.'

The pair continued with their meal while gazing at the road with large raindrops bouncing and water flowing heavily to the drains. It hadn't ceased all morning. Raymond hadn't bothered going to fetch the morning paper. He had some repotting to do in the shed, but the thought of even a few paces in the downpour had doused his enthusiasm.

On Radio 2, Jeremy Vine was in discussion with several victims of recent flooding, one in North Yorkshire and another in Worcestershire. Nowadays, it seemed that as one major storm passed another was soon on its way. Towns and villages were not getting time to recover from one flooding incident before another compounded their problems. Mary and Raymond listened without any great concern for their area. Nothing like that had ever happened on Treadwater. And yet, Mary thought, there must come a time when even the drains on the estate could no longer cope with incessant rain.

Mary, a bright-faced woman of sixty-eight, never had much to be proud of and had little to complain about either. Her daughter had emigrated to Australia at the age of twenty-six and, nine years on, was hardly likely to ever come home to Liverpool, not now with two young girls to raise and a divorce in progress. Raymond's son from his first, albeit brief, marriage had died while at university. Consequently, they had no close family coming to visit or stay with them.

Little education for Mary had resulted in factory work until a final cleaning job at a local primary school. There had been a time when she liked to get dressed up and she and Raymond would go out with friends on a Saturday night. But those times dried up and the friends dwindled away. Soon it was Raymond and her alone in the house they had shared since the day they married, forty-six years ago. She had been good-looking then, a real seventies girl, but now plain was hardly a dull enough word to describe her appearance or her mood. She and Raymond had both needed something new, something fresh in their lives. It seemed a silly idea at first but worth a try. They responded to the leaflet dropped through their front door. 'You don't have to be a great singer to be in a choir,' the flier read. With nothing else to fill their Wednesday, Mary and Raymond went along to the practice. Three years on, it was now the highlight of their week. Strange that something so basic as singing had given them a new outlook on life.

'Nothing on the news about young Mandy,' Mary said, drinking the last of her tea. 'I hope it wasn't her that was killed on the motorway.'

'I don't think we'll hear anything on TV or the radio. I reckon she's just taken off with some lad, scarpered. People are making too much of the whole thing.'

CHAPTER 8

Danni

There was a dip in the road right below her flat, and Danni could see that the drains were struggling to cope with the flow of water as the rain poured down and spilled over the tarmac. For twenty-four hours it had rained non-stop. Drivers didn't bother to slow as they passed by and huge splashes of dirty water cascaded across the pavement. At least she felt safer on the first floor, but old Mr Johnston in the ground-floor flat would be in a fix if the water started to come in. He was mostly bedridden with carers attending him in the morning and evenings.

Screams rang out from the kids' bedroom.

'Mikaela, darling, please keep the noise down, mummy can't hear the TV.'

Her daughter, four years old with strings of blonde hair and ruddy cheeks trotted into the room still squealing as her twin brother, Bradley, pursued her with a toilet brush.

'Mummy, help me! He's trying to get me!'

Danni removed her eyes from *Poirot* on the TV and yelled at her son.

'Bradley! Not the toilet brush. It's disgusting. Put it back right now.'

The boy, with hair as long as his sister's and cheeks as flushed, charged out of the room, the toilet brush hoisted in the air.

'Mummy, can we go to the park?' Mikaela pleaded. It was the fourth time in the last hour that she had made the same request. She draped her arms over Danni's legs and looked at her mother with a pained expression.

'Not now. It's raining,' said Danni.

'But when?'

'Whenever it stops raining.'

'When will that be? Mummy? When?'

'Mikaela, I'm trying to listen to my programme.'

'But, Mummy!'

'Be quiet, Mikaela, or I'll put you to bed.'

Bradley raced back into the room flinging toilet roll at Mikaela. Both children squealed in delight. Danni felt the four walls closing in.

Danni was twenty-three, born and raised on Treadwater. She had never been further than North Wales in her life. Youthful mistakes had brought her adult regrets. A wasted education, dull jobs, a spate of unreliable boyfriends, two kids, and now depression, alcohol and benefits.

When she looked outside, she noticed the water level rising, the dip in the road was submerged, the pavements covered and water, she reckoned, was now seeping into Mr Johnston's flat. People were gathering on the street watching the floodwater rise. She hoped at least one of them had telephoned for help.

It hadn't taken long for rescue to arrive. Danni stood with others on the street, her kids, hopefully, asleep indoors. A couple of neighbours had broken open Mr Johnston's front door, got inside and lifted the old man from his chair as the water lapped at his feet. They carried him to a nearby house, while social services were notified.

The dozen or so people who had gathered outside in the rain stepped back as a Merseyside Utilities lorry pulled up. It was a tanker capable of pumping out blocked drains and sewers. Danni overheard one of the workers talking to a neighbour.

'Must be a blocked drain,' he said, 'hasn't been raining long or hard enough to cause this flood without there being a blockage. No doubt we'll find something's been trapped in the drain.'

'Fatberg, usually,' said one of the bystanders.

Danni, her long pink hair covered by the flimsy hood of her anorak, looked on as the men attempted to clear the water from a drain at the side of the road. Initially, it seemed to be successful, but soon the water gathered again, and a strong smell of sewage emerged. The workmen decided to open a manhole to inspect the main sewer.

The nearest manhole cover was located just beyond the dip in the road. It lay above the level of dirty floodwater which now contained raw sewage. Once the metal cover was raised, a workman shone a torch into the hole.

Immediately, he called to his colleague who came to see for himself. Danni, her slight figure in leggings and trainers, stepped forward hoping to hear what was being said. The one phrase she did manage to hear was 'better call the police'.

CHAPTER 9

Tara

Much to her chagrin, Tara was the first detective at the scene. There was no place other than Treadwater that evoked such a feeling of desperation in the pit of her stomach. In her policing experience, nothing good had ever happened here. Nothing had ever ended well.

She parked her car a little way off from the melee of other police vehicles, utility company vans, and a queue of motorists waiting to drive through but having encountered the flood and the subsequent disruption. Retrieving an umbrella from the back seat, she pushed open the car door and stepped out. Heavy raindrops pelted down, drumming on her umbrella as she walked to the scene. The road was covered in slimy mud and a stench hung in the air. She felt eyes upon her. Kids charged around splashing in filthy puddles. Several men had their attention piqued by the sight of a pretty woman arriving. Wearing slim jeans, heeled ankle boots and a denim jacket, Tara perhaps did not fit the image of a detective inspector. Such had been her experience since her first day working for Merseyside Police.

A uniformed constable raised a stretch of incident tape to allow her to pass underneath.

'Ma'am.'

'Thank you,' she replied.

Two more uniforms stood next to the manhole as a forensics photographer tried his best to capture the view of what lay inside. Tara stepped close to the edge and peered into the hole. At first glance, it seemed like a huge boulder or a ball of sticky clay was wedged at the bottom. Everything appeared dark brown, but she noticed a pair of feet in black shoes. Tara immediately took charge.

'Move all of these people further back,' she said to a uniform. 'Can we get this area screened off?' she shouted to another.

'We're waiting for SOCO to show up, ma'am,' the constable replied.

'As soon as we have a screen in place, we can get the body out of there.'

Tara allowed the uniforms to get on with things and called Murray on her mobile. She already had a peculiar feeling about this find and wanted Murray to be present. Sometimes she needed the reassurance of a colleague. When she finished her call, she shouted a question. 'Who opened the drain?'

'That would be me,' said a cheerful-faced man wearing a yellow high-vis waterproof coat and wellingtons.

'Tell me what happened,' she said bluntly. Her heart was racing at the thought of what they were about to discover.

'The road was flooded,' the man explained. 'Water was getting into some of the properties hereabouts. We didn't think there was such a heavy flow of water from the rain. More likely that there was a blockage somewhere. I lifted the cover so we could put a camera down to check the sewer. Soon as I opened it up, I knew I didn't need any camera. What's a body doing in there anyway?'

'Your guess is as good as mine, Mr…?'

'Cummings. Bob Cummings.'

Tara wrote his name into her notebook.

'Mr Cummings, thank you for your help. If you don't mind waiting, we may need your assistance in retrieving the body.'

The smile dropped from Cummings' face at the idea of removing a corpse from a sewer.

An hour or so later, Tara stood within an area enclosed by a white shelter as three men – two uniforms and a forensic assistant – grappled with the muddied body. A tripod with a pulley and chain was positioned over the manhole. Slowly, the body was hoisted until it hung above the opening. Bob Cummings, fortunately for him, had not been required, and he sat in the cab of his lorry parked beyond the scene.

The medical officer, Brian Witney, waited to provide his first response to the state of the corpse. As the body was placed on the road a few feet from the opening of the sewer, Tara immediately noticed the similarity to her most recent murder case. The body of a man, she assumed from the shoes, was encased in plastic film. This became more apparent as a forensic officer, using a hose, washed the mud and sewage from the package. The entire body was wrapped in plastic film. Only from seeing the protruding feet could anyone surmise that it was human remains.

Question after question arose in Tara's mind, but for now she stood silently and allowed the medical officer to do his job.

Murray stood beside her. Give it a few minutes and she would be bouncing all her ideas off him. He would also do the same with her.

'A fairly sound connection, don't you think?' Tara said.

'Absolutely, ma'am,' Murray replied. 'And now we have somewhere to begin asking questions. Is it just me, or do you hate this bloody place?'

'Honestly? You're asking me that question? Just think what's happened to us on this estate, Alan. My blood is curdling at the thought of another damned investigation here. No good will come of it.'

Now they had two bodies. Tara could only hope that this latest find came with more answers than the first.

CHAPTER 10

Dinah, Marcus and Sheena

His grey hoodie was soaked through, and he pulled it off as he came into the kitchen. He'd stood all afternoon watching the goings-on in Trent Lane. The story was that a body had been pulled out of the sewer. That was the cause of the flooding in the Lane.

'Pasta for tea, Marcus,' said Dinah, his mother, standing over a pot simmering on the cooker.

'Great. I'm starving.'

Marcus, nineteen, thin-framed and swarthy complexion, his mother second-generation West Indian, his father a long-forgotten Irish seaman, helped himself to a large glass of tap water. 'You should've seen, Mam. A dead body in the sewer.'

'Nothing surprises me these days.'

Dinah was not yet forty, had been a teenage mother to Marcus, who was followed closely by Sheena a year later. Their father, Gerry, took his leave shortly after Sheena's first birthday. The lure of the oceans, he claimed, while Dinah knew it was the lure of his wife in Dublin that caused Gerry to abscond.

'Somebody said it was the same as that stiff they found on the M57 last week.'

'Don't call it a stiff, Marcus. That's so disrespectful. They are human beings like you and me.'

'I know that, Mam.'

Dinah set a large serving bowl of spaghetti and meatballs on the kitchen table. As Marcus gathered plates and cutlery, Dinah went to the bottom of the stairs in the hall and called out.

'Sheena, dinner's ready.'

There was no immediate reply, but Dinah didn't linger. She didn't have time. All three of them had choir practice this evening. They had to be out by half past six. Choir was the one activity they did together as a family. It had brought them closer in recent months and, Dinah believed, it was keeping her kids out of trouble. Eighteen months ago, Marcus was roaming the estate with a bunch of young lads, and heaven knows what they got up to. Drinking, certainly; drugs, most likely, and then there was stealing cars and racing them around the estate. She had prayed long and hard for change in the area, and with the choir it seemed to be happening. Instead of knife fights on the playing fields or wild parties in one of the empty flats, half of Marcus' old crew were now choir members. And at last, her son had an outlet for his talents. He sang well, but he also played piano, and now he was composing his own songs, and he and his mates had formed a band.

Sheena also had thrived. Her work at college had improved since she started singing, and now she was talking about going to university.

Since last week, however, Dinah had noted a change in her daughter's mood. At first, she put it down to a particularly heavy period but then remembered that Mandy had been a close friend. Sheena was upset by Mandy's sudden departure.

When they had finished dinner and cleared away their plates, all three got ready to leave for choir practice. Dinah felt a pleasant buzz walking through the estate with her two children. She had even cut down on the anti-depressants and had virtually stopped drinking. The odd glass of white wine when she got together with Esther and some of the other girls from choir was all she seemed to need now. Her newly restored faith in Jesus had brought her peace. Sheena also had found renewed faith in God. Dinah was confident that her daughter would soon get over Mandy's departure from the estate.

Their house sat at the north-western side of Treadwater, and the roads created a labyrinth of passageways, cul-de-sacs and alleys through and across the estate with some shops located at the south-eastern edge. The community centre and library were close by and overlooked the park. A group of town-planners, back in the late fifties and early sixties, were perhaps the only people satisfied with their work. Treadwater was intended to represent a new age in social housing with areas of open space, houses accessed at the front via walkways, while to the rear there were parking areas and lock-up garages. The estate had been the future of community living in Liverpool, with similar projects scattered about the city and in many others across Britain. Despite the careful planning, no one foresaw the social ills that would eventually turn some of them into ghettos and hotbeds of unemployment, drug dealing and reckless vandalism. Council attempts to improve matters stuttered along, resulting in a patchwork of new housing initiatives splattered across the bleak remnants of earlier times. Many of the older houses, thanks to the Thatcher years, were privately owned and boasted kitchen extensions, conservatories and driveways, many installed without planning permission.

Each road had been named, without regard to local history, after rivers of the British Isles, an idea probably hatched over tea break in the planners' site office. Dinah, Sheena and Marcus walked along Shannon Lane, Severn Way and Ribble Crescent. They emerged on Trent Lane which remained cordoned off while police and forensic personnel completed their work. Dinah paused to have a look. The thought that a lost soul had been killed then dumped into a drain filled her with sadness.

'I wonder if they know who it is yet?' Marcus asked.

Dinah merely gazed at the white screen blocking the road.

'Been down there for years, I heard,' said Sheena.

'We'll find out soon enough,' said Dinah.

Dinah and Sheena exchanged a look but said nothing. They hurried on by and joined several others all eager to escape the rain and get inside the community centre. As Dinah entered the hall, she overheard Esther speaking quietly to Raymond.

'We'll have to do something about it now,' said Esther.

Dinah had no clue of the context, but she felt it to be rather conspiratorial. Raymond walked away from Esther, a wry grin on his face.

CHAPTER 11

Beth

Beth ran her tongue along the edge of the cigarette paper and sealed it over the meagre portion of cheap tobacco. Her disposable lighter was empty, so she had to make do with a match. Once lit, she took a long deep draw and held it in before slowly exhaling. It felt good. It wasn't weed, but it was all she could afford. Her benefits were well fucked up through her inability to fill out the damn forms properly. She would have to ask that slimy git from social services to help resubmit them. For now, she had no money and had to rely on the food bank on the estate just to survive.

There were times in the last four months when she regretted ever coming back here, but would it have made much difference if she'd gone somewhere else:

Manchester, Leeds or even London? She had no income except the fucked-up benefits, no job and no family, at least no family who would have anything to do with her. At thirty-nine, Beth had poor complexion and teeth, mousey hair, a decrepit look, and a body in need of nourishment or another hit. She felt more like a woman of sixty. Since the age of twenty-two she had known only prison. There had been two: New Hall and Styal. She was scarred as a murderer. Two pensioners in Bootle had been killed and robbed of their pensions so her boyfriend at the time could afford his next fix. She had not done the actual stabbing, but she'd been there, in the pensioners' home, watching and egging on Bryn who had been off his head on glue.

He died years ago, having managed to OD in Strangeways. Lucky sod. She'd survived and was now back where she started her miserable life. Back on Treadwater, where her father had made a despicable effort in raising her and her sister Martha. Her mother had scarpered before she even knew her. At least Martha had been lucky. She was taken into care at the age of five and then adopted by a well-off family. Beth was happy for her. Her sister had gone to university and had a good job and a husband and three kids. Beth had seen her only once since the day they were parted. Martha had visited her at Styal, but only to warn her that when she was released, she was to stay out of her life. She didn't need or want a jailbird sister. Fair enough, not like they were ever close – complete strangers really.

The curtains in the flat were grimy and thin, the original colour faded and long obscured by dirt. She didn't bother to pull them closed at night. She didn't bother to switch on her lights either. When darkness fell, she sat on her single armchair, smoked fags and gazed out the window. A television was her only company.

In Styal, she had taken to reading for the first time since getting expelled from school at the age of fifteen. She read non-fiction mainly: travel books, history and politics. Couldn't be arsed with made-up stories. Too many of them had happy endings. That wasn't real life, not in her experience anyway. She joined the library next to the community centre. At first, the snotty-nosed bitch of a librarian wasn't too keen on allowing her to borrow any books. The woman probably thought she would use them for lighting the fire. She insisted that Beth produced two forms of ID and a utility bill. She had utility bills but no proper ID except for her signing on card. And so, for the first couple of visits, Beth had remained in the library and flicked through some books there. Then, on her third visit, the librarian seemed to have a change of heart, perhaps when she saw the kind of books Beth was reading. That maybe behind that downtrodden appearance there was a functioning brain. On that day, she had returned home with four books: biographies of Michelle Obama and Hillary Clinton, a walking tour of Italy, and a history of the Norman Conquest. Now at least she could read in her flat.

It was amazing what information you could gather simply by watching people from your window. She'd heard about the body found in the sewer and had ventured down to the scene. No one took much notice of her, not with her beanie hat on and hood pulled up. She listened to their chit-chat, their speculating on who the dead guy was and the reason why he had been dumped in a sewer. There was other stuff talked about such as the flooding on Trent Lane and the people who were having to move out of their homes. Then a girl was mentioned. She couldn't recall hearing her name, but someone said that a body had been found a week earlier on the M57. Whoever this girl was, some folk had decided that she was the person found on the motorway. It didn't seem that she was popular on the estate, though. There was a lot of mumbling and whispering, especially when a young lad realised that Beth might be listening to their discussion.

There was talk also of a choir on the estate, but she couldn't figure out what that was all about. Then she overheard two men, one of whom was old enough to be her father, discussing this girl who had left the estate. It wasn't their mention of the girl but more what they agreed in general that gave her something to think about, something perhaps to fear. The old guy whispered to the younger man that the best thing happening round here in the last while had been the clearing out of useless twats, those with no job, squatters, drunks and druggies, paedos and gangs. The sooner they got rid of them all, the better, he'd said. The final words were loud enough for all those standing close by to hear. Beth glared at the old man, and he returned her stare with a disparaging look.

One guy she noticed seemed friendly if a tad strange. He smiled at her more than once, and she remembered having passed him several times in the street. He was in his early thirties, tall and slim, short brown hair and smooth skin as if he had no need to shave. She couldn't help noticing that his jeans were tight, like a pair of women's leggings, and his fingernails had a gloss to them as if he'd had a French manicure. Beyond that, he seemed all right.

This evening, as she smoked her second and last roll-up, watching the world go by from her dismal flat, she saw him sidle past. He was aware that she'd been watching him, for as he passed her window, he peered in, waved and smiled. She had no instinctive reaction but to sit rigid. She wasn't used to friendliness.

CHAPTER 12

Tara

Tara and Murray were in late-evening discussions with the head of their team Detective Superintendent Harold Tweedy, an officer of long, hard experience and exemplary record. Over the years his Christian faith helped keep him grounded and caused him also to adopt a deep concern over each of his murder investigations. That same attitude, although not necessarily the religious devotion, rubbed off on the members of his team.

'Hopefully, DNA matching between this latest victim and police records will tell us something,' he said.

Tara was not convinced.

'Still a long shot, sir,' said Tara. 'This man may never have had his DNA on file as was the case with the woman found on the M57.'

'The answers to both killings lie in Treadwater,' said Murray with certainty in his tone and stretching his arms skywards.

'Then we need footsloggers on the estate asking questions,' said Tara. 'I mean, how do you put a body down a manhole in the middle of the busiest road in the area and no one notices?'

'Or did notice but isn't telling,' suggested Murray.

'Peculiar MO,' said Tweedy. He was tall, thin and frequently looked pensive. 'Both methods of disposal suggest that the perpetrator was not particularly concerned about getting caught.'

'Clever enough not to leave much by way of incriminating evidence,' said Tara.

'Except for a lot of cling film.'

Tara glared at Murray; she knew when he was being flippant.

Tweedy rose from his chair and checked his watch.

'Twenty past seven. I'm late for my dinner again. Eleanor will not be a happy woman when I get home.'

As Tara and then Murray also stood, Tweedy pulled on his overcoat and lifted his leather-bound Bible from the corner of his desk. It travelled to and from work every day. Tweedy was often to be seen reading from it during quieter moments in his day.

'Goodnight, folks. Tomorrow, I think we should set about an extensive door-to-door on that estate and pray also for something useful to come out of the lab.'

'Goodnight, sir,' Tara replied as she left Tweedy's office and made for her own desk.

She gathered her bag and coat, took a final glance at her screen, then joined Murray to exit the office.

'So, how are you getting on with Kate?' Murray enquired.

'We're fine. It's great to have some company when I get home. And I can help with looking after Adele when Kate is on shifts at the hospital. Can't get too used to it, though, she might end up back with her fella.'

'I see a return to the old Tara.'

'Well, it is the one good thing that has happened to me in the last few years. If it hadn't been for Kate moving in, I don't think I would still be a police officer. She's helped me deal with things.' Tara had reached her car and was relieved to end the conversation. It was hard enough these days to keep the past resigned to the past without having to discuss it with a colleague. 'Goodnight, Alan.'

'Night, ma'am.'

Saying goodnight didn't mean that she could just switch off from her job. Tara had always found difficulty in that respect. Now, even with company at home, she would mull over her cases until eventually a mundane subject suppressed it.

The prospect of going door-to-door on the Treadwater Estate filled her with dread. She had convinced herself through time and experience that the kind of people living on council estates in this day and age were a peculiar breed. All of them had one social ill or another. If it wasn't unemployment or a broken home then it was old age, poor health, alcohol or drugs. The people had a look about them. Their troubles were branded in their facial expressions, their unhealthy living evident by a grey pallor, sunken eyes and weakened gait. Tara couldn't recall ever meeting an individual on Treadwater who was free of all shackles. Every person she had ever dealt with had an issue in their lives, young and old, male and female.

Now there might well be a serial killer living among them. Another ill for the melting pot of social behaviours.

On the drive home to her flat at Wapping Dock, she pictured a face for the killer, or perhaps killers. So far, they had no motive, no identities for the victims and no confirmed cause of death except that the female had been cut to pieces by traffic on the M57. Was it merely coincidence that the second victim had been found on Treadwater? Was it possible that the body had been washed through the sewers by floodwater? If that were true, then they would be wasting valuable time on door-to-door inquiries on the estate. The body may have been disposed of somewhere beyond Treadwater.

As she entered her flat to hear CBeebies on TV, she realised, trying to be honest with herself, that she would do anything to avoid having to work in that dreadful estate.

CHAPTER 13

Esther

Practice had gone well. They'd managed to get through all the songs intended for their upcoming concert at Netherton Leisure Centre. The date was drawing near, and it gave a fresh impetus to the evening's practice. Even the songs that were causing Esther some concern sounded much improved. *Take Me to the River* was better than the previous week, although, of all the songs in the list it was the one most at risk of being dropped. She had several others in mind as replacements. *Shine Jesus Shine* was a favourite of hers from singing in church although she realised many of the members would fail to identify with anything religious.

A few weeks ago, she'd asked for suggestions of song favourites, hoping to get some of the more reluctant members to step forward. All sorts had been submitted, from *Smoke on the Water* to *Rehab* by Amy Winehouse. Now *Rehab* was a must. Esther reckoned the song resonated with several choir members. It wasn't the kind of music that did anything for her, but she wanted inclusiveness in this venture. Without it, people would lose interest and the project would gradually fall apart. Which was why, this evening, she continued to have concerns about the choir's committee. She had already refused outright to allow the musical direction to become the responsibility of this committee. She was the musical director, and that's how it was going to stay. But foolishly perhaps, she had acquiesced when it came to the general matters of organisation: fundraising, promotions and recruitment. She had thought it best to stay out of it, to let them get on with things. For some, the committee had taken on greater prominence than the actual singing.

This evening, as the others tidied the room and put away the chairs, she watched the committee members scurry to one of the smaller rooms in the building to hold a meeting. She wondered what on earth they had to discuss that took so much of their time. She'd heard that there were frequent gatherings also at the homes of members. Now she regretted giving them a free rein. What were they discussing? Was it her? Were they unhappy about Mandy leaving? Were they now planning to oust her from her own choir?

For a while, after most choristers had left, Esther remained at her piano, playing over some of the tunes on the performance list, thinking of how to improve the arrangements, pondering the abilities of her soloists and thinking ahead to the proposed concert of Christmas music. Really, she was waiting for the committee to finish their meeting, to gauge the mood as they came out of the room and maybe to strike up a casual chat in the hope of discovering what had been discussed.

Raymond and Mary Glover were first to emerge. Mary smiled weakly then lowered her head.

'Goodnight, Esther,' said Raymond, ushering his wife to the door.

Dinah and her daughter, Sheena, came out next, closely followed by Nathan who looked ashen. He did have a difficult time living on the estate with so many intolerant people mocking him. He was a fantastic tenor, though.

Danni appeared, taking Hannah by the arm. Her husband, Stan, followed behind them, switching off the light in the meeting room as he left. Stan was just a few months younger than Hannah. They appeared a devoted couple, a real Darby and Joan. She didn't say much, but Hannah still retained a good alto voice. She was rather stooped now, noticeably worsening in the time that Esther had known her. Hannah dressed plainly in contrast to Stan who always looked quite dapper in a suit or sports jacket and well-polished shoes. Esther guessed that he was of a military background, but she had never inquired. He seemed to order Hannah around everywhere.

'Good night, folks,' Esther called.

'Good night, Esther,' two of them replied.

In the silence, and now alone in the community centre, Esther wondered again what had been discussed in the meeting. Nothing that was any of her business, it seemed. She gathered her papers and music together and packed away her piano. Usually, a male chorister would stay behind to carry her instrument to her car, but not tonight. She knew that Billy, the centre caretaker, would be along shortly to lock up and he would oblige.

Fifteen minutes later, Esther lifted her bag into her Fiat hatchback, while Billy, a stocky man of sixty-two, puffed and panted as he eventually eased her piano onto the back seat.

'Thanks, Billy.'

'No problem, Esther love.'

As Esther was about to drive away, she noticed a car sitting at the far end of the centre's car park. She knew it wasn't Billy's because he lived just across the road from the centre and would walk home. The car's tail lights were on and she saw two people inside. The passenger side was nearest for Esther to see as she drove away, and a face turned to look as she went by. It was young Carrie Dobson. She didn't recognise the driver, but she noted the car and intended to check who it belonged to at the next practice.

CHAPTER 14

Stan and Hannah

Hannah had never needed much sleep. It had been that way for years, dating to when she was first married. That came, she supposed, from her living on an army base, one after another, from Aldershot to Germany, to Cyprus and Northern Ireland. She'd never known a settled home. Her father, too, had been a soldier, although things were much different way back then. It was war and he was in North Africa with Monty, while she, her mother and three sisters sheltered from Luftwaffe bombing raids on Liverpool.

All were memories now and she was grateful she still had them. She felt so alone in the house on this damned estate. Years of moving around, bringing up a family, while Stan played soldiers, then finally when the army was done with Stan, he brought her to live in this godforsaken place. They had no savings, just an army pension. They couldn't afford to buy a big house somewhere nice, close to the sea or in the countryside. No, it was a council house with little choice of where it would be.

Worse than all the disappointment was that while Stan left the army, the army didn't leave him. He ran the house military style. Not for any noble purpose but simply for him to rule over her, to dish out orders, for her to do as he commanded. God forbid if she stepped out of line. His punishments, too, were of military standard.

Lights out – 22:45. If she were not tired and didn't need to sleep, she would have to sit in the darkness. Breakfast – 07:15. And she had to have it ready and on the table for him at precisely that time. Hungry or not, she would have to eat with him. On Saturday afternoons, while he went to the match at Goodison, she must devise the menu for the forthcoming week. On Monday mornings, he took her shopping, leaving her at Morrisons, while he went for coffee at Costa with his old army pal, Ronnie. She had to be ready and waiting for him when he returned to pick her up an hour later. There was hell to pay if she wasn't standing with her trolley of groceries ready to be loaded into the car. He could be up to an hour late in returning but that didn't matter.

On Tuesdays, the house was cleaned from top to bottom. During cleaning time, Stan worked in his shed in the garden, playing with his model trains. Every Wednesday they attended choir practice, the one concession he'd made to her in the last twenty-five years since leaving the army.

At eighty-one, Hannah was the oldest member of the choir, Stan a few months younger. She loved singing; she cherished the opportunity, albeit briefly, to mix with people, to chat and smile and laugh. There was no chance of that at home except when the children came to stay. Mark, her eldest, had joined the army. He was a major and the apple of Stan's eye. He was married to Rachel, and they had two kids. Hannah pitied Rachel, who seemed to have the same lifestyle that she had once endured, moving from base to base, never knowing a settled home.

Susan was Stan and Hannah's daughter. She only visited if she wanted something, a loan usually, or a place to stay until she got back on her feet after another relationship breakdown. Hannah loved her dearly, but Stan could hardly find a civil word to say to her. Sadly, Susan had never known a place to really call home. Now in her fifties, her third divorce recently finalised, it was unlikely she ever would.

Hannah hadn't yet discovered why Stan had permitted her to join a choir and had also become a member of it. He had a reasonable singing voice as a bass, but he had never expressed enjoyment from the activity. Her only conclusion was that he came to practice merely to keep an eye on her.

She worried that since joining the choir, Stan's control over her had deepened. The routine at home remained as tight as ever, but now she was forbidden to leave the house alone. She was ordered not to speak to anyone unless Stan was with her. Hannah had dared question him, asking why she couldn't speak to a living soul.

'I don't want my business discussed in public,' he said coldly over the dinner table.

'But what is so important in this house that I can't have a chat with friends at choir or with our neighbours?'

'I don't want you talking to people and that's final.'

'But, Stan, if someone speaks to me it's rude not to answer.'

Stan rose from the table. Hannah knew from his expression that something bad was about to happen. He moved behind her, grasped her left wrist and twisted her arm behind her back. She cried out as he tugged her hair, pulling her head backwards.

'You heard what I said. Just do as you're told.' He pushed her away and her face crashed into her dinner plate. 'Lights out at nine,' he said. 'I think I'll have an early night.'

'But my programme is on at nine,' she sobbed.

'Should have thought of that before you gave me all that cheek.'

He walked out of the kitchen, leaving her to clear away the dishes.

The clock on the mantelpiece chimed two o'clock, and she had yet to venture to her bedroom. She slept alone at the back of the house. Her one successful disobedience to Stan had come fifteen years ago when she refused him sex and left the bed they shared. He had tried to coax her back, trying to be romantic and loving when behind it all she knew his military habits simply needed satisfying. For nearly a year, he came to her room twice a week and forced himself on her. His longings eventually waned. She believed he had encountered a male problem, common for men of his age. He hadn't touched her sexually for over twelve years.

She was used to the darkness now. In a way, she took comfort from it. Alone in the lounge, she quietly sang through her favourite songs, over and over, straining every ounce of joy she could from each melody and line. Her left arm still throbbed from his latest assault on her, and her right hand held a tissue that she used to dab the tears at her eyes.

CHAPTER 15

Tara

Although the floodwater on Trent Lane had seeped away, the rain still pelted down on police officers going from one door to the next gathering information on the finding of a body in the sewer. Tara and Murray were having to do their share of interviewing. So far, they had acquired little information on the male victim or on the woman killed on the M57. They must get something from this campaign, or their investigation would grind to a halt.

Tara was unable to carry an umbrella and her warrant card and write in her notebook, so she got soaked in a short anorak with a flimsy hood that kept blowing off in the wind. She entered a building that housed four flats and was close to the manhole where the body had been found. It was also the first property to be flooded and one of the residents evacuated. As she knocked on the frosted glass door of the ground-floor flat, a voice shouted down from the landing above.

'He won't be there, love,' said a woman. 'The place got flooded. They moved old Mr Johnston to a care home for a few days until they get his flat sorted.'

Tara stood at the foot of the concrete staircase listening to a woman, still in her dressing gown, with straggly pink hair. At the mention of the ground-floor flat being flooded, Tara gazed around the hallway. The concrete floor was damp and muddied with a watermark on the wall nine inches above the floor.

Tara made her way up the stairs to the woman.

'Can I ask you some questions?'

'Ask away, love, don't know if I can help you. Didn't know Mr Johnston that well. Are you from the council?'

'No, I'm Detective Inspector Grogan, Merseyside Police.'

Tara stood opposite the woman on the landing. The door of her flat was ajar, and Tara heard a television playing inside. Self-consciously, the woman gathered the two sides of her dressing gown together. Tara asked for the woman's name.

'It's Danni Pearce.'

'Well, Danni, we're looking for information relating to the finding of a body in the sewer outside yesterday afternoon. Have you noticed anything odd or suspicious recently?'

Danni was shaking her head.

'Did you see anyone working at the manhole?'

'Not till yesterday.'

'Have you noticed any strangers moving around the estate, people you might think were not what they seemed?'

Again, Danni shook her head.

Mikaela emerged from the flat eating cheese strings and watching the lady talking to her mam.

'Do you know of anyone who has gone missing off the estate recently, someone perhaps who hasn't been reported as such?'

'What do you mean?' she sounded indignant.

'Well, anyone you've not seen around, and you're concerned for?'

'No one like that except for my bastard of a boyfriend who scarpered a year ago and is not paying me a penny. Don't suppose you can do anything about that?'

'I'm sorry, but this is a murder inquiry.'

'I'll leave you to it then. Come on, Mikaela, let's go see what Bradley's up to.' Danni turned away and closed her door behind her.

Tara paused for a second, unsure what to make of the woman's attitude. It certainly wasn't helpful.

She noticed another door to the rear of the landing. Approaching, she saw that the frosted glass was adorned with stickers and slogans, the biggest one reading 'No cold callers.'

Beneath it, the message was more tersely stated. 'If you're not the postman, fuck off!'

Ignoring the message, she pounded on the door with her fist. A dog barked inside as she read another sign, 'The dog is always hungry.'

She read the others as she waited for her knock not to be answered: 'Hitler was a nice guy!' 'Brits in, immigrants can fuck off somewhere else.' She knocked again with growing eagerness to meet the person who lived inside. After a third attempt, she thumped harder on the glass and called out, 'Police. Open up please!'

The dog became more excited, and Tara heard its paws scraping on the inside of the door. At last, it opened, and the face of a young man glared angrily at her.

'What?'

'Merseyside Police. I take it you're aware of a body being found yesterday in the street outside?'

'Yeah, so?'

He was a slight-framed guy, a little taller than her, with a pimple-dotted face and shaven head. He wore a black sleeveless T-shirt allowing him to display both arms adorned in tattoos of skulls, motorbikes and machine guns. His eyes were dull and held a defensive stare. Beyond that, Tara didn't find him quite so intimidating as she'd expected.

'We're seeking information in connection with the body found yesterday in Trent Lane. Have you noticed anything suspicious lately on the estate?'

'Na.'

The dog, trapped in another room of the flat, was going berserk. Without another word, the youth slammed his front door. Tara noticed another sticker, 'England expects.'

'England is bloody disappointed,' she mumbled.

Outside on the street, Tara sighed and looked around for sight of Murray. She was already frustrated with her lack of success. Rain was beating down as she stepped into the road and entered the cordon where a team of sewage workers were inspecting the drain using a video camera. Tara asked a question and one of the three men glanced around in surprise.

'Sorry to interrupt,' she said, showing her warrant card, 'DI Grogan, Merseyside Police. I'm wondering if it is possible that the body got washed along the drain to this point before getting stuck.'

A man in a high-vis jacket and waterproof trousers straightened up. It was the chap named Cummings from the day before.

'It's possible,' he said, 'but it wouldn't have travelled far. The drain is only wide enough along this section because it carries waste from more than one street.' He walked from the shelter with Tara following. He was a man in his forties, tall and broad-shouldered with a fuzzy beard gathering beads of rain. He pointed along Trent Lane. 'The flow comes from where Trent Lane, Ribble and

Severn converge. The body might have been placed in a manhole between that point and this one.'

'Thanks. Where do you think was most likely?'

'I'd say the first one. All the others are in the middle of the road. Surely somebody would have seen if a body were being dropped down a manhole.'

'Why the first one?'

'It's on the parkland, close to the path. Less likely to be noticed from the road.'

'Could you nice men open the drain for me?'

'Sure, love. Give us a few minutes to finish up here.'

Tara wandered along the street towards the park. The intention to call door-to-door had temporarily slipped from her mind.

The park on Treadwater occupied the centre of the estate. She recalled hearing a tale of how, back in the mid-sixties, the residents, with their children at the forefront, protested to stop further building on the estate and to have the central area developed as parkland. Clearly, it had been and remained a successful campaign. The expanse of green held two football pitches, a children's play park and several tarmac footpaths, criss-crossing areas of shrubs and bushes and linking the upper and lower regions of Treadwater Estate. The upper portion of the estate was beset with blocks of flats, not high-rise, but hardly the most attractive architecture. To the west, and beyond the boundary of the housing, lay an area of undeveloped land. At one time, a property developer had begun the construction of private houses, but this was halted when his company went into receivership. Eventually, the land was restored to its original state.

The eastern area of the estate was most embossed on Tara's memory. It was where she had investigated the murder of a Lithuanian girl, Audra Bagdonas, and had encountered the ill-fated Callum Armour. She shivered at the memory. The roads and cul-de-sacs in that area were named after trees: Sycamore Gardens, Broad Oak Lane and Birchwood Drive. There was not a real tree apparent in any of them. It was another town planners' tea break decision.

A few yards along a footpath winding through the park, Tara located a manhole cover. She paused and gazed towards Trent Lane, hoping the workmen would soon come to open the drain. It lay in open ground – quite visible, she presumed, from the houses that bordered the playing fields. The only advantage over the manholes in the road for disposing of a body, was that someone could probably work uninterrupted by cars passing, and if it were done in the dead of night then unseen by people living nearby.

'Sorry to keep you, love,' said Cummings. 'We wanted to get finished down there so that the road could reopen.'

'No problem,' Tara replied, smiling thinly as she continued to get drenched in the downpour.

Two workmen were quick to attach the metal hooks that allowed them to lift the wrought-iron drain cover and slide it to the side. The instinct to lean over and peer in afflicted all those present. There was little to be seen but sufficient for Tara to immediately use her mobile to call for a forensics team.

CHAPTER 16

Sheena

Sheena's mind was elsewhere as she stepped off the bus. But Carrie had spotted her.

'Hi, Sheena.'

'Oh hiya, Carrie. How are things at my old school?'

Carrie was dressed mostly in school uniform – blouse, skirt and school tie of navy, yellow and purple. The one dissension was a black leather biker jacket rather than a school blazer. Despite the uniform, Carrie looked older than the sixth-form girl Sheena, dressed in black jeans and a thick jumper.

'Same as ever,' Carrie replied with a sigh. 'Mr Collins is still a pain and Miss Hartley is still a first-class bitch.'

'Nothing changed then. This is a bit out of your way home, walking down here?'

'I just had to call with a friend.'

The pair of them ambled in the direction of Sheena's road which was taking Carrie even further from her home on Broad Oak Lane.

'Are you looking forward to the concert?' Sheena asked.

'Yes. Some of the songs are a bit dull, but I suppose Esther has to get some variety into the show.'

'Can't please everyone. This is your first concert; you'll enjoy it. All the practicing will seem worthwhile when you hear the audience cheering at the end.'

Carrie stopped abruptly, looking dead ahead. Sheena spotted Ian Bankhead getting out of his car. She glanced at Carrie, who seemed hesitant about walking on. Her eyes seemed fixed upon Ian, but her face was a picture of fright.

'Are you all right, Carrie?'

The question seemed to prod her onwards.

'I'm fine.'

'Hi, girls,' Ian called. 'Are you two rehearsing a duet I don't know about?'

'Not likely to without Esther's permission,' Sheena replied.

Ian was quite tall, at least six foot. He was dressed in gym gear, grey vest and jogging trousers, and his hair was still wet from having showered. Sheena had always found him attractive but didn't suppose for a second that an older man like Ian would even notice her. Besides, lately it wasn't her habit to make herself look particularly appealing to boys, never mind grown men. She wore little make-up, except on special occasions, her dark hair was usually in a ponytail and her clothes were not at all daring, which was a pity because she did have a shapely figure.

Ian didn't stop to chat. He pulled his bag from the boot of his car and walked briskly to his front door. Sheena noticed that Carrie's eyes never left him. Carrie was just like her, Sheena thought. She had a futile crush on a man who wouldn't think twice about either of them.

As they walked on by, however, Carrie glanced behind. Then Sheena thought she saw Ian and Carrie exchanging a look that was more than a mere greeting. There was something in his smile, and something in Carrie's eyes that said they were more than just friends from choir. Sheena wondered.

'So, where does your friend live?'

The question took Carrie by surprise, and she had no immediate answer.

'Ribble Drive,' she replied at last.

'But, Carrie, you're going the wrong way.' The teenager looked dumbfounded.

'Silly me,' she said, 'I don't know what I was thinking. I'll see you, Sheena.' She turned and hurried away, past Ian's house, quickening her step as she went.

'Take care, Carrie.'

Sheena watched her go, wondering if there was anything to what she had just witnessed. But the notion soon left her. She had more important matters to claim her thoughts.

CHAPTER 17

Tara

Tara sat next to a radiator, drying her wet jeans and boots. She and Murray discussed their progress so far, but there was little to say on the case. Murray sat at the desk next to Tara's, munching on a BLT sandwich and drinking from a can of Coke. He was less concerned with drying off, more imperative that he filled his stomach.

'We have nothing worth talking about concerning the woman found on the M57,' said Tara, leafing through the meagre file.

'Not a soul on Treadwater even wants to discuss it,' Murray replied.

'Do you think that some people have information they aren't sharing, or do they really know nothing?'

'They may know nothing of the woman on the motorway, but surely somebody has information about the guy who was dumped in the sewer. I mean, it happened right in the middle of the bloody estate.'

'Forensics examined the manhole at the park,' said Tara. 'Wasn't much to find but it is likely that the body was dumped there rather than in Trent Lane. There was a strip of plastic film stuck to the wall and there were scrape marks as if a large object had rubbed against the mud on the bricks.'

'It might have been left by a workman.'

'I asked Cummings, the foreman, to check when the cover had last been opened. He has to get back to me.'

A silence ensued, while Murray finished off his sandwich and then started into a KitKat.

Tara read over the initial post-mortem report on the male victim. In this instance, the body had decomposed to some extent. The cause of death could not be established, although there was a likelihood that the victim had been asphyxiated by the covering of his nose and mouth with the plastic film. There were no other injuries detected, no stab wounds, bullets or broken bones. They had yet to identify the victim, but DNA samples had been collected for profiling and were being compared for matches on the police DNA database. That was their only hope, a match with an individual on police file. Tara found it hard to believe that there were no current listings of missing persons to fit the profile of either victim. Didn't these poor souls have family or friends who were worried about them?

'We could do a search of the estate,' Murray suggested when he'd finished eating.

'What do you mean?'

'Well, both victims were wrapped in this cling film stuff. Presumably, that was done in the same place, either by hand or machine. Witney reckoned it was industrial strength, like the material used for packaging boxes in factories.'

'That shouldn't take us long. I can't think of any factories on the Treadwater Estate.'

'No, but it may have been somewhere nearby, or someone on the estate might have access to a machine that does that kind of thing.'

'Which still leaves us with the problem of where to look.'

Tara's desk phone rang, and she answered straight away.

'Ah, Mr Cummings.'

Murray waited as Tara listened to her caller.

'Thanks for letting me know. Bye,' she said.

'Well, anything interesting?' Murray asked.

'According to the utilities company, the manhole in the park has not been opened by them since June of last year.'

'That would mean our victim died sometime between then and a few days ago. PM report suggests that he has been dead for approximately a year. So, he must have died soon after the manhole was last opened by the utilities company.'

Tara called across the room.

'John, any success with a match on the DNA?'

Wilson rose from his desk, gathered a page from the printer in the centre of the office and came over.

'Just as you speak, ma'am,' he said, placing the sheet of paper in front of her.

She glanced down the page then read aloud for Murray's benefit.

'Olev Eesmaa, 22, of no fixed abode. Estonian national. Entered the UK on 15 March 2014. Two arrests, one by Greater Manchester for alleged assault, May 2015. Second arrest, also by Greater Manchester for possession of Class A drug, October 2016. Released on bail pending hearing. Failed to appear in court. Arrest warrant issued February 2017.'

'So, how did he end up in Treadwater?' Murray asked.

'Maybe he was mixed up with a drug gang,' said Wilson. 'Ventured too far off his turf.'

'Perhaps,' said Tara. 'Wouldn't surprise me in Liverpool.'

'So, you reckon he was a victim of drug running?' Murray asked.

'Doesn't explain any link to the dead woman on the M57,' said Tara.

'Unless she was also involved,' said Wilson.

CHAPTER 18

Beth

Beth struggled to motivate herself to leave the relative safety of her flat. But today was the best time to visit the food bank. She'd discovered a couple of weeks earlier that on a Tuesday evening the food bank took delivery of near end-of-date fresh food from a supermarket. By early Wednesday, the goods had been sorted and were made available. It meant that she could get her hands on ready meals such as chicken curry, lasagne and slow-cooked pork or lamb shanks. At least these were tastier than tinned soup, savoury rice and pot noodles. The incentive to go out, therefore, was greater than her fear of walking through the estate. She was certain there were those around who knew of her past, and one or two who might even remember her living here with her father and sister. People were naturally suspicious of strangers, and her appearance was less than appealing. But she wasn't here to make friends; she was here simply to live in a place that wasn't prison. Beyond that, she had no aspirations. Her probation officer had suggested that she should find a job, but she'd never had one, except in jail. She worked in the laundry at first, then in the kitchen at Styal. She doubted anyone would give her a job and besides, she had enough problems sorting out her benefits never mind going through the whole process again if she did find one.

The day looked bright and perhaps warm. At least the rain had stopped. The weather didn't influence her decision of what to wear. She didn't have such choice. It was jeans or leggings; T-shirt or sweatshirt; hoodie or anorak; and no choice of footwear; trainers or barefoot. She lifted two carrier bags from the kitchen, unlocked her front door and stepped into the bare hallway.

Outside, it felt like the eyes of the world were on her, and yet the road was deserted. She walked to the end of the street, through an alley at the rear of a cul-de-sac, emerging on Severn Way with the park directly ahead. She crossed the road and took the path across the open space, leading to the shops and the food bank. The premises were formerly a newsagent's that had closed, unable to compete after the mini-market had expanded into a second shop unit. Now, within the row of four shop units, the mini-market occupied two, the food bank one, and the fourth was a Chinese takeaway. A mile down the road was a large retail park with a supermarket and several large stores. Beth didn't think she would be going there anytime soon.

When she was halfway across the park, instinctively, she glanced behind her. A man had joined the path and was heading in her direction. At first sight she didn't recognise him, but after a second look she realised it was the guy who had smiled and waved as he walked past her flat. She felt nerves rising in her stomach. Her step quickened until she crossed the road and entered the food bank.

A young lad, late teens, in a beige jumper and jeans, smiled at her then asked for her ID and proof that she was on assisted living allowance. Beth pulled the creased documents from her anorak pocket and handed them over.

'Thanks,' said the youth, handing them back.

Without a word, she lifted a plastic shopping basket from the stack and wandered into the aisle, making directly for the only refrigerated cabinet. Already, the goods had been well rummaged, and little choice remained. She lifted a potato dish, the name of which she did not recognise, nor could she pronounce. She placed a single-serving pack of sweet 'n' sour prawns with jasmine rice into her basket.

That was all the luxury available. Finally, she chose a can of tomato soup, baked beans, a small loaf and a tub of spread.

At the counter, the teenager looked on but didn't help as Beth packed her groceries into her bags.

'Bye, have a nice day,' he said as if she had just spent a fortune in his exclusive store.

She had enough money to buy some rolling tobacco and a few cans of cheap lager from the mini-market. As she browsed the shelves, she noticed the guy who had followed behind her as she'd crossed the park. He was perusing the magazines, leafing through a *Woman's Weekly*. She noticed his clothing and thought it a strange mix. His jeans with rips at the knees were a slim fit, his T-shirt was a baby pink with Vogue printed across the chest in a glittery blue, and his nails were painted purple. Gay, she decided and instantly the feelings she had of threat and danger subsided, and she drew nearer to him to reach the alcohol.

'Hiya,' he said in a shrill voice. He replaced the magazine in the stand. 'Are you all right?'

'Fine,' Beth replied and went to walk on by.

'You're new round here, aren't you, love?' His voice was softer than she had imagined, proper Scouse and a little camp. His face was bright, and he wore eyeliner. She couldn't ignore his friendly smile. Here seemed to be a guy with no ulterior motive, a lad who was only being friendly.

'Yes,' she answered. 'Just moved in a couple of weeks ago.'

'You on your own then?'

'Yep.'

'I've seen you about. I'm Nathan.' He smiled again and waited for her to reciprocate.

She walked on by to choose from the cans of lager on offer.

Nathan did not seem put off by her unfriendliness. He pulled a copy of the *Echo* from a stand and sashayed up to her. She could smell his scent, not at all masculine but very pleasant.

'Can you sing?' he asked.

'What?'

'Can you sing?'

He smiled broadly, and she noticed his white teeth, smooth skin and the outline of a bra beneath his T-shirt. All Beth could do was shrug a reply.

'We have a community choir on the estate,' he said. 'If you're looking for something to do and a chance to make friends, you could come along to practice.'

'Why would your choir want the likes of me?' It was the first time she'd said something about herself to a stranger on this estate.

'Why not? We're always looking for new members. Don't have to be a great singer. We can't all be Beyoncé.' He struck a Beyoncé-style pose.

Beth managed to smile. Nathan watched her lifting a four-can pack of Dutch lager from the shelf. He wasn't to be put off and offered to carry her drink.

For reasons that she couldn't fathom, Beth allowed Nathan to continue his chat, while she feigned a browse of the shop, although she couldn't afford to buy anything else other than tobacco.

'Come on, give it a go. It's lonely being on your own. You might even enjoy it. You can come with me, if you like, so you will already know somebody.'

Beth couldn't help herself. She felt her face warming, and she was smiling constantly in the company of this cheerful man who wouldn't leave her alone.

She paid for her beer, bought her tobacco and left the shop as Nathan continued to joke with her, walking backwards and pleading with her to enjoy herself.

'Fuck. Do you never let up?' Beth said, exasperated.

'Ooh! A touch of angst in there, I think.'

She laughed at his use of the word angst when really, he should have sworn back at her. Suddenly, they laughed at each other.

'So, does that mean yes? You'll come?' Nathan asked.

'Fuck's sake, all right, anything to shut you the fuck up.'

They strolled back to her flat, Nathan laughing, cracking jokes and Beth unable to resist his good humour. As she left him to go indoors, he called after her.

'You didn't tell me your name.'

'Beth.' She slammed her door. God, what had she let herself in for?

CHAPTER 19

Tara

'All reports on door-to-door inquiries have yielded little,' said Tweedy, seated at his desk and looking grave.

Tara and Murray could only nod in agreement.

'Now that we have an ID for the male victim we can go back and ask again,' suggested Murray.

'Yes. Also, I am going to issue a public appeal for information. Hopefully, that will bring some positive results,' Tweedy said.

'If we're repeating the door-to-door inquiries,' said Tara, 'it might be useful to set up an incident room on the estate. A definite police presence may help jog a few memories.'

'How about someone going undercover, living on the estate, see what's going on?' said Murray.

'Is that necessary?' said Tara. 'Other than reluctant witnesses, we can't say that anything untoward is going on.'

'Do you have someone in mind for the role, Alan?' Tweedy asked.

Murray grinned and couldn't help gazing at Tara.

'Me?' she asked.

'I could do it, ma'am, but I think I'd be easily recognised. John grew up in Treadwater, so he's a non-starter.'

'But we've covered so many cases on the estate in recent years. I would be recognised just as easily.'

'Dye your hair, don't wear make-up, and you'll look entirely different,' Murray said.

'Oh, thanks very much, Alan. Is that all it takes? We could just as easily put you in a dress and slap on some face paint!'

'All right,' said Tweedy, 'that's quite enough. I don't think we need to resort to personal insults. Let's keep it as an option for now. If we have no success from the public appeal, then we can reconsider.'

Tara left Tweedy's office fuming. When Murray got to his desk, she crossed the room in a determined stride.

'What the hell do you think you're playing at?'

'It was only a suggestion, Tara.'

Her eyes bulged at his reply.

'It's "ma'am" to you. And it's not for you to go volunteering me for anything, do you understand? I'm not some wet-behind-the-ears rookie you're trying to impress. I'm your superior.'

'Yes, ma'am. Sorry, ma'am.'

'No one in this unit has any experience of undercover work. We could do more harm than good and completely destroy public relations.'

She marched back to her desk. Murray, she hoped, was now feeling admonished.

Within her tangled thoughts on the case there lurked some agreement with what had been suggested. But not yet. It was too soon. Going undercover on Treadwater suggested there was a conspiracy among residents. They had no evidence of such activity. All they had so far was either a reluctance to assist the police or else there was truly a lack of information about the murders.

CHAPTER 20

Danni

Danni rushed them through their tea. Mikaela was her usual stroppy self, while Bradley threw his fish fingers in her direction, oblivious to Danni's scolding. Recently, she'd been thinking that her social worker was right. That Bradley was showing signs of ADHD. She didn't need a professional diagnosis to know that he was a bloody handful. And he was getting worse.

Tonight was choir night. Not only was she getting out for the evening, but she wouldn't have her blinking kids howling in her ear. And they stayed over at their gran's. She got a break for one night in the week. It wasn't entirely ideal. Her mother came to choir also. That meant leaving her kids in the care of her mother's boyfriend, Barry. Danni didn't like him, much less trust him. But what could she do? Valerie, her mum, was fine about it. She and Barry had been living together for two years now. You were supposed to know someone well in that length of time.

She had a child at each hand as she rushed them across the park to her mum's house on Broad Oak Lane. The children knew where they were going, knew that their mum was leaving them for the night, and it seemed that they were trying everything to make her late. Mikaela's screeches could be heard all over the park. Danni didn't like to swear in front of them, but she failed to hold her temper.

'Come on, you little shit!' she shouted at Bradley. 'Mikaela, stop that fucking squealing, or so help me–'

Barry Sugden, ten years younger than Valerie, stood on the doorstep smoking a fag. He was a big lump of man, untidy and sporting a beer gut that he fed several nights a week at home, and on weekends when he went to the match. Danni couldn't think what her mum saw in him. Companionship, she surmised, for he didn't have a penny except benefits, and surely the sex could not be great. As Danni hurried to the door, Barry ignored both children entirely, raised his arms and grasped Danni on either side of her face to force a kiss on her lips. She fucking hated that, but her mum said that Barry was just being affectionate. His breath stank of tobacco and frequently of stale beer.

'Looking gorgeous, as ever,' he said with a lurid smile on his fat gob.

Danni barged inside with her children. Valerie stood before a wall mirror in the lounge applying mascara. It might only be choir practice, but she turned up as if for a night on the town. Danni felt odd and quite inferior walking beside her, wearing plain black leggings, trainers and a puffer jacket.

'Are you ready, mum? We're five minutes late. You know what Esther will say.'

'I'm coming, love.'

'I wish,' quipped Barry standing rather too close to Danni.

'Don't talk like that in front of the kids, Barry,' said Valerie, pulling on her long coat.

The children were chasing each other around an armchair, Mikaela screaming at the top of her voice. Usually, Danni was shouting at her to stop but, knowing she was about to leave them in the care of Barry, she was quite happy for the rumpus to continue all night.

'No more of those DVDs of yours, Barry,' Danni warned. 'Mikaela had nightmares last week.'

'OK. No more violence. I'll just stick to the porn this evening.'

He thought he was funny, but Danni fired him an icy look. She reckoned he was quite capable of watching dirty movies in front of the children.

'Behave yourself, love,' said Valerie, leaning over and giving him a kiss.

Danni reckoned he was expecting one from her too, but she stepped outside quickly.

'Hope my two are not too much of a handful for Barry,' said Danni as they hurried along the street.

'They're fine. Barry loves kids.'

That's what worried Danni. He was a man she could never trust.

CHAPTER 21

The choir

Dinah, Marcus and Sheena were first to arrive at the community centre. The teenagers helped Billy to set out the chairs for practice. Then Marcus hurried outside to help Esther with her piano and boxes of music.

'Hi, Esther,' he said as she climbed out of her car. He felt a slight tinge of fantasy when he saw her legs in black stockings beneath a short, body-contour dress. Her hair was swept back into a ponytail. With such a bright face, she looked like a girl closer to his own age.

'Hello, Marcus,' she answered with a smile from red-painted lips. 'I'll need you to play for me this evening. I want to be able to conduct and listen to how everyone is singing. The concert is coming up in a few weeks. We've still got a lot of work to do.'

'Sure, no problem.'

He lifted the piano from the back seat then waited for Esther to bend over and pick up a plastic box containing sheet music. Suddenly, she stopped to watch as a car drove into the car park. Marcus looked on for a moment, then carried the piano into the building.

As Esther directed operations, Marcus, knowing all the current songs they intended to use for the concert, played the piano. She may have looked stunning this evening, but Esther's temper was short, her nerves too easily frayed. Several times she stopped the choir during the first song, *Lifted*, only to be restarted from the beginning.

'Come on, folks, this sounds terrible. You're not together. Carrie, you're flat. Sheena, so are you. I need the basses to lighten up, you're drowning out the other parts. Let's start again. We must get this one right before we do anything else. Marcus, play us in again.'

Esther halted the singing of *Lifted* twice more before she grudgingly moved on to the next song.

Dinah eventually relaxed as they sang through *Penny Lane, Good Day Sunshine* and *Rehab*. She could see that Esther was stressed, and young Carrie was bearing the brunt of her wrath. At least, this evening it was all about the music and singing. Talk had petered out regarding Mandy and whatever had happened or didn't happen to her. No one mentioned the finding of the man in the sewer. Perhaps they were all spooked when the bizzies came knocking at their doors.

Of course, tonight Nathan was playing as his other self, or herself. Dinah found it disgusting, a man dressed as a woman. That's all he was, as far as she was concerned. He may be taking hormones and planning to have a sex change, but to her the whole idea was revolting. She was certain it was against God's will. But what could she say about it? Nothing. Not in these times with all this political correctness about discrimination. She would be the one out of order, not some lad in a dress. By now, they should be used to seeing him, Nathan, or Katrina as she called herself, prancing into the hall, but the sight never failed to turn heads. The females looked bemused, while the older men had disbelief smeared across their faces. And to top it all, this evening, Nathan lolloped in with a new girl in tow.

CHAPTER 22

Beth

Beth's hand was shaking as she smoked another fag. What the hell had she been thinking, agreeing to sing in a bloody choir? Of all the whacky things to do. And yet she had washed her hair and put on the best clothes she possessed: a fresh pair of jeans and a plain woollen jumper. She had never really worn make-up; never had the need when she'd spent most of her adult life in prison. There was some facial cleansing fluid in her bathroom, and she used that with some bog roll to remove the blackheads on her cheeks and nose. Her dirty fair hair needed cutting, never mind styling, and she didn't own a hair dryer. She had to potter about the flat until it dried on its own.

She brushed her teeth twice to kill the smell of tobacco. Beth could hardly believe she was going to so much trouble for a lad to walk her across the estate to a bloody choir practice. Surprisingly, she felt butterflies in her tummy. She felt elated that someone had found her friend-worthy.

There was a knock on the door, and God, she checked herself in the mirror for the umpteenth time. When she opened the door Beth jumped back, startled by the person smiling at her.

'Hiya! All set?'

'Fuck, Nathan, is that you?' she said, unable to prevent the smirk overtaking her face.

'Yep, it's me, love. I prefer Katrina when I'm dressed like this.'

Katrina wore a short tunic-style dress in a black floral print, fine tights and a pair of black ankle boots with a Cuban heel. Her wig was a blend of blond and dark brown in a pixie style, and she topped off her look with a black denim jacket and a strap bag.

'You look…'

'What? Say it, Beth love, don't be shy.'

'Fucking amazing!'

Aside from the clothing, Beth was taken by the quality of Katrina's make-up. It had taken skill to achieve such a look. The voice was still a giveaway, but if they were meeting for the first time, Beth would have no suspicions that Katrina was not a woman.

'I try my best. Haven't had the op yet, obviously.' She clasped her crotch to emphasise the point. 'But someday the NHS will call my name.'

Beth's previous encounter with a transgender person had been in Styal Prison, but Angie had never looked like this, more like a sheep farmer in a cheap dress.

'Are you going to stand and gawp at me all bloody night, or are you ready to go?'

Beth closed her door behind her, and Katrina took her by the arm as they headed for the community centre. When they entered the single-storey building, Beth was not surprised to see heads turning. Katrina was obviously a sight to behold – she was probably the hottest-looking female in the room. Then she realised that Katrina's arrival was not what had people staring. It was her. She was the stranger. They were well used to seeing Katrina but not hanging on the arm of a plainly dressed woman. Suddenly, Beth felt self-conscious, her cheeks warmed, and her gaze met the floor. She hadn't felt this awkward since her first day at New Hall Prison when she was greeted by catcalls, hisses and threats of what they were going to do with fresh pussy.

'Esther, this is Beth. She's new on the estate. She'd like to join us.'

Beth stood next to Katrina and before a glamorous woman who gradually summoned a smile.

'Beth, you're very welcome to join us. Nathan, I mean Katrina, might have told you already that we are rehearsing for a concert. It's a bit late for you to get to know all the songs but if you can catch up, you will be welcome to take part. How does that sound?'

'Great.' Beth remembered to smile. She was not standing before a cop or a prison governor and therefore a smile was quite appropriate.

Katrina led her to a chair in the back row and sat next to her. Beth felt a peculiar comfort when Katrina took her hand and squeezed it gently. Then a woman seated in front turned around and spoke to her.

'Where are you, love?'

Beth offered a confused stare.

'Where are you living?'

'Oh, Deeside Crescent,' she replied.

'Not far from me then. I'm in Ribble Lane. I'm Mary.'

'Beth.'

'Nice to meet you, love.'

Several more introductions followed, and each name and face began to merge with another until Esther brought the whole choir to order and Katrina handed her several sheets of music. At first, she was self-conscious about raising her voice to sing and so merely listened to the others. Gradually, in songs that she recognised, she felt herself singing along and suddenly she was enjoying herself. Esther glanced at her several times, although Beth thought she was a rather stern-looking woman.

By the end of practice, Beth was inwardly pleased that she had come along. It was the most joyous experience she'd had in years.

'OMG,' said Katrina in a more camp tone than Beth had so far heard from her, 'you have a fantastic voice. You were great!' Katrina waved her hand in front of her face as if to quell her tears. 'And Esther loves you. I can tell. She kept looking over at you.'

'Maybe she thought I sounded rubbish.'

'No, love, she knows we've found a singer in you, a real Cilla.'

Beth wasn't used to praise. Who in her life had ever said well done? Not a fucking soul. And here was a lad, a girl or whatever, whom she'd only just met, telling her she had a great voice. She thought she was a hardened woman, but she couldn't help the tears welling in her eyes.

'Bloody hell, Beth, I didn't mean to make you cry, love.' Katrina carefully wiped Beth's cheeks with her fingers and thumbs.

Beth tried to laugh them away.

'It's all right, I'm fine.'

They walked together across the park, Katrina once again hanging on Beth's arm like a schoolgirl.

'Everyone seems nice.'

'Most of them are,' said Katrina, 'but there are a few you have to watch out for. I'll tell you more as you get to know them. There are things on this estate that you need to know about.'

'What kind of things?'

They had reached the centre of the park where several paths intersected. As they turned left, a figure appeared in front of them. Until that moment, he had been hidden by several bushes.

'Well, if it isn't the tranny, all dolled-up with no one to blow,' he said.

'Leave us alone, Justin,' Katrina said.

'Who's your mate?'

Justin was not tall, but he carried a lad's swagger, like a football hooligan backed by a hundred mates.

'None of your business.'

Katrina attempted to hurry Beth away. Beth was not frightened of a lad with a mouth on him.

'What do you call yourself this week? Eh? Kylie? Britney? Sexy Cindy?' he said.

'Fuck off, will ya?' Katrina said.

Justin was now blocking their path. Beth watched his eyes, at first mocking Katrina then looking disparagingly at her.

'We don't need perverts round here,' he continued. 'One minute you're dressed as a slag, the next you'll be fondling the kids in the play park.'

'Why don't you fuck off, son?' snapped Beth. 'Go home and play with yourself.'

'Who the fuck are you? Telling me what to do. You think I don't know what you are?'

Katrina's head jerked backwards as Justin's fist caught her nose and mouth and blood spewed over her dress. Beth was about to retaliate, but Katrina held firm to her arm.

'Don't, Beth. Not worth it,' Katrina cried, as Justin's spittle landed on her face.

'We don't need your sort in Treadwater. Both of you.' Justin, hands in his pockets, walked nonchalantly away.

'Come on, Katrina. Let's get you cleaned up,' Beth said.

'I told you there were people to look out for on this estate.'

As they continued their journey home, Beth was irked by Justin's claim that he knew what she was.

CHAPTER 23

Stan and Hannah

Hannah enjoyed meeting the new girl. It was great to see more people joining the choir. She hadn't got to say much more than her name to Beth when she noticed Stan glaring at her. She wasn't supposed to chat with the other women, and certainly not to a stranger. She knew that Stan was scared in case she told someone what he did to her. But it was too late now just to tell on him. It was way past the time when she craved help and rescue. She was too old and had suffered for too many years. Long gone were the times when she'd considered running away from him and starting a new life with someone who would love and care for her. She had given up on the notion that Mark or Susan would finally see that their father was a brute and come to save her. Mark was seldom home, but on his visits, he only saw the upbeat Stan eager to talk about the army. Like father like son, she prayed that wasn't so. Susan took her parents for granted. She was self-absorbed and would never notice that anything was wrong with her mother. Even in those days when she came home from school to see her mother in tears and nursing a bruise on her cheek, her father could never be to blame for it; not a clean, tidy and upright soldier.

'Who is she?' Stan asked coldly as they walked home.

Their house wasn't far from the community centre on the eastern side of the park. Stan usually walked much faster than Hannah could manage, but he slowed to her pace to pursue his interrogation.

'Beth,' she said.

'What else?'

'What do you mean?'

'What is she?'

'I don't know, Stan. She seems nice.'

Hannah's feet were hurting. She struggled to keep up with his pace but knew there would be trouble if she let go of his arm. He'd promised to buy her new shoes six months ago, but she was too frightened to remind him.

'What did you tell her?' he asked.

'Nothing.'

'Are you sure? Don't lie to me.'

'I'm not lying, Stan. Esther started the practice. I didn't tell the girl anything.'

'You'd better not. Too much talk on this estate causes trouble.'

He brushed her away and hurried on at his own pace. Hannah, at last, could slow down and pause for a breath. There was nothing new in him asking what she had talked about with a stranger, but he had never expressed a concern before about causing trouble on the estate. She wondered what he meant by it.

CHAPTER 24

Esther

It niggled Esther all the way through choir practice. She had seen him arrive in that car. The same car she'd noticed a week ago with young Carrie sitting inside. It was Ian Bankhead's car. He was at least forty years old. Carrie, surely, was only fifteen.

She couldn't get it out of her mind during the singing and realised that she'd taken it out on Carrie, as if it was her fault. But Ian should know better. As far as she knew he had children of Carrie's age. She tried telling herself that it must've been quite innocent, there was nothing in it, but then she recalled the look on Carrie's face when she saw her. A rabbit caught in the headlights, startled from whatever she had been saying to Ian Bankhead.

By the end of practice, Esther had decided to have a quiet word with Ian about Carrie. If there was nothing between them that was fine, but God, he was breaking the law if he had laid a hand on her. Then she considered telling someone on the choir's committee. Did they even deal with this kind of issue? Surely, the answer to that question was yes. As a community organisation the choir must adhere to child protection rules. They should be safeguarding the lives of children who were members of the choir.

Despite her growing anxiety, the singing tonight had been impressive. It was hard to believe how far they had come in a few short years. This evening they had once again sung through the entire song list she intended for the concert. Old songs as well as the modern all sounded great. They had even taken to the couple of hymns she had tentatively introduced, *Shine Jesus Shine* and *Amazing Grace*. Their singing would rival any bespoke gospel choir. If they kept this up, she would think about them entering competitions; regionals at first, obviously, but who knows, by next year they could be singing in a national festival.

The new girl, Beth, was a bit timid at first, but by the end of the night she was singing her heart out. She had a reasonable voice and was worth considering as a future soloist. Esther had hoped to have a chat with Beth, but she left straight away with Katrina. There was always someone wanting to have their say to Esther at the end of practice, while she had been hoping to speak with Dinah. She thought that Dinah might be the most discrete person to discuss the Carrie-Ian situation with. But she missed her leaving the hall too.

Marcus was the only member who had stayed behind to tidy up and to carry her piano out to the car. She was very fond of the teenager. One of the great success stories of the Treadwater Community Choir. He had real musical talent, both singing and playing instruments, and she knew that choir involvement had rescued him from street gangs and probably drugs too. She was aware also that he had a crush on her. Other members joked and teased him about being the teacher's pet, and she saw how he looked at her and how he always hung behind at night to help her clear up. But she was more than thirty years older, older than his mother, Dinah. Besides, she wasn't looking for romance of any kind. Her one obsession nowadays was this damned choir.

Struggling to carry her box of sheet music, her handbag and her car keys, Marcus came to her rescue. As he took the box from her, behind him she saw Ian getting into his car and Carrie opening the passenger door. Quite deliberately, Esther called out.

'Goodnight, Carrie, see you on Sunday!'

Carrie looked over and nervously ran her hand through her hair. She didn't reply, but Esther had demonstrated that she knew what Carrie was doing. When she had thanked Marcus and said goodnight, she climbed into her car but waited for Ian to drive away. Tonight, she thought, I'm going to follow this pair and find out exactly what is going on.

CHAPTER 25

Tara

Tara watched from the side of the room, within earshot but out of sight of the journalists. She had been asked to do so. Tweedy did not want his DI to be on show to the public. He was considering another direction for her regarding this case, and being easily recognisable would jeopardise his plans. She listened as Tweedy and Murray faced the media.

'We are appealing for information,' Tweedy began in his usual sedate tone, 'in relation to the finding of a woman's body on the M57, westbound carriageway close to junction seven on the evening of Tuesday, 3 March. If you were driving on the M57 at any time that evening, did you see anything that seemed peculiar? Did you see any vehicles stopped on the hard shoulder at any time that day? Does anyone have dashcam footage of driving on that carriageway on the evening of Tuesday, 3 March?

'We are also interested to hear from any member of the public who may have information relating to the identity of the woman found on the motorway. If someone you know has gone missing and their disappearance has not been reported to police, I would urge you to get in touch with us at St Anne Street station. If anyone has information regarding the leaving of the body on the M57, please pass that information on to us too.

'I would like to move on to the finding of a man's body on the Treadwater Estate on Wednesday, 11 March. The man has been identified using DNA records as Olev Eesmaa, aged twenty-two, and of no known address. Mr

Eesmaa was an Estonian national and had been living in the UK since June 2014. As far as we are aware, the deceased had spent time living in the Greater Manchester area.'

Murray, seated next to Tweedy, held up an A4-sized photo of the victim. The picture had been taken from police records.

'Does anyone recognise this man?' Murray said. 'If so, please contact us here at St Anne Street. Does anyone know where Mr Eesmaa had been staying in Liverpool or why he might have been on the Treadwater Estate? I would like to make a special appeal to residents of the Treadwater Estate. Did anyone notice suspicious activity recently, particularly in the Trent Lane area and the adjacent park?

'To conclude, if any member of the public has information that could lead us to apprehending the perpetrators of these vile murders, please get in touch with Merseyside Police. Thank you.'

A barrage of shouted questions followed, but Tweedy was unfazed and merely selected a television reporter seated close by.

'Are these deaths related?' a young woman asked, after identifying herself as a reporter for BBC Merseyside.

'That is one line of inquiry, but at this time we are not ruling anything out,' Tweedy answered.

The questions continued.

'Are the deaths drug-related?'

'Gang related?'

'Are both victims foreign nationals?'

Tweedy raised an eyebrow at that question. It never failed to amaze him how professional journalists did not listen to facts when presented to them. He'd told them at the outset that they had no information on the ID of the female victim. He called a halt to proceedings, thanked everyone for their time then left the room with Murray following.

Tara caught up with them back in the operations room. Telephones were already ringing around the office.

'I have arranged for a mobile incident room to be set up on the Treadwater Estate,' Tweedy announced to his team of detectives. 'I want this picture of Mr Eesmaa circulated with an appeal for information. Surely somebody on that estate knows about this killing. Even if the victim had been killed elsewhere, someone on the estate must know why he was dumped in a sewer on Trent Lane. Tara, may I have a word in private?'

She followed her boss into his office and sat down. She wasn't sure whether she was in for a telling off about her lack of progress in the case or if another task was about to be piled on top of her current workload. Tweedy sat at his desk with his hands folded in front of him. Tara was always taken by the man's old-fashioned traits. The word gentleman seldom applied nowadays, but Tweedy displayed a genteel manner despite the horrid circumstances in which they had to work.

'Tara, I've been thinking about the suggestion that Alan made the other day.'

'Sir?'

'The idea of placing an officer on the Treadwater Estate to see if we can unlock what seems to be going on there.'

'Yes, sir.'

'I haven't decided yet, but if it would be advantageous to have an officer on the inside then you would be my obvious choice.'

'Yes, sir.'

'You know the place well, have experience of working along with the public and you understand exactly what is required of the operation. What do you think?'

'I'm worried that I might be recognised, sir. I was the first detective at the scene last week, I've already done some door-to-door inquiries and, besides this case, I've dealt with several other high-profile incidents on Treadwater.'

'I understand that, Tara, but I think it best if you do it rather than Alan or John. You're more likely to strike up contacts with people. And you would be more discrete than anyone else. There would be too much work involved in bringing another officer onto the case even with experience of working undercover.'

'I understand that, sir, but I'm not convinced that an undercover operation will be of much benefit to us. We're still not sure who or what we are looking for. Treadwater may not be at the centre of these crimes.'

'Well, let's just keep it as an option for now. We'll see how the mobile incident room performs and whether we get much response from the public appeal.'

'Yes, sir.'

She breathed a sigh on leaving Tweedy's office. Her mood wasn't helped by walking into Murray as he played havoc with their new photocopier. He was attempting to run off 300 copies of the photo and the appeal for information on Olev Eesmaa.

'I hear you're not coming with us to Treadwater tomorrow, ma'am,' he said, randomly pressing buttons on the machine with no effect.

'No thanks to you,' she snapped. 'How the hell am I going to live on Treadwater without being recognised as a bizzie?'

'You could always dye your hair or wear a wig.'

'Oh, that's great. Maybe a pair of sunglasses and a trench coat?'

The photocopier burst into life and blank pages began piling into the tray. Tara smirked then walked on.

By late afternoon, the team of detectives had fielded two-dozen phone calls, most of them from cranks, a couple from psychics claiming to know the location of more bodies, several complaints about the police presence in the Netherton area, and only three that were of interest.

One call, taken by Tara, came from a witness to the incident on the M57. The woman, a sales representative, had been driving home late and recalled overtaking a white van as it swerved onto the motorway from a slip road. She noticed that one of the rear doors was open. Tara thanked the woman and noted her contact details in case they needed to speak with her again.

Two further calls, one taken by Murray, the other by Wilson, were anonymous callers. Both claimed that there was a connection between the female found on the M57 and the Treadwater Estate, and Wilson got a suggested name for the female victim – Mandy Wright had recently disappeared from her home on the estate. The detectives looked at each other in amazement when they related similar information from their callers. Murray delivered the news to Tara in the style of a stand-up comedian hitting the punchline.

'So, we at last have a connection to the estate and between both victims,' said Tara.

CHAPTER 26

Justin

There were times when Justin wandered as far as Formby and Southport. He would hop on a bus and get off in a quiet district with big houses – not too big, just a better standard than he was used to on Treadwater. In the mornings, he could start off at Aintree or Melling, then meander to Maghull, Sefton and Lydiate, and by late afternoon he was beside the sea at Crosby. The area wasn't so important just so long as there were big houses, with postboxes attached to walls or gateposts. People were so fucking careless. If he followed the postman on his rounds, keeping a discreet distance, he could have the mail back out of those damned boxes and sometimes it would lead to money. He knew a guy up in town who would pay for information taken from credit card statements or anything with bank details.

Justin was amazed to discover how many people there were who still put cash in the mail. Mostly, he found it in a birthday card from a gran to her grandchild, but some businesses were daft enough to post cash. On a good week, with finds of cash and maybe a few bank details to sell, Justin could make three hundred quid. He spent most of it on blow, but it was easy money.

For more than a year, he'd had to venture further from Treadwater. There had been a crackdown on his kind of pursuits on the estate. It hadn't come from the bizzies either. No, there were folks living around him who had decided to kick all the pushers, gangs, whores and hooligans out of Treadwater. He didn't know who they were, these self-appointed lawmen, but some of his mates had been threatened and had to clear off the estate. There were rumours also that the guy they fished out of the drain had crossed somebody on the estate. The woman killed on the motorway may also have come from Treadwater.

Justin sifted through his takings as he walked along. Anything of interest, he stuffed into a rucksack. Envelopes and junk mail were dumped in litter bins as he passed them on the street. He worked alone. All his mates had fled the estate, and his girlfriend, Karen, had gone off with some guy she'd met at college. Now he had to fend for himself. There was no one to watch his back.

He would be happy to do his bit for these mysterious vigilantes. Shit like that guy Nathan, who thinks he's a girl, should be put down. Fucking weirdo, prancing around the streets in a dress. Smacking him in the face wasn't enough for the likes of him or the cheeky cow who was with him. He hadn't seen her before, but she needed to be taught a lesson. The rumour was that she was an ex-con, a resettled offender as they described them nowadays. He didn't need her kind in Treadwater.

He bought two bottles of cider from the shop and a special fried rice from the Chinese takeaway then hurried home to his flat. Once indoors, he opened one of the bottles and took a drink. He hadn't had anything to eat or drink since leaving home at ten that morning. Buster, his bull terrier, sniffed around his feet. He needed to be fed. There was only one tin of dog food left in the cupboard, so he mixed it with some of his fried rice and set it on the kitchen floor.

'There you go, Buster, get that into ya.'

He didn't bother with a plate and scoffed the remainder of his meal directly from the plastic carton. This evening, he had the cider to enjoy and a match on the telly. There was nothing else to do round here anymore.

Outside his flat, a man strolling by glanced at the curtainless window and saw the glare of a television within a darkened room. He knew who lived inside. Another candidate worthy of consideration.

CHAPTER 27

Tara

Tara was ensconced at St Anne Street station reviewing the information received from the public appeal. Several colleagues, including Murray and Wilson, were operating from the mobile incident room set up on the Treadwater Estate. She was hoping for a breakthrough from their endeavours, anything to avoid her having to live undercover in the place. A flat had already been acquired for her should Tweedy decide that the operation was necessary.

This morning, however, she had insisted on visiting the address they had for the alleged victim from the M57. Murray and Wilson had accompanied her to Sycamore Drive, to an end-of-terrace house next to a row of lock-up garages. Climbing from the unmarked car, Tara was struck by the thought of how close the house sat to the scene of her first murder investigation on this estate. It was only a few yards from where the teenager, Audra Bagdonas, had been found. Shivers coursed through her slight frame just thinking of it.

Wilson carried a ram for breaking into the house if they did not get a reply. So far, they knew little about Mandy Wright except that she lived in Sycamore Drive and had gone missing. Apparently, no one they knew of had seen her for several weeks. Her name had drawn a blank on the missing persons database.

Murray banged on the front door. At the lounge window vertical blinds were closed. The three officers did little but stare at each other as they awaited a reply. Murray tried again with his fist on the door.

'Police! Open the door please.'

Tara repeated the call through the letter box. She couldn't see any signs of life within the house.

'Right, John. Break it open.'

Wilson thrust the heavy ram at the door, just below the lock. A single strike and the door swung open and bounced off the inner wall.

'Hello! Police!' Tara marched into the hall and thrust open the first door she came to.

Murray stepped ahead of her into the lounge.

'Clear,' he said.

Wilson proceeded to the kitchen. He shouted that it also was clear. The upstairs was deserted. The entire house held an aroma of stale cigarette smoke. The walls of the lounge and hall were stained brown with nicotine. A layer of dust covered the wooden furniture in the lounge and the glass table upon which sat a large-screen television. The house was reasonably tidy. There were no signs of a hasty exit by the occupant or occupants.

It was soon established that Mandy had lived alone. In the master bedroom, Tara noted a double bed, standalone wardrobe and a set of drawers. Clothes hanging inside the wardrobe were female, quite trendy, but not expensive labels. In two of the drawers, she found rather more adventurous lingerie and a couple of sex toys. She replaced them before her colleagues had a chance to do their usual sniggering at such things.

Above the bed, a large frame held an array of photographs. Two holiday shots showed a pretty girl, mid-twenties, wearing summer clothes. Others depicted several groups of young people and there was one of a toddler walking unaided. Tara guessed that at least one of the photos contained Mandy, but they had no conclusive ID. At this stage, she could not be certain that this was the home of the woman who was found on the M57.

Murray called from downstairs.

'Ma'am, you should look at this.'

Tara and Wilson came into the lounge. Murray stood next to a wooden display unit, the shelves empty but for several glass vases and a pile of *Reader's Digest* magazines. He had opened the drawer at the base of the unit. It was brimming with papers, letters, junk mail and envelopes. In his hand he held what looked like a security pass.

'A gym membership card for Mandy Wright.' He handed it to Tara.

It held a photograph, and the membership was still current. Now she knew what Mandy looked like, but she wasn't convinced that this was a picture of the woman lying in the city morgue.

'I can't say for sure that it's our murder victim. The face of the woman from the motorway was so badly crushed,' said Tara, passing the card to Wilson. 'I think we'll need to get some of Mandy's DNA from here to be certain.'

In the master bedroom Murray found a hairbrush from which they could get a hair sample for DNA comparison with the dead woman. They brought all the paperwork they'd found back to the station. Wilson volunteered to sift through it for any clues to the whereabouts of Mandy Wright.

At her desk, Tara studied the information passed to her by Murray and Wilson. It was the lack of something useful that worried her. What was going on within that estate that people were not coming forward, even now when they had identified Olev Eesmaa and perhaps Mandy Wright? Mandy lived in Treadwater, and yet no one was willing to talk about it.

CHAPTER 28

Carrie, Ian and Esther

They shared a can of cola and a bag of salt and vinegar crisps. The car windows were lowered to dispel the condensation from inside after their lovemaking. Ian's car was partially hidden by trees and bushes in the deserted country lane. In the closing darkness, Carrie rested her head on Ian's shoulder and dreamed of a time when they could be together permanently, without the secrecy and the danger that he could be arrested for having sex with an underage girl. She loved the idea of becoming Mrs Bankhead, having his children and living in a nice house far away from Treadwater. But Ian refused to discuss it. He told her that his ex-wife would raise merry hell if she even got a hint that he had found someone else. Carrie then worried if things would ever change. Would they still be coming out here to shag after she had turned sixteen? She ventured another thought that had been troubling her.

'I think Esther knows about us.'

Ian shifted abruptly, and Carrie had to lift her head from his shoulder.

'Why do you say that?' He sounded alarmed, more than she would have expected. He was always such a cool guy, confident with her, relaxed and in control.

'She saw us the other night, after practice, getting into the car.'

'So? I was just giving you a lift home. That's our story, remember? You haven't told anyone, have you?'

'No, but it was the way that Esther looked at me.'

'What do you mean? She wasn't happy with your singing, maybe she was still cross.'

'She looked like my mum would look when I go out in a short dress, or I'm wearing too much make-up. Like she doesn't approve.'

'I told you we need to be careful,' said Ian. 'Maybe it's best not to see each other after choir practice. If Esther has noticed, you can bet some of those nosey gits in the choir have noticed too.'

'But that means we only see each other once a week. You're busy the rest of the time.'

'It's only for a few months until you're sixteen.'

'And what about your ex, won't she still cause trouble for us after that?'

Ian paused for a second and looked intently into the teenager's eyes. They were eyes that trusted him, that loved him, so young, and still quite innocent. He smiled and stroked her hair.

'I was thinking that once you're sixteen we could go away together. We could get a place of our own in Manchester or Leeds. Would you like that?'

A smile broke on her face and eagerly she leaned over and kissed him.

'Yes. That would be lovely.'

They hugged each other.

'So, for now let's just cool things a bit. It won't be long.'

Ian raised the windows but as he turned to start the engine Carrie had removed her top waiting for him to love her once more.

* * *

Esther arrived home, tossed her keys on the kitchen bench and went straight for her open bottle of gin. Her worst fears had been confirmed. She'd waited outside Carrie's school. Ian Bankhead's car was parked a little way off on the opposite side of the road. It had taken three days and three attempts to time it right. Then Carrie came hurrying through the school gates, rushing past the other pupils, oblivious to Esther looking on. She went directly to Ian's Volvo, jumped in and a few moments later they drove off.

She had followed, no real need to keep her distance, because she didn't believe that Ian would recognise her car. They drove into the countryside, towards Sefton Village; then on Lunt Road, Ian turned onto a narrow lane, a secluded spot in amongst trees and surrounded by fields. Esther didn't bother to follow; she had enough proof. Ian Bankhead should have more sense. She'd checked her choir records to confirm that Carrie was under sixteen.

Nursing a generous pouring of gin and tonic, Esther wondered what to do next. There weren't many options. She wasn't intent on ruining someone's life, but she didn't want scandal within her choir. Either she would have a word with Ian, or if that did no good, she would speak to Carrie's parents.

CHAPTER 29

Raymond and Mary

Mary answered the ringing of her doorbell to be confronted by a burly man in a grey suit.

'Detective Sergeant Murray, Merseyside Police. Sorry to disturb you, but we are conducting house-to-house inquiries regarding the two incidents of murder in the area.'

Mary froze. The very idea of a policeman calling at her door was enough to get her nerves going without being asked about murder. She turned around and called for Raymond.

Murray held out an A4 sheet of paper showing a picture of Olev Eesmaa.

'Do you know this man, or have you seen him around the estate?'

Mary was shaking her head doubtfully when Raymond came and stood beside her. Murray repeated his introduction and asked Raymond if he recognised Olev Eesmaa.

'Can't say that I do,' said Raymond.

'His body was recovered from the sewer just around the corner in Trent Lane.'

Raymond shook his head.

'Heard about it, but I don't know him. Never saw him around the place.'

Murray then produced a second picture, this time of Mandy Wright.

'Do either of you recognise this person?'

Mary breathed in sharply. Her hand went to her mouth. Murray noted her reaction, but Raymond jumped in.

'Don't know her.'

'Is it possible that you've seen her around the estate?'

Raymond shook his head, and now he held Mary firmly by the wrist.

'Don't think so,' he said. 'Is she the woman who was found on the motorway?'

'Can't say at the moment, sir. Her name is Mandy Wright. She lives in Sycamore Drive but has gone missing. You're sure you don't recognise her?' Murray was looking at Mary as he asked the question. She seemed a woman afraid to speak out of turn.

'No, never seen her before,' said Raymond.

'If you do have any information that could help us find this woman, or if you know anything regarding this man please contact us. We have a mobile incident room just down the street from here, or you can phone this number.' Murray handed Raymond a card.

Raymond closed the door and was fully intent on resuming his gardening, but Mary blocked his way.

'Why didn't you tell him?' Her face had paled, her eyes watering.

'Mary, we don't want to get involved.'

'But the police, surely we can tell them what we know?'

'No. Stay out of it, Mary. If we tell the police that we know her, they'll start asking more questions. We're not getting involved. It'll only cause more trouble.'

'But, Raymond–'

'No, Mary! Enough! There's people on this estate who wouldn't like it if we talked to the bizzies.' He barged past her and resumed his potting in the garden.

Mary broke down in tears. She went to the lounge window and looked outside. The policeman was slowly walking along, noting something down as he went. She was tempted to go after him, to tell him what she knew about Mandy, but Raymond would be furious. Perhaps he was right. Better to stay out of it. Besides, what exactly did she know? She knew Mandy well enough from around the estate, even before they had joined the choir. Mandy was a great singer; she had a soulful voice and a fantastic range. But she didn't seem to get along with Esther. It started as friendly banter during practice, then open criticism of each other and finally a blazing row one morning in the mini-market. The two of them were yelling obscenities at each other.

Mary hadn't been a witness to it, but it was the talk of the choir. She never saw Mandy after that. Mandy didn't attend practices and Esther refused to say whether she had resigned or not. It was Raymond who told her that Mandy was gone. She'd taken off somewhere, he'd told her. But then a woman's body was found on the motorway and Mary immediately thought of poor Mandy. Now Raymond had ordered her not to say anything to the police. They didn't even talk about Mandy now at choir practice. It was as if she had never existed, had never been their friend. Mary didn't like it; it wasn't right.

CHAPTER 30

Wilson

DC John Wilson wandered across the football pitch in the park and couldn't help reminiscing of his childhood days when he seemed to spend every hour out here playing football with his mates. They dreamed, of course, of one day playing at Anfield or Goodison depending on whether you were red or blue. Today the pitches were deserted. Kids didn't seem to play outdoors anymore, not even a game of football. He felt old.

Up ahead, and coming towards him, he saw a mother with two young kids, one pushing a doll in a buggy, the other making a hard job of moving on his bicycle fitted with stabilisers. The mother wasn't unattractive, but she looked fraught. Her pink hair sailed in the breeze. She looked tiny when she reached Wilson.

'Hi, there. I'm Detective Constable Wilson.'

'I know who you are,' said Danni with a wry smile. She ran her fingers through her hair, an attempt to control it, and smiled again.

'You do?'

'It's me, Danni Pearce? We were in the same class at school. You used to chase me and my friends off your sodding football pitch!' She waved her hand over the green space where they stood.

'Ah, Danni! I didn't know you.'

'No kidding. Must be my pink hair. But look at you. You've done well for yourself.'

Wilson smiled as his mind skipped back ten years, trying to picture the younger Danni Pearce. He couldn't quite recall if they had ever gone out together. At the age of fourteen there were loads of girls to choose from. Could be they may have got together at a party, got drunk on cider, and had a quick snog before traipsing home. He wondered if that's how Danni remembered him.

'It's a job,' he replied, 'pays the bills. And how about you? These two yours?'

'Oh, they're mine all right. No one else would have them.'

Both kids were now moving ahead of their mother for the first time since coming out, just when she would have preferred them to wait for her.

'You still living round here?' Wilson asked.

'Yes. Didn't make it far. From Broad Oak to Trent Lane. That's the wrong direction even on this estate. You married now, John?'

'Divorced. Didn't work out, me a bizzie and her a nurse. We hardly saw each other. And what about you? Who's the proud dad of these two?'

'He's a prick by the name of Wayne Bennett. Didn't come from round here. Said he couldn't settle and took off back to Luton. Arsehole!'

'You're not bitter then?'

'How would you feel, left with two kids and no money?'

Wilson sensed it was getting too hot and personal. He asked the question he had originally intended before he discovered that he and Danni knew each other. From a loose-leaf folder he produced the photocopied picture of Olev Eesmaa and showed it to her.

'Do you recognise this bloke?'

Danni studied the page then shook her head.

'No, don't think so. Who is he?'

'He's the guy who was fished out of the sewer in Trent Lane. His name was Olev Eesmaa. We're trying to find out if he had a connection to Treadwater. Maybe he'd been staying with someone on the estate.'

'Can't help, sorry.'

'How about this woman?' Wilson showed a similar photocopy to Danni. 'Her name is Mandy Wright, lived on Sycamore Drive.'

Danni studied the picture but said nothing. Her hand went to her earlobe and fidgeted with a small gold stud.

'Is she familiar?'

'I've seen her about the place and that, but I don't know her. I'll have to go. The kids are getting too far ahead. I don't want them going on the road.' She hurried on.

Wilson watched her go and sensed that he had touched a nerve with Danni Pearce. She seemed glad to see him after all these years, but she could hardly get away fast enough. She was nice, though, despite the pink hair.

CHAPTER 31

Tara

The news from Treadwater was less than promising. A whole day with a mobile unit on site and not one resident from that damned estate had even stepped inside. Between them, Murray and Wilson had kept up house-to-house inquiries. They'd been armed with pictures of the two murder victims and had posted leaflets through the doors of those houses where they got no reply.

No one claimed to recognise the young Estonian Olev Eesmaa. No one remembered ever having seen him on the estate. Tara could understand that response because Olev may never have set foot in Treadwater until the time when he was killed. What flummoxed her was that no one claimed to know Mandy Wright. A few said that they had seen her around but had never spoken to her. Not one contact in the four years that Mandy had lived in Treadwater. Tara could not believe that was true. Somebody must know her. Even her next-door neighbours denied having ever spoken with her. Murray and Wilson had commented on the reactions of residents when they were shown Mandy's photo. They had cut short their discussion with the detectives, making some excuse to get away or to close their doors. One woman had seemed shocked and obviously recognised Mandy Wright. Her husband, however, spoke over his wife and denied any knowledge. Time and again this was the reaction they had encountered. Residents were not simply uncooperative, they were either frightened, or they were hiding something.

This view was shared by Murray, Wilson and Tweedy. Something weird was going on, Tara was convinced of it.

The number of phone calls in response to the public appeal for information had tailed off. It, too, had not been a roaring success. Yes, they got the name of Mandy Wright as a missing person, but it was not yet confirmed she was the woman found on the M57. Most of the calls they had received concerned the motorway death. Dozens of cars, lorries and vans had driven on the stretch of the M57 before the incident occurred. Unfortunately, they still had not identified the vehicle involved in transporting the victim. They had no information on how she came to be lying in the centre lane of the motorway. Had she been placed there deliberately? Was she thrown off a vehicle when it was moving, or had she fallen off in trying to escape? They had no answers.

She arrived home to laughter from Adele who was being chased around the living room by Kate. Tara dropped her coat and bag and joined in the fun.

'Tara!' Adele squealed. 'Help me. Mummy's trying to get me.'

The child ran behind the sofa then behind the curtains. Kate was bearing down on her.

'I'm trying to catch her so I can wash her hair,' said Kate. 'It's filthy. We've been baking and she's covered in flour and dough.'

'Come to me, Adele,' said Tara.

'Don't you dare take her side,' said Kate.

Adele's laughter filled the room as Tara jostled Kate out of the way. Then the child bolted from behind the curtains into Tara's arms.

'Yay! Can't get me now, Mummy.'

Tara swung her around while Kate stood watching, hands on hips.

'How about me washing your hair?' said Tara. 'Let Mummy have a rest, she is really old, you know.'

'OK, but no soap in my eyes.'

'I'll try.'

Tara carried her god-daughter to the bathroom, while Kate finished preparing the dinner. When the hair washing was complete, Adele was given her dinner then allowed to watch some DVDs in her room before finally, a 'lights out' and off to sleep. Kate and Tara sat down to a meal of baked salmon, spicy potato wedges and garden peas, washed down by a chardonnay. She was glad of a quiet moment to ask Kate's advice on something that was posing a problem for her.

'How do you think I could change my appearance?'

CHAPTER 32

Esther and Dinah

Esther phoned Dinah at work and invited her for coffee that same afternoon. Of all the choir members, Dinah was probably Esther's closest friend.

Dinah worked until three o'clock as a secretary at Treadwater Primary School. When she finished work, she hurried through a fine drizzle to Ribble Lane. As was her habit, Esther had the coffee ready to pour and a light snack of chicken tikka wraps, crisps and chocolate chip cookies laid out on the kitchen table. Dinah was always impressed by Esther's level of organisation. It was the reason why she had been so successful with the choir.

Despite no longer having to work full-time, although she did give private music tuition, Esther always looked immaculate even when merely pottering around her home. This afternoon, she wore a pair of trendy print leggings and a red tunic.

'Thanks for coming, Dinah,' she said warmly, kissing her friend on the cheek.

'No problem, love. It sounded very urgent this morning.'

'Let's get some coffee first and we can talk.'

Dinah removed her waterproof hoodie and sat down at the table. Esther poured the coffee into two mugs and sat opposite her friend. Neither the kitchen nor the table was at all spacious. Everything in a council house on Treadwater, no matter how skilfully designed, always appeared cramped. The table was squeezed between the fridge and the kitchen door.

'So, what's been happening?' Dinah asked. 'You haven't changed your mind on the song list for the concert, have you?'

'No… well yes, but that's not why I asked you here.' Esther sipped her coffee and watched Dinah saying a silent Grace before tucking into a chicken wrap. 'I want to tell you something that's been bothering me and to get your advice on what to do about it.'

Dinah waited for Esther to continue. She couldn't imagine what was coming next. She felt a slight twinge of nerves wondering if it concerned Marcus or Sheena.

'Young Carrie, she is only fifteen. She looks much older – her build and that wonderful hair she has, but she is definitely still a child.'

'Yes, I suppose she is.'

'I am fairly certain she is having a relationship with a man, a much older man.'

'Do you mean a sexual relationship?'

'Exactly that. What should I do, Dinah? Should I tell her parents? Should I speak to her alone?'

'You could have a word with her, but you're only her choir mistress, Esther. You shouldn't be the one having to deal with this.'

‘I know, but I feel that I do have a duty of care. She is a child, and if she’s having sex with an adult man then that person is breaking the law. He is a paedophile.’

‘Do you know this man?’ Suddenly Dinah was thinking again of her Marcus. But surely not. She would have noticed something. She’d never seen Marcus look particularly interested in Carrie or in any girl in the choir.

‘I do,’ Esther replied. ‘And that’s why I’m doubly concerned about how to deal with this.’

Dinah could hardly wait and yet dreaded to hear the name spoken. Surely not her Marcus.

‘It’s Ian Bankhead.’

‘Ian? But…’

‘What?’

‘It can’t be Ian,’ said Dinah, amazed. ‘Everyone is always hinting that he’s the most likely man for you, Esther.’

‘For me? What makes you think that, for goodness sake?’ Esther’s cheeks glowed red. Embarrassment replaced doubts over what to do. ‘Do you think I’m a cougar now? I must be at least ten years older than Ian.’

‘I’m sorry. I didn’t mean that anyone believes Ian and you… I’m sorry. Are you sure Ian and Carrie are seeing each other?’

‘Fairly sure, yes. She leaves choir practice with him. And I have followed them when he picked her up from school. They drove out by Sefton and turned into a country lane.’

‘Maybe it is quite innocent.’

‘Oh, come on, Dinah. No adult man should be alone in his car with a child who is not a relative. Even if they are not having sex, this kind of meeting should not be happening.’

‘In that case, it is not Carrie that we need to speak to, it’s Ian. We need to warn him about what he is doing.’

‘I don’t want a scandal, Dinah. I know it sounds selfish, but I am proud of my choir. I don’t want anything like this to spoil things.' Esther wiped a tear from her eyes with a napkin.

'If you'd prefer, I can speak to Ian. It won't seem like a choir issue then.'

'Would you? Dinah, that would be great.'

'Let's hope he sees the error of his ways. If not, then we will have to make him see.'

CHAPTER 33

Beth

It was almost noon. Beth was not an early riser when there was little to look forward to in the day. The room was bare. Her possessions amounted to a single bed and a set of drawers. Several nails in the wall allowed her to keep a few clothes on hangers. The floor was laminate, cold and hard; the walls, in need of painting, were a dull beige with numerous scuff marks. She felt relative comfort under a cheap duvet. There would be reason to get up if she thought a benefit payment would come today. Fat chance, more likely to be another letter requesting further information to complete the assessment. What was she supposed to do in the meantime? Food, she could get from the food bank, but what about money for booze and drugs?

Succumbing to another doze, she was startled awake by noises outside. It sounded like the door of a van closing. Then she heard raised voices, not angry, more of instruction followed by cheerful banter. The front door of her block squeaked open and banged against the inner wall. Male voices reverberated in the stairwell. She couldn't resist temptation any longer, rose from her bed and peered out of the window. A white van was parked outside, and furniture was being unloaded. In her pyjamas, she traipsed barefoot to her front door. When she opened it, a figure was standing with her back to her. Only when she spun around was Beth certain it was a female.

'Hi,' said the woman.

She looked of a similar age to Beth, quite short with a shapely petite body. She wore stressed blue jeans and a faded grey T-shirt. Her face was pretty with no make-up, her eyes blue, but most striking of all was her shaven head.

'Hi,' Beth replied. 'Are you moving in?'

'Yes, upstairs, 23c. I'm Claire.'

'Beth.'

They watched as two men carried a brown sofa up the stairwell. Then Claire followed, carrying two seat cushions.

'See you later, Beth.'

She closed her door and went back to bed. Seemed like the social used this place to house ex-offenders. That Claire looked every bit the jail candy as she had ever come across.

CHAPTER 34

Tara

Furniture had been delivered and some personal items, including carefully selected clothes. Tara placed them in the single wardrobe and set of drawers. She tried to make the place seem liveable, but it was gloomy, and it stank of stale tobacco and poo. Animal or human, she couldn't tell. No sooner had she closed the door on her colleagues who had helped her move in, and she was on her phone to St Anne Street station.

'I have some news for you, ma'am,' said Wilson. 'DNA results from samples taken at Mandy Wright's house – they do not match our victim from the M57.'

Bloody piss-poor timing.

'Bugger!' said Tara. 'So, we still don't know who she is. Now we have two murder victims and a missing person. What the hell am I doing here?'

'Ma'am, just putting you on speaker. Superintendent Tweedy and Murray are here.'

'If you're all there at the station then who is manning the mobile unit here on Treadwater?'

'All under control, Tara,' said Tweedy in his usual saintly tone. 'I take it you have settled in safe and sound?'

'Yes, sir. Can't help wondering just why I'm here now.'

'Why is that?'

'Well, sir, if Mandy Wright is not the woman lying in the morgue then there is precious little connection between this case and the Treadwater Estate.'

'But Olev Eesmaa's body was found there.'

'He didn't live here. No one seems to know him. The only link to the place is that his body was dumped in a sewer in Trent Lane. Apart from that the entire case has no connection to Treadwater. I could be wasting my time living here.'

'I would like you to give it a go for now, Tara,' said Tweedy. 'The feeling is that the residents on the estate seem reluctant to pass on information to us. It feels rather sinister to me. See if you can test the temperature of the place, as it were. I'll leave you now to get settled in. Take care, Tara.'

'Thank you, sir.'

She ended the call and couldn't help a petulant sigh as she flopped onto the well-worn sofa. The thought of having to live here for months or even weeks merely added to the frustration she felt over this damn case. This morning her main lead had been Mandy Wright. Now that she was not the body from the M57 meant that Tara had nothing. Mandy Wright's disappearance, it seemed, was not linked to the murders.

Her hand, instinctively, went to her head, her now bald head. What the hell had she been thinking, allowing Kate to do this to her?

'It's the only way, Tara,' Kate had said. 'Your hair is too short. If we dye it another colour, you'll still be easily recognisable. But if we shave it all off, it gives you a whole new persona, like you're a girl with attitude or someone who has been through a tough time.'

When Kate had finished, Tara had to agree. Either she wore a wig, or it all came off. A wig would be too risky. With a bald head she could pass herself as an ex-con.

Kate had suggested an ear or lip piercing to add to the bold appearance, but Tara refused. That was taking her job way too far. Without any make-up, however, she was less recognisable as Detective Inspector Grogan. Kate, though, wasn't finished. Rather than a complete absence of make-up, she suggested that Tara wore a very pale foundation and some greyish contouring below the eyes. When they had finished, Tara looked a sad person with a drug habit who had not known fresh air for months.

She hoped the ex-con role would help her burrow into the minds of some individuals on Treadwater. Her confidence increased when Murray told her that her new neighbour, Beth Chapman, was an ex-offender released on licence. If Tara could wheedle her way into Beth's confidence, then maybe it was a route to others on the estate and eventually a road to the truth. She realised it was a difficult first test to pass. Beth would detect any slip-up in Tara's ex-offender story because she was the one with experience of prison.

CHAPTER 35

Stan and Hannah

Hannah liked these moments in the day best. Stan was in his garden shed with his trains. A new model of some kind had arrived in the post this morning and it put him in a good mood. After lunch, he went outside to play with it. Alone in the lounge, Hannah could watch afternoon TV, a Father Brown mystery was on. She did some knitting and hummed one of the songs they'd been rehearsing at choir. It was a modern pop song, not something she would usually listen to, but it had a pleasant melody, and it suited her mood.

The doorbell rang. Suddenly, her period of tranquillity vanished. A shock rippled through her body. Close to panic, she hurried to the back door and was about to step outside to call Stan. But Stan hated to be disturbed. He would emerge from his shed in a foul temper, and she would bear the brunt of it.

The doorbell rang again. She closed the back door and went into the hall. Through the frosted glass of the door, two figures were visible. She didn't know what to do. The bell sounded again, and with each chime an indecision pulsed through her. Her hands trembled. She prayed for Stan to come back indoors. Then it would not be her fault. The figures remained at the door. She heard the muffled voices of two men.

Finally, she could no longer bear the anxiety. She put the chain on the door, opened it a crack and peered out. Two large men in suits smiled at her.

'Merseyside Police, love,' said Murray. 'Can we have a quick word?' He showed his warrant card to Hannah.

'Em, my husband is…'

'It's all right, we just want to ask a couple of questions. We're calling at every house. Would you mind opening your door?'

Hannah closed the door, released the chain, and reopened it although hardly much wider than before. Wilson showed Hannah the picture of Olev Eesmaa.

'Do you know this man, or have you seen him around the estate?'

Hannah's eyes widened in staring at the photo. The image meant nothing to her, but the fear on her face was giving them an entirely different view.

'His name is Olev Eesmaa, a young man from Estonia. His body was found in the sewer in Trent Lane. You may have heard about it.'

Hannah covered her mouth with her hand, and her face grew pale.

'No,' was all she managed to say.

'How about this woman?' asked Murray, holding out a picture of Mandy Wright.

Hannah trembled. She knew Mandy, of course she did. She looked behind her in hope, yet fearful too, that Stan would come to rescue her. The two policemen waited for her answer. Her only thought was that they had to go. They must leave before Stan came in. He would not be happy.

'No. I don't know anything.' She closed the door and leaned against it scarcely able to breathe.

Suddenly, the back door opened, and Stan came in. He saw her from the kitchen.

'What are you doing, Hannah?'

'Nothing, just catching my breath.' She prayed that the two policemen had gone, but she remained by the door to prevent Stan from seeing beyond her and through the window.

'Time for a cuppa,' he said.

She knew well that he wasn't going to make it.

'OK, I'll put the kettle on.' Still, she had not moved.

'What have you been doing to get out of breath? Was there someone at the door?'

She found it hard to lie, but she did not want to tell him.

'Well?' he said.

'Yes. Two policemen.'

'Police!'

Stan bounded down the hall and stood before her.

'What did they want? What did you tell them?'

Hannah could no longer contain herself; her nerves took over.

'Nothing, Stan. I didn't say anything, honest I didn't. They asked about the man that was found in Trent Lane. Then about Mandy. But I didn't say anything, please believe me!'

Hannah knew her tears meant little to him. He was well used to them. But she couldn't help herself. How else could she cope with his questioning? He slapped her on the face, and she cried out.

'Get the damned tea. If I find out you've told them anything, I'll give you a bloody good thumping.'

He pulled her arm and thrust her towards the kitchen. She staggered from one wall to another in the narrow hallway.

'When you've made my tea, you can go to your room. I don't want to see your ugly face again this day. And you just think about what you've done.'

'But, Stan, I haven't done anything.'

In the kitchen as the tea brewed in the pot, she cut the ham sandwiches in two with a bread knife. She hated Stan more than anything in the world.

CHAPTER 36

Katrina

Quite often late in the evening and if the weather was dry, Nathan, en femme as Katrina, ventured for a walk through the estate. It was quieter and safer now that the gangs had been cleared out. A few hellions remained, xenos she called them, xenophobic, homophobic bastards who believed that if you were homosexual you must be a child molester; if you were transgender you must be homosexual and therefore a child molester; if you were different you were weird and weird meant paedophile. Thugs, like Justin Boyle, were quick to use their fists, to spit and to threaten, but in Treadwater, thankfully, they were literally a dying breed. There were people on the estate who wouldn't tolerate Justin's behaviour. Nowadays, it was a case of reform or clear off. Ordinary people were at last standing up for the weak and vulnerable and she, Katrina, was the better for it. At times, though, she couldn't help wondering how long it would be before the old scum were replaced by new scum.

Tonight, she strolled through the lanes and drives on the western side of the estate, the places named after rivers. Whoever thought up the name Treadwater had not been far wrong. That's about all you could do here to survive, and survival was the only life on offer.

She wore a pair of five-inch heels – no point in anything less if she wanted to practice walking like a woman. The colour, neon pink, was chosen on a whim. Her legs were her best feature, and better looking than most of the women around Treadwater. She showed them off in sheer tights and a miniskirt of pale pink. Her silk blouse, with a keyhole front, wasn't sufficient to keep her warm, so a long woollen cardigan finished off her look. She'd spent an hour on her make-up. It was good practice for when she ventured to a club in the city. That only happened when she had the money and was feeling particularly daring.

It was after nine, but the streets were quiet. Several cars drove by, and a few dog walkers passed her on their way to the park. Katrina felt liberated. If only she could begin her transition for real – hormone treatment followed by the surgery. Then she would be the person she was always meant to be.

Katrina passed by the homes of fellow choristers. In a strange way, they were like family to her. The choir had been the saviour on this estate. Young and old had been brought together and respect had blossomed among them. She reached the house where Stan and Hannah lived. It was already in darkness. Some older people went to bed early. From Conwy Drive, she moved into Cherwell Avenue where Marcus and Sheena lived with their mum, Dinah. At Trent Lane, the place where they had found the bloke's body in the manhole, she shivered. Overlooking the spot was Danni's first-floor flat. The lights were still on. Maybe the kids hadn't gone to sleep. When she turned into Severn Way, her toes nipping in her shoes, Katrina passed Mary and Raymond's home, sitting immaculate between two drab properties. They always seemed a nice couple and had always been polite to him as Nathan but also to Katrina. Further along the street on the opposite side, she noticed the figure of a woman stepping out of a house. As Katrina drew nearer, she realised that it was Ian Bankhead's home. She didn't care much for him. He was a bit of a lad and fancied himself, although he had never upset her in any way. When the woman reached the pavement, Katrina couldn't help making eye contact. She smiled and called out.

'Hiya, Dinah love.'

'Hello, Nathan,' Dinah replied in a surly voice, hurrying on with her head down.

Katrina watched her rush away. At first, Katrina did not think anything of Dinah having just left Ian's house. But with her hurrying away, without any chat, she wondered what Dinah might have been doing there. Perhaps there was something going on between them.

As she headed towards home, she wondered if Dinah would ever manage to address her as Katrina. She was the only choir member reluctant to recognise her as a woman. Some people could never overcome their prejudice.

CHAPTER 37

Tara

Tara awoke surprised that she had managed any sleep at all, never mind eight and a half hours of it. She knew she had to get out and about on the estate. The answers she sought were not going to come knocking on the door. The temptation was to get showered and dressed and head off to St Anne Street station, but reality fell over her like a net dropped from above. Firstly, there was no shower in this flat, just a bath in need of scouring, if not replacing. Secondly, she would not be going to the station. The most she could do in that regard was to phone Murray for an update on the case.

After a stand-up wash at the basin and donning a pair of grey sweatpants and black vest, she had a breakfast of cornflakes followed by tea and a slice of toast. She listened intently for any movement within the building. She hoped that someone would stir, head out perhaps, and she could hurry after them to get her investigation started. While she breakfasted, she made the call to Murray. He was at his desk at St Anne Street.

'How was your first night?' he asked.

'Fine. Managed to sleep at least.'

'Made any new friends?'

'I met the ex-offender from downstairs, Beth. Seems all right, although she didn't say much.'

'You'll have to be careful if you're going to play the jailbird. She'll try to sniff you out.'

Tara laughed nervously.

'I hope that's not a euphemism.'

'Glad to hear you're in fine fettle, ma'am.'

'I will be as soon as I get some scented candles lit in this place. It stinks in here.'

'What's your plan for today?'

'Well, hopefully, I can have a conversation with someone. It's easy to see how people get lonely living alone in these places…'

She cut the call short when, from her window, she noticed Beth heading out. Grabbing her bag, then thinking the better of it, she took some cash and the flat key from her purse, left the bag and hurried outside. She walked briskly and soon caught up with Beth as she neared the junction of Deeside Crescent with Severn Way. Tara had rehearsed a habit of dispensing with pleasantries. Straight to the point with these people.

'Food bank on this estate?'

Beth, drawing on a roll-up and squinting through the smoke, turned to look at her. Tara felt straight away that she was being examined. She imagined Beth absorbing every inch of her: her look, her stance, her voice, even her smell. At least she was confident that she looked terrible. And her shaven head was stinging in the cold morning air.

Beth wore a navy puffer jacket, the worse for wear, and ripped jeans. Tara knew her to be just thirty-nine, but she didn't look well for it. She seemed malnourished.

In response to Tara's question, Beth pointed with fag in hand.

'This way,' she said.

Tara accepted it as an invitation to walk with her.

They'd covered the length of Severn Way, and Beth had said nothing more. If she was adopting an aloof attitude, then Tara would too.

'Where you from?' Beth said at last.

'Birkenhead.'

'Don't sound like you're from Birkenhead.'

'Spent a long time down south.'

'You got any gear?'

'No. Just about to ask you. Know anywhere round here I can get some?'

Beth didn't answer. They'd reached Trent Lane, the park ahead of them, the scene of the gruesome find in the sewer behind them. Tara took the chance.

'I heard a body was found in a sewer around here.'

'Don't know nothing about that. Been down there for ages, is all I heard.'

Another silence ensued, while Tara thought of the next question to get the conversation flowing. Beth was proving hard work.

'How long have you lived here?'

Beth disposed of her fag butt, flicking it on the grass.

'Not long. A few weeks.'

She walked on, as if Tara wasn't with her. When they entered the food bank, Beth wandered in among the shelves leaving Tara to speak with the young lad at the counter. Tara had fake ID and benefits papers with her so that she could use the store. Beth ignored her and concentrated on choosing food. Tara watched her. It was sad to see someone selecting food through sheer necessity rather than choosing for pleasure. She realised that she would have to do the same. She couldn't be seen to be acting fussy. The young lad handed back her papers, all in the name of Claire Brady.

'Have a nice day,' he said without conviction.

Tara lifted a plastic basket and went exploring. It didn't take her long to notice that there would have been little choice even if she had been fussy. She hurried when she saw Beth finish and go to the counter. By the time she'd finished, Beth had already left.

Outside, Tara peered into her carrier bag. Two cans of chicken soup, a can of baked beans, butter and a frozen meal of chilli con carne. She gazed around for sight of Beth. Getting to know people around here was going to be difficult. She was about to enter the mini-market to buy things to supplement the rations from the food bank when a man rounded the corner and went inside ahead of her. He didn't even take her under his notice.

Ian Bankhead had more to be worried about.

CHAPTER 38

Esther

The Blue Danube Waltz was playing in the background. Soothing music, however, did nothing to cool the tempers of Esther and her visitor, Ian Bankhead.

'My concern is for the reputation of the choir and for the safety of that young girl.'

'Safety? What the hell do you mean by that, Esther? Do you think I'm going to hurt her?'

'She's fifteen, Ian. Anything you do with her in a sexual relationship is illegal. And yes, in the long run, you're going to hurt her.'

'I love her, and she loves me.'

'Stop it now, before it's too late. You'll end up in jail, and when you get out, you'll be labelled a sex offender for the rest of your life. Think about that.'

'While all you think about, Esther, is the reputation of your damned choir.'

'Yes, I do think about the choir. Don't forget that you and Carrie are members. The choir has done a lot to improve the lives of the people round here. I want it to go on doing that.'

'Who do you think you are, Mother Teresa of Treadwater? And I don't like you sending other people round to my house to accuse me.'

Esther didn't appreciate the remark, but she could hold back her tears. She had to be strong. A choir mistress always had to be strong.

'Please take my advice, Ian. It's for your own good and Carrie's. Think of her; if all this gets out.'

'Is that a threat, Esther? If I don't break it off, you'll go to the police?'

Esther stared coldly at the man she had always regarded as a pleasant member of her choir.

'Not the police,' she said. 'Not round here. You should know that. There are other ways to deal with these matters.'

'Just like Mandy, eh?'

'Need I say more?'

Ian stepped closer to Esther. His eyes bore down on her, but she matched his glare. Without another word, he turned and headed for the door. Esther called after him.

'Please, Ian, think about it, for all of our sakes.'

He slammed the door behind him. Esther flopped into an armchair. Her entire body trembled. So much for Dinah being discreet, she thought. Now, it seemed, the problem of Ian and Carrie was entirely an issue for her choir to overcome.

CHAPTER 39

Tara

Tara donned a black baseball cap, lifted a four-pack of Newcastle Brown from her table and went downstairs. She knocked on Beth's door, but was surprised by the person who answered.

'Hi, I was looking for Beth?'

'Oh, she's here, darling,' said Katrina. 'Come in, love.'

She opened the door wide for Tara to enter. Tara saw Beth ensconced in an armchair, her feet dangling over the side. A book rested in her lap. It seemed Beth had now been interrupted twice from her reading. Resigned to having company, she set *A Life on Our Planet* by David Attenborough on the floor.

The interior was remarkably similar in décor to her flat, drab-painted walls and laminate flooring. The place even smelled the same, of tobacco and stale air.

'I thought you might like to share a beer,' said Tara, too formally and suddenly conscious of it. She held the cans aloft. 'It's all I could afford.'

Beth didn't reply, but merely acknowledged her visitor with a flick of her head. Tara stepped further into the living room with Katrina following. She hadn't immediately deduced that Katrina was a fella; it took a while longer. Katrina wore a short metallic-gold skirt, knee boots and a black top. Tara was struck by her exquisitely made-up face.

'I'm Katrina, love.'

'Claire. I've just moved in,' replied Tara.

Katrina extended her rather bony hand.

'Pleased to meet you, love. I just called to see Beth. She's not been here long either. You have to get to know people round here, or else you'd just be staring at four walls all bloody day.'

Without invitation, Tara sat on the sofa and reached a can to Beth and one to Katrina. She clicked one open also.

'Cheers!' she said.

'Cheers,' Katrina and Beth replied in unison.

'Well, this is nice,' said Beth, sardonically, 'all girls together.'

'So, where're you from, Claire?' Katrina asked.

'Birkenhead, but I've spent a long time down south.' She thought it best to add the disclaimer to avoid a repeat of Beth's question earlier in the day.

'What were you doing down there?' Katrina continued.

Tara cleared her throat. She thought it best to come out with her fake background even though Beth hadn't yet admitted to being an ex-offender.

'This and that. Did some time.'

Tara saw Beth's eyes widen at the remark, but it was Katrina who continued with the questions.

'Oh, my goodness. What did you do?'

'Class A.'

'Dealing?' Beth suddenly asked.

Tara nodded and took a sip of beer. She hoped she'd revealed enough of herself to get Beth joining in the chat. It was a bonus to have Katrina present to keep the conversation going. Also, she now had another Treadwater resident to examine more closely.

'What do you do, Katrina?' Tara asked.

'Me?' She seemed bemused by the question. 'Don't work, if that's what you mean. Depression, stress and benefits: that's me, love.'

'Are you…?'

'A tranny? Haven't had the op yet, so I still have a couple of unwanted parts.'

'You two ask an awful lot of bloody questions,' Beth snapped.

'Just getting to know each other, Beth love,' Katrina struck back.

Tara had an instant liking of Katrina. She'd never heard such a cheerful soul on this estate before. In her experience, everything had always been murder and mayhem. It was clear, though, that Beth was uncomfortable with company, or perhaps just with Tara's company.

'Can you sing, Claire?' Katrina asked.

CHAPTER 40

Justin

It was a dry Tuesday morning, and he'd made his way to Thornton, walking along Lydiate Lane, Green Lane and into Ince Road. There were big houses around here, leafy lanes and letter boxes not easily spotted from the road. Justin needed cash. He needed to score some crack or blow. If he didn't get off soon, he would go fucking nuts.

So far, he'd managed twenty quid. A kid's eighth birthday card from Gran had been inside a wall-mounted postbox of a house in Lydiate, and it had not been locked. This granny was a tight bitch, though. Surely, the kid was worth more than a measly twenty quid. Two further postboxes had provided him with the bank details of the house occupants. From another letter, he had obtained a credit card number and expiry date. He could earn a tenner for that when he sold the details to Raj in Toxteth.

Justin was growing bored, and his feet were sore. It didn't help that he'd now strayed quite far from

Treadwater, and he didn't want to spend his cash on a bus fare home. He halted in the road and gazed at a house, the final one for today, he'd decided. It was a large, detached house, a modern build and nicely concealed behind trees and bushes. There was a separate double garage with a room above, but there were no cars parked in the drive. He padded towards the front door, watching intently for any signs of life. The windows were free of blinds and all the curtains were open. If anyone were watching him, hopefully, he would spot them and get offside. He had to pass the lounge window to reach the front door. When he peered inside, he saw the room furnished with a plush suite, coffee table and bookshelves. He had a gut feeling that the house was not currently occupied. It seemed deserted. Maybe the owners were on holiday, he thought. Nothing seemed out of place. There were no newspapers, coffee cups or even a pair of slippers lying around. The room was clean and tidy. He was confident that no one would notice him breaking into the postbox.

It was yet another house with an external box mounted on the wall next to the door. To his delight, it was bursting with mail. It didn't matter if the box was locked. He had simply to pull the envelopes from the opening. At first glance, there were a variety of letters: junk mail, bills and a couple of handwritten envelopes. Personal correspondence was usually the most likely to contain cash.

He dropped the junk mail on the doorstep, and held on to the official-looking letters, while he tore open a handwritten envelope. There was no money inside, and he didn't bother reading the typed note within. As he ripped open the second handwritten envelope, Justin noticed that it had a foreign stamp. Inside, there was no money.

'Aw man!' He walked away, still holding the letter and the remainder of the mail. Disappointed by his lack of success, he traipsed back to the road. As he walked, he read the letter from the envelope with the foreign stamp. It was printed on two sheets of stiff paper and was addressed to Dr P Hazzard. At the end of the letter, the name Isaac Dahan was signed and typed. By the time Justin had read the contents, he had reached the road. He took a final look at the house. There may not have been cash in the envelope, but Justin was certain he could earn some dosh from what he had just read.

CHAPTER 41

Tara

Tara watched as the mobile response unit was towed away from its site near the play park. From what Murray had told her by phone the previous evening, they'd had zero success. Not a soul on the estate had come forward with information about Olev Eesmaa, Mandy Wright or the still unidentified woman found on the M57. So now, it was up to her. She would have to wangle her way into the fabric of this estate, gain confidences, search for clues and listen for slip-ups from the mouths of those who might be involved. She kept telling herself that the answers lay on Treadwater. If she didn't believe that then there was no point to her being here. She had already voiced an opinion to Murray and Tweedy that the whole sorry mess might have nothing to do with the place at all. Mandy Wright may have simply left her home for an indefinite period. She didn't have to tell anyone where she was going. Olev Eesmaa may have met his death somewhere other than Treadwater and his body was then dumped in the sewer on Trent Lane. The woman found on the motorway had not been identified. There was nothing linking her to the estate. The only connection between the two murders was the damned plastic film encasing both bodies.

But why hadn't people come forward with information?

From the park, Tara strolled into the area of the estate nicknamed the forest, the place where all streets were named after trees. She thought of the kids who used to hang around here, those she had encountered in her first case in Treadwater, the murder of Audra Bagdonas. Some of them had probably moved on. Mark Crawley certainly had, having been found guilty of the killing and now serving life in Liverpool Prison. Others, she guessed, might still live around the estate. They might be potential sources of information. Then again, she could not afford to be recognised by any of them. Self-consciously, she pulled down the peak of her baseball cap and walked on.

She reached the home on Sycamore Drive of Mandy Wright, stopped and inspected the outside. The small square patch of lawn was overrun with dandelions and nettles. To the right of the windowed front door, was a plastic tub of winter flowers well past their best. She pushed open the picket gate, and ventured down the path. She noticed the padlock fitted to the front door following their first visit when it had to be forced open.

'Are you looking for Mandy?'

Startled by the voice, Tara spun around to face a tall girl standing by the gate. She wore light blue jeans and a long dark shirt. Carrie's long fair hair was tossed in the breeze, and her cheeks were rosy from the cold.

'Yes. Do you know where she is?' Tara asked.

'She's gone.'

'Gone? What do you mean?'

'Are you a mate of hers?'

'Yeah. Haven't seen her for ages. I've been away. When is she coming back?'

Carrie shrugged.

'Dunno. She took off a couple of weeks back. The bizzies have been looking for her.'

'Sounds like Mandy, all right,' said Tara. 'Any idea where she went?'

Tara came down the path and stood before Carrie Dobson.

'Nobody knows. She just buggered off,' said Carrie.

'Are you a friend of hers?'

'Not really, I just knew her from choir.'

'Is that the community choir?'

'That's right. See ya.'

Carrie walked on, leaving Tara to ponder the piece of information that had just launched a shiver down her back. Now she had a link to Mandy Wright. She wondered, though, why the hell no one else from the choir had come forward to say that they knew Mandy.

CHAPTER 42

Danni

Danni had always fancied John Wilson. So had many of her mates, but as a teenager John was a quiet, shy type, more interested in football than girls. Then, in a flash he was grown-up and married to a girl from Wavertree, and he'd become a bizzie. Occasionally, she would see him around the estate on police business or visiting his mother when she still lived in Treadwater.

She hadn't felt this nervous in years and all because of a fella. The day after their meeting in the park, John had found out where she was living, knocked on her door and asked her on a date.

She had taken Mikaela and Bradley to her mum's in the afternoon and, for once, was less concerned about leaving them in the care of that sod Barry. This evening, she felt she had the best chance in years to change her life. She didn't want to think ahead too far, and yet she couldn't help dreaming of her future with John Wilson.

When she got back from her mother's, she soaked in the bath for an hour, shaved her legs and shampooed her pink hair. It was the first time she'd regretted the colour – now it looked trashy. She tidied it up using straighteners then applied make-up to her face. God, she hadn't done that in ages. There had been no point when the only place she went was choir practice on a Wednesday, and it was clear that no man there was interested in her. She once thought that she might have a chance with Ian Bankhead, but he never showed any interest. There was no one else as far as choir was concerned, unless she fancied a toy boy like Marcus, or a man old enough to be her father.

Nice clothes were also a problem this evening. When she called at her mum's, she borrowed a couple of Valerie's dresses. Her mum always looked better than she did. Valerie had more money to spend on herself and always tried to look her best. Danni decided on a blue fitted dress with a little bling on the front, rather than a green one which did not go well with pink hair. There was no choice in shoes. She owned only one decent pair, black patents with four-inch heels. Jewellery was also limited: a gold chain bracelet, her twenty-first birthday present from her mum, and a ring that had belonged to her gran.

When she had finished getting ready, she darted about the flat tidying up in case she brought John back after their date.

Danni hadn't called an outing a date for years and, even then, there hadn't been many. Maybe her life was on the up. She was going on a date with a cop. She had learned to cope with two lively kids. Aside from the recent murders, the estate was improving, becoming a safer place to live. She had choir too, although this evening she was crying-off in favour of a night out with John Wilson.

By seven o'clock, she couldn't help sitting by her window watching the street below for his arrival. He drove up bang on time at seven-thirty, and her nerves tingled again. She thought it a good omen that he wasn't late. He jumped out of his car and walked sprightly to her building. Pulling on her coat, also borrowed from Valerie, she rushed to open her door.

'Hiya!' he said, cheerfully.

She stepped back into her living room, not wishing to appear too eager.

'Hiya,' she replied. 'Come in, I'm almost ready.'

'God, you clean up well,' he said.

She saw him look her up and down. It made her feel great. He also looked well: a sports jacket, open-neck shirt, navy chinos and brown shoes.

'Ta very much,' she said with a smile. 'Right, I'm all set.'

Wilson was also nervous about the evening. Divorced for more than a year, he hadn't dated many women since. When he got home after meeting Danni in the park, he recalled the times when he was a teenager. Danni was one of the girls on the estate he would have loved to have called his girlfriend, but she'd seemed way out of his league. To him, she had the pick of the lads, while he was too shy to even approach her. The notion that he may once have snogged her at a party was far from the truth, he realised. It was more likely that he'd watched a mate snog her at a party.

Wilson had made a reservation at a good restaurant in the city. It wasn't too flash because he didn't want to seem like a pretentious prick. He simply hoped for an evening where he could get to know Danni all over again.

It hadn't crossed his mind, however, that his date with Danni could potentially conflict with his duties as a police detective who was embroiled in a murder investigation on Treadwater Estate.

CHAPTER 43

Tara

Tara was anxious about the evening ahead. She hoped there were answers to be had within this choir, but she must be careful how she set about getting them. Wearing jeans, T-shirt, trainers and the baseball cap, she ventured downstairs and met Katrina and Beth waiting by the door.

Katrina was dressed in all her finery: a leather miniskirt, black tights and black ankle boots with stiletto heels. Her wig was neatly curled around her face which was exquisitely made-up, including a glittery eyeshadow. She was overdressed for the occasion but, for her, trapped in a bubble on the estate, choir practices were special occasions. Besides, she liked to turn heads.

'All set?' asked Katrina, cheerfully.

Beth managed to smile, revealing the gap left by a missing front tooth.

'I think so,' Tara replied.

'Let's go, girls!' chirped Katrina, as she opened the door and stepped outside.

Tara gave Beth an amused smile as they followed.

This evening, it appeared that Beth had thought of some questions. Tara got the impression that there was a devilish intent behind them.

'So, where did you do your time?'

'Bronzefield,' Tara replied.

'Where's that?'

'Near London. I told you I spent a lot of time living down there.'

Tara felt good about her answers to Beth. It seemed clear that Beth had never heard of the place and therefore was less likely to press Tara on the subject.

'Why come to Treadwater?' Beth continued.

'No reason. I'm hoping it's temporary.'

'Are you thinking of going down south again?'

'Maybe.'

When they entered the community centre, all heads turned. Whether it was to view Katrina's latest outfit or to take note of another new face, Tara wasn't certain.

'Esther, love, this is Claire,' said Katrina. 'She would like to join us.'

Tara smiled and said hello to the smartly dressed woman.

'Hello, Claire, nice to meet you.'

'Don't worry,' said Katrina, 'she can sing.'

Tara was surprised by Katrina's remark but supposed that she was simply putting in a good word for her.

'Great,' said Esther. 'We'll see how you get on then. We have a concert coming up soon, so if you can learn the songs in time you and Beth should be able to take part.'

Tara sat between Beth and Katrina and was soon introduced to several of the women seated around them.

'This is Valerie,' said Katrina. 'Danni not coming tonight?'

Valerie had a tanned face and drawn eyebrows. Her hair was currently a deep brown.

'No. She's gone on a date,' Valerie replied.

Tara noticed that Valerie seemed pleased to be telling that news.

'Valerie is Danni's mum,' Katrina explained. 'She's trying to get her daughter married off.'

Tara recalled having spoken to a Danni Pearce, a woman with long pink hair.

'About time she found herself a decent fella,' Valerie continued, 'not one who's gonna piss off and leave her with two kids.'

'So, who is the lucky man this evening?' Katrina asked.

'He's a nice policeman. Grew up round here. John Wilson's his name.'

Tara's face reddened. She could do nothing to stop it. What the hell was Wilson playing at? Going on a date with a girl from the very estate that was under investigation. She would have a word with him about that. Her attention, though, was quickly redirected to another choir member.

'Mary, this is Claire,' said Katrina.

Tara shook hands with the bright-faced lady and then turned around to be greeted by the young girl she'd met outside the home of Mandy Wright.

'Hiya,' said Carrie. 'I didn't realise you were from round here.'

'I've just moved in,' said Tara. 'I'm Claire.'

'I'm sorry about Mandy.'

Katrina was listening and couldn't resist butting in.

'Mandy? What about her?'

'Oh,' said Carrie, 'I met Claire yesterday outside Mandy's house. She and Mandy are friends.'

'OMG, how do you know our Mandy?' Katrina asked loudly.

Everyone within earshot of the conversation suddenly fixed their eyes on Tara.

'I know her from years ago, before I went down south. When I heard I'd be moving into Treadwater, I had her address, so I thought I'd catch up with her.'

'Were you at school together?' Mary asked.

Several members were still focused on Tara, although Beth looked bored with the subject.

'No, we met in our late teens. We sort of hung out together for a while.' Tara was fast running out of detail to embellish her background story. She'd expected to be questioned on her fictional background but not on the background of another individual, one who lay at the centre of her investigation. Tara's explanation, however, seemed to have satisfied those sitting around her. But she wasn't finished. This was her opportunity to find out what had happened to Mandy Wright. It seemed that Mandy was well known in this choir, and yet not one person had offered information to the police.

'I hear that Mandy was a member of the choir.'

Several women turned away. Katrina cleared her throat, but Carrie was first to reply.

'Yep. Good singer was our Mandy. She was supposed to be one of the soloists for the concert. Sheena had to take her place.' Carrie pointed to a girl who had just entered the room. She had an attractive face but looked rather glum as she spoke with Esther.

'Has Mandy left Treadwater for good? When I spoke to you yesterday, Carrie, I assumed she'd just gone away for a while. Has she actually moved out?'

The question brought down a veil upon the conversation. No one offered an opinion, and the choir practice was brought to order by Esther.

'Right, folks, to warm us up, let's run through *Oh Boy*. I know we're not doing this song for the concert, but it will give our new members a taste of what we're about.'

Esther began playing her piano, and everyone joined in singing the Buddy Holly song.

Tara thought the sound and tone were excellent, and soon she was singing along, a less confident Beth singing beside her.

Before the choir dispersed at the end of practice, Tara again ventured a question regarding Mandy Wright.

'So, does anyone know what's happened to my old friend, Mandy?' She tried to sound jovial, as if it weren't really that important. There was no response, as the older women donned their coats, while the men and some younger members cleared away the chairs. As Tara got to her feet, an elderly man stepped close and whispered in her ear.

'The subject of Mandy Wright is closed round here, love. Best you leave it.'

Tara watched the man, who continued stacking chairs as if nothing had happened.

'Katrina, who is that?' Tara asked quietly, pointing to a man in grey trousers and green jumper.

'That's Raymond, Mary's husband.'

Tara continued watching him. He seemed ordinary, exchanging jovial words with other members. He never once looked in her direction.

As they left the community centre, Tara, with a bundle of music under her arm, songs to learn for the concert, was not content to let the subject of Mandy rest. She told Katrina and Beth what Raymond had said.

'Take no notice, Tara love,' said Katrina. 'He's probably fed-up hearing about Mandy.'

'Why would that be?'

'Raymond and Mary are incredibly supportive of Esther and what she has achieved with this choir. Mandy, before she left, caused a bit of a row.'

'With Esther?'

'Yes. During practice, she used to moan about the songs Esther had chosen. Then one night they had words after choir when everyone had gone home. It all came to a head when they had a shouting match in the mini-market. Esther was terribly upset.'

'Was that the reason Mandy left?'

Katrina paused and dropped eye contact with Tara.

'I'm just puzzled by Mandy going off without a word to anyone,' said Tara. That was as far as she thought she could push it.

Katrina sighed then stopped walking. She turned to Tara, while Beth trudged on.

'Listen, love, your mate Mandy pissed off a lot of people round here. It was better that she left.'

As Katrina walked on, Tara pondered those last words. What if Mandy hadn't left Treadwater voluntarily? What if she was hounded out, or worse still if she hadn't made it out of the estate at all?

CHAPTER 44

Danni

Danni hadn't been on many proper dates, so the idea of sleeping with someone on the first one had never really presented itself before. Previous boyfriends had picked her up in a nightclub and had sex with her in a car or against an alley wall before she even got home. It was hardly a romantic experience. With John there had been no decision to make. They had a nice meal in town, a few drinks, and when he drove her home, she invited him in. That was it, simple but also wonderful. She was so glad to have changed the bedding and tidied the room.

When she awoke in the morning, John had already gone, leaving a scribbled note on the pillow, a promise to see her again soon. She was ecstatic and couldn't help racing ahead to the next time, the time after that, and to the point where he moved in, and finally to the day when they got married. She chuckled at the thought and swooned at the memory of what they had just shared.

Rising from the bed, she pulled on a dressing gown and opened the blinds to a damp morning. For a while she stayed put, elbows resting on the windowsill, watching her little piece of the world go by. Vans and trucks of the utility company were driving along the street. She counted four and then a huge flatbed lorry with a digger on the back eased between the parked cars at the roadside. Men in high-vis jackets and hard hats gathered on a path leading through the park. The scene sparked her into action. Bradley and Mikaela had to be picked up from her mother's. Quickly, she dressed in jogging pants and a hoodie and rushed out of the flat. On the landing, she heard that damned dog of Justin's barking madly.

With her head down against the drizzle, and hands secreted in the pockets of her hoodie, she walked briskly towards the park. Men were already lifting a manhole cover and one of them climbed inside. At the side of the road the digger was being unloaded from the trailer. She hurried on by, then cut across the football pitch to reach Broad Oak Lane. Her children had spent the night at her mum's, but she didn't want them to be there all day. Not with that knobhead Barry. Memories of her wonderful night were greatly suppressed just thinking about having to deal with him.

CHAPTER 45

Tara

First thing in the morning, they held a conference call. Tweedy, Murray and Wilson were at St Anne Street station, and Tara was in the flat on Treadwater. At least she could eat toast and drink tea, while they discussed the developments in the case of Olev Eesmaa et al. Tara related her experience at the choir practice the night before.

'I really couldn't believe it,' she said. 'Mandy Wright was a member of this community choir, and yet not one member came to us with that information.'

'Why do you think that is, Tara?' Tweedy asked.

'Don't know, sir. There was a row and falling out between Mandy and the choir's leader, Esther Dodds. That might explain why Mandy left the choir, but it's stretching things a bit to think she fled the estate because of it.

According to my new friend, Katrina, aka Nathan, it seems that Mandy upset quite a few people around here. Again, was that so grave that she left her home?'

Tweedy baulked at hearing Katrina was also known as Nathan. Murray delicately explained the situation and Tweedy merely nodded his understanding.

'Also, sir,' Tara continued. 'I was warned not to persist with my questions about Mandy. An elderly member of the choir suggested that I leave it.'

'Did you get his name?' Murray asked.

'Only that he's called Raymond, and that he's married to Mary. No surname yet, but it won't be hard to find out.'

'I'll check my notes,' said Murray. 'I may have come across them on the house-to house calls.'

'Anything on our murder victims, Tara?' Tweedy asked.

'Not a word, sir. My closest contact, Beth, hasn't lived here long, and she's generally disinterested in what goes on.'

'Well, keep at it and take care.'

'Yes, sir. Can I have a word with John, in private?'

Murray and Tweedy said their goodbyes, and she assumed John was left alone in Tweedy's office.

'John?'

'Yes, ma'am?'

'I gather you've been seeing Danni Pearce from the estate.'

'Yes, ma'am.'

'Not such a bright idea considering we're in the middle of an investigation. What if she's involved?'

There was silence. Tara waited.

'Do you think that's likely, ma'am?'

'Why not? Something strange is going on here and she is a member of the choir.'

'I didn't think. I've known Danni since schooldays. She grew up on Treadwater.'

'Just be careful, please. Your date was the talk of the choir last night. I learned also that Danni and her mother are choir members.'

'That's strange, ma'am.'

'What do you mean?'

'When I showed Danni a picture of Mandy Wright, she denied knowing her.'

'In that case, you must tread very carefully, John.'

Tara ended the call, relieved that she hadn't vented anger on Wilson but instead issued him with a warning to be careful.

After clearing up the few breakfast dishes in her sparse kitchen, she ventured out. There was nothing to be gained by staying indoors. She needed to engage with more people on this estate if she were to make progress with this case. On her way to the mini-market, she witnessed the arrival of water utility vehicles and a team of workmen, including Mr Cummings who had been so helpful when recovering the body of Olev Eesmaa.

A woman in a grey hoodie scurried by on the same side of the road. Tara noticed the pink hair protruding from under the hood and realised it was Danni Pearce.

Frustratingly, her shopping trip to the mini-market, followed by a browse in the library, did not provide opportunities to chat with residents of the estate. The teenage girl working in the shop looked bored to tears with her lot, and Tara counted it a success to even raise a smile from her. The librarian was efficient, polite but far from friendly when Tara inquired about joining. Tara realised that her own appearance probably had not impressed the surly woman. She had deliberately removed her cap to reveal her shaven head and had chewed gum during their exchange. She spent an hour browsing the bookshelves and leafing through women's magazines, hoping that a friendly face might enter the library, and she could find an excuse for a chat. During that hour not another human being came or went from the place.

She returned to the flat, bored like the girl from the mini-market, and at a loss for what to do next. Esther Dodds should be her intended focus, she thought. By rehearsing the songs given to her, she had an excuse for calling with the woman.

By late afternoon, however, life for Tara on Treadwater suddenly became more exciting.

CHAPTER 46

Justin

'Sorry, mate. I'm not touching that. Way too hot.'

'C'mon, Raj,' Justin pleaded. 'It must be worth something?'

'It's not worth the hassle. If I tried to move that one, I'd have bizzies down on me, not to mention the guys involved. You need to be careful, mate.' Raj handed the letter back.

'What am I supposed to do with it?'

'Burn it,' said Raj. 'Pretend you never set eyes on it. I'll give you thirty quid for the other bank details.'

'Fuck! Is that all?' Justin was desperate. He thought he would be in the money when he'd sold the letter taken from the house on Ince Road.

Raj knew when to leave well alone. He was a scrawny guy, born in Toxteth in the eighties, he made his living in electronics, cameras, phones and game stations. His lucrative sideline was trading in personal details: bank account numbers, emails, PINs and passwords. Talented hackers used him to eke their way into the private lives of anyone, ignorant, careless or foolish enough to disregard their personal security. Justin was one of his low-life suppliers.

Despondent, Justin stepped from Raj's shop into pouring rain. It was not the kind of weather conducive to his thieving activities. As he tramped along the pavement from Toxteth towards the city centre, he had a difficult decision to make. He could do as Raj had advised and destroy the letter, or he could go it alone and perhaps make a fortune from this Dr Hazzard. That would involve contacting the man and suggesting that the doctor pay to have his letter returned, or risk it falling into the hands of the bizzies. The letter that came from Isaac Dahan contained delivery dates and product details for materials requested by Hazzard. Even a loser like Justin recognised the sale of illegal weapons when he saw it. If this doctor was buying guns, what was he up to?

Justin rounded the corner by the library and entered Treadwater. Gazing ahead, he saw a flurry of activity. The fucking bizzies were everywhere.

CHAPTER 47

Carrie and Ian

Ian Bankhead knew many of those who stood on one side of the police tape stretched across the path leading to the play park. Within the cordon was a melee of uniformed police, plain-clothes detectives and a dozen or more water utility workers. A JCB digger sat idle by the edge of a trench it had just dug on the football pitch. It was twenty feet long, and four wide. From where Ian stood, it was impossible to see what lay within the trench that was causing such consternation among those peering into it.

Three figures in high-vis hard hats were standing inside. The men were digging with spades and under instruction from a supervisor standing at the edge.

Two forensics vans drove onto the field. Personnel in white hazmat suits emerged ready to climb into the trench.

Carrie, just out of school, eased her way through the clusters of onlookers and stood beside Ian. She gently squeezed his arm, and he jumped. Immediately, he seemed conscious of those around him, and he stepped away from the girl. Carrie maintained her smile. She was oblivious to the significance of their situation.

'Don't, Carrie. People are watching,' Ian whispered.

'It's all right, they're not watching us.'

'Just leave it, Carrie.' He stepped away from her and stood next to a group of men.

Barry Sugden had strolled down to the park to see what all the commotion was about. He plonked himself on a bench beside the kids' play park. Deliberately so. From here, he saw the activity by the trench but, more importantly, he could indulge himself by watching a group of teenage girls playing on the swings. Valerie was at work. He was bored and, when he got bored, he started thinking darker thoughts. He preferred young women like Danni, and he had a depraved fantasy of screwing daughter and mother at the same time. Today, though, his mind was on girls much younger and easier to handle. He flicked his fag butt on the grass and watched the girls playing together.

A young lass in school uniform strolled by. Barry smiled.

'All right, love?' he said.

Carrie smiled at the slovenly figure sprawled on the bench, but she didn't reply.

'What's happening down there?' Barry asked.

'I think they found a body,' Carrie answered over her shoulder as she kept on walking.

'I think I'm looking at a great body right now.' Barry winked and smiled, but Carrie hurried on. He watched her go, lusting after her fine legs and wonderful hair. He would have to keep an eye out for her.

CHAPTER 48

Tara

Tara, much to her frustration, could only watch as the police went about their business on the field. She saw Murray and Tweedy arrive together and go directly to the open trench. When she noticed Brian Witney join them, she had confirmation that a body lay within it. While she watched the police activity, she also took note of the reactions of onlookers. She recognised several faces from the choir. Another murder would mean the entire process of house-to-house inquiries being repeated, except that now she was living as a resident of the estate and would not be conducting any interviews. Not official ones.

At that moment, she stood alone, so she quickly composed a text and sent it to Murray.

'Hey, bizzie, what's going on?'

She waited for him to glance at his phone. It took more than five minutes, while Tara grew impatient with her DS.

'C'mon, Alan, look at your phone,' she mumbled.

At last, she saw Murray checking his mobile but, to her frustration, he quickly replaced it in his pocket. He then proceeded to have an intense-looking conversation with Tweedy.

Tara examined the faces of those she knew around her. Esther, whom she had met only briefly at the choir practice, stood at the roadside on Trent Lane. Beneath a large umbrella and wearing jeans, boots and a pink anorak, her expression was sullen. To Esther's right, a cluster of people spoke quietly to each other. Tara knew the name of just one of them. Mary had sat close to her during the choir practice, and she had seemed a pleasant lady. This afternoon, she looked shocked and frequently dabbed her eyes with a tissue. Tara then spotted Mary's husband, Raymond, the man who'd told her to stop asking questions about Mandy Wright. She couldn't help wondering if Mandy's body had just been discovered.

A young man Tara instantly remembered, came and stood next to her. It was the cheeky-faced lad who had the nasty slogans on his front door. She hoped that he would not recognise her. She removed her cap. Her shaven head might deflect his attention from her face. But her phone beeped, and Justin looked at her. Tara read the brief text from Murray.

'Three bodies so far,' was all it said. As Tara slipped her phone into her pocket, Justin stepped closer.

'Any news?' he asked.

She glanced nervously at him. He had a sly grin on his face. She feared that he'd recognised her.

'Nope,' she replied without looking at him.

Despite her attempt to ignore him, Justin remained at her side. He lit a roll-up and blew the smoke in her direction. Tara felt that she was under his scrutiny. Her eyes continued to scan the crowd. She saw Beth arrive, looking curious, the most interest she'd expressed in anything since Tara had known her.

Katrina, wearing jeans, trainers and a dark wig, chatted with teenage girls who watched the activity with their arms folded. Tara had observed many people at a crime scene before, but for some reason this felt different. Would this be another investigation that attracted zero response from the residents?

'Fancy going to a party?'

Tara glared at the grinning face beside her.

'Who has a party at three in the afternoon?'

'Me and you,' said Justin.

'In your dreams.'

Without warning, Justin ran his hand over Tara's head. She backed away.

'Had to cop a feel, love. Never had a girl with no hair before.'

'You're not having this one.'

Katrina saw what was happening and hurried over to Tara.

'Leave her alone, Justin,' she said.

'Keep your nose out, ladyboy!'

'She wouldn't be interested in the likes of you,' Katrina said. 'So, do us a favour, and piss off home.'

Justin stood face to face with Katrina. They were of equal height, and he smiled mischievously at her.

'How about you go play with your balls and stop pretending to be something you're not.' Suddenly he smacked his head into her face.

Katrina reeled backwards, blood pouring from her nose. Tara caught her before she collapsed.

'Why don't you fuck off before I call the bizzies?' Tara shouted, her arm around Katrina.

Justin scoffed a laugh.

'I've told you before, Justin,' said Katrina, now on her knees and searching in her bag for a tissue. 'You need to be careful round here.'

'Yeah? I'm quaking in my fucking boots.'

He sidled away. Tara retrieved a tissue from her pocket and used it to stem the blood dripping from Katrina's nose. Several women, including Mary and Esther approached, offering to help.

'I'm all right, girls, thank you,' Katrina said.

Unable to find tissues in her bag, Katrina accepted a pack from Esther.

'What did you mean by that?' Tara asked.

'What?'

'It sounded like you were threatening him, telling him he needed to be careful.'

'Didn't mean anything, love. Just banter.'

As Tara walked from the park with Katrina taking her arm, she wasn't so sure that they were empty words.

CHAPTER 49

Stan and Hannah

Stan spent most days in his shed. He was working on a new track layout and creating landscape from papier mâché. The shed measured twelve by fourteen feet and the table he'd constructed for his layout was eight feet by ten. He had little room to move between the table and his workbench, but he was alone, a solitary figure with a solitary kind of hobby. Locked away in his private world, he was engrossed in his task and thought little of anything else. That's how he liked it. He'd escaped from the world outside and didn't even concern himself with Hannah. The only thing they shared nowadays was the house. At times, though, he grew uneasy thinking about what she might be capable of. Her talking to the bizzies was one thing he could do without.

Hannah sat by her front window staring vacantly into the road. She had noticed a lot of activity, people hurrying towards the park and police vehicles going by, but she had no idea what was unfolding around the corner. She was able to listen to the radio while Stan was in his shed. But she longed to be out in the fresh air, even now as it rained. She longed to chat with neighbours and to go shopping in the city. She wanted freedom. She wanted a life, what little was left to her, away from Stan and Treadwater. So much time had been wasted through her empty thoughts.

This afternoon, she wondered why Stan had been on edge lately. He was furious with her for speaking to those policemen. He didn't approve of her speaking to anyone, but why was he so angry this time? She touched the side of her face where he had slapped her. It was no longer painful, but she knew the colour of the bruise hadn't gone. Aside from his anger, she had the feeling that Stan was frightened by the police asking questions. Perhaps he knew something about Mandy leaving the estate. It was strange how everyone at choir no longer spoke of her, except for that new girl. Claire was Mandy's friend, and yet no one was prepared to tell her what had happened.

Hannah was struck by a notion. Stan was locked in his shed. He hated being disturbed and wasn't likely to emerge until it was time for his tea.

She went to the cupboard under the stairs and removed her overcoat. Her entire body tingled with the thrill of what she intended. Gathering her purse and house key, she opened the front door and stepped outside. Hannah was slow on her feet, but within a few minutes, she stood in Trent Lane taking in the scene before her. Police were everywhere, her neighbours were standing around chatting, while she tried to settle her nerves after escaping from her home.

Easing herself along the pavement between the spectators, she met a friendly face.

'Hello, Hannah, love.'

'Katrina! What's happened? You're bleeding.'

Hannah recognised the woman with her arm around Katrina's waist. It was the new girl Claire from choir.

'Just a wee barney with that Justin Boyle.'

Hannah tutted.

'Never mind me, Hannah love,' Katrina said. 'What have you done to your face? Purple's not a good colour.'

Hannah's frail hand went to her bruise. She composed a hesitant answer.

'Oh, I bumped into a cupboard door in the kitchen.'

'You need to be more careful. I'll have a word with Stan, tell him to look after you better.'

Hannah moved on. She was intrigued by all the activity on the football pitch. She asked questions from those she knew around her. Mary, perhaps the nearest person she had to a friend, looked upset.

'What if they've found Mandy?' she whispered to Hannah.

That was something Hannah had not contemplated. When Mary then asked about the bruise on her face, she quickly supplied the same answer as before and moved away. She saw Raymond talking with Dinah, and she noticed Esther looking forlorn.

Esther's expression changed instantly when Hannah approached her.

'Hiya, Hannah, love. Where's Stan?'

'Left him to his trains, I needed fresh air, Esther. Had to get out of the house.'

'I know, love.' Esther placed her hand on Hannah's arm. 'Can't be easy for you. If you ever need to get out for a chat you can call round to me. We can have a nice lunch and a G&T.'

'Thanks, Esther. I don't know what I'd do without the choir, you know.'

'Thank you, Hannah. It's good to know we're making a difference.'

Both women had tears in their eyes. For Esther they came from the fear that all was about to change on this estate. Whatever was happening before them was going to ruin everything she'd worked for. With Hannah, the tears were deep set. Stan was always the cause of them.

CHAPTER 50

The committee

They always met in the same house and always after nightfall. Tea and biscuits would be served, there was some idle chat and then the serious business ensued. Tonight, however, was yet another emergency gathering, following the discovery in the park earlier in the day. All their hard work was now under police investigation. First, it was the girl on the M57, then the bloke in the sewer and now the bizzies had dug up four bodies. Seated around a coffee table on a sofa and two armchairs, were several worried faces. The chairperson had called the meeting as an attempt to put minds at rest.

'There's no difference now,' said the chairperson, 'than when they pulled the Estonian out of the manhole. The bizzies have nothing except the body.'

'But this time there's four of them!' said one member. 'The cops won't rest until they get a result.'

'As I said,' the chairperson continued, 'they have nothing that can lead to us. No one else on the estate even knows who we are, so they are never going to grass. Life is better for everyone since we started this. No gangs, no hooligans racing cars through the streets, no pushers and no paedos.'

'But we have to take more care of getting rid of the bodies,' said the secretary. 'I mean, losing one on the motorway was plain reckless.'

'An accident,' said the chairperson. 'But you're right. We must be more careful.'

'Who'd have thought they would dig up the football pitch again after putting in the new drainage?' said another member of the committee.

'Yeah, but how daft was it putting the Estonian into the sewer?' said the treasurer of the committee.

'Again,' said the chairperson, remaining composed, 'it was expedient at the time. It was either that or get caught in possession, thanks to that bizzie patrol car venturing into Treadwater at eleven o'clock at night. But let's get real, folks. Everything will be fine if we keep our heads. And don't go talking to journalists or TV crews. There'll be plenty of those around the estate in the next few days.'

The room fell silent as the chairperson gazed from one member to another to gauge agreement.

'Right, any further business?' asked the chairperson.

Two members slid folded pieces of paper onto the coffee table. Not a word was exchanged, nor would there be until the chair had examined the notes.

'I hope we're not getting beyond ourselves,' said the chairperson in a concerned tone, having read the first note.

'Definitely not,' replied the member who'd contributed the slip of paper.

'We have Stan Oldfield,' the chairperson announced.

Gasps erupted from others around the table.

'What's the charge?' asked the treasurer.

The chairperson read the charge from the same piece of paper.

'Wife battering, bullying and abuse.'

'We can't confirm that!' said a member, incredulously.

'Nope. Can't go there,' said the treasurer.

'He's an old man, for goodness sake,' voiced a third.

The member who had submitted the name and the charge spoke up.

'And Hannah is an old woman. It's obvious to me that she is controlled by Stan. She's not allowed to go out without him. She can't speak for herself. She's a frightened woman, and she bears the marks of a violent man.'

'I saw her out today,' said the chairperson. 'She was down at the park. She had a huge bruise on her face.'

Heads were shaking. This would not be a unanimous decision and the group rarely acted upon a majority vote. It was written in the constitution of the group that they must always be in complete agreement before any action was taken. While the debate continued regarding Stan Oldfield, the chairperson lifted the second piece of paper from the table.

'The name is Justin Boyle. The charge is drug possession, bullying, thieving and most recently, assault.'

This time, there were no dissenters.

CHAPTER 51

Tara

Tara was summoned to St Anne Street station. She took a bus from the main road outside the estate to the city centre. Wilson picked her up from Liverpool One and drove her to St Anne Street. Hopefully, she had done enough to avoid being followed. A volley of whistles and cheers erupted when she entered the operations room revealing her shaven head. She behaved magnanimously and, using the language of the streets, showed them the finger.

Seated in Tweedy's office with Murray and Wilson, she was brought up to date on the recent events occurring on the Treadwater Estate.

'Four bodies, all of them young adult male, were recovered yesterday from a trench on the football pitch,' said Tweedy, displaying a grave expression. 'The condition of the bodies is similar to the previous finds of Olev

Eesmaa and of the unidentified female from the M57. Plastic film had been wrapped around each victim.'

'Any idea how long they have been dead?' Tara asked.

'Estimated between six months to two years,' said Murray. 'The exact time of death will be difficult to establish. The bodies are essentially mummified, so the usual decay processes have been slowed considerably.'

'How were they discovered, sir?'

'Utility company workmen were digging on the pitch to inspect a drainage pipe, a follow-up operation after the recent flooding on Trent Lane, I believe. The bodies were lying side by side, presumably killed and buried at the same time.'

Murray related his findings from interviews carried out at the scene.

'Your friend Mr Cummings, ma'am, made the discovery. Poor guy, second time in a month. According to him that area of land was excavated about eighteen months ago when new sewer pipes were laid for the proposed building of houses on the waste ground nearby. The new building hasn't yet occurred. It seems likely that the bodies were placed in the ground at that time and covered in. Anyway, as you might have expected by now, not one resident who was at the scene yesterday was forthcoming with information. No one recalls seeing anything strange on the football pitch at any time in the past. No one heard anything, no one knows who the victims are, and no one would even guess at who was responsible. A completely closed shop on that estate.'

'John,' said Tweedy, 'you have some news on post-mortems?'

'Sir, the four bodies were removed from Treadwater during the night. Post-mortems are to begin this afternoon. Also, full post-mortem reports and lab results on the earlier victims have been received.'

'Can you summarise for us, please?'

'Well, sir, the female is still unidentified. There are no DNA matches with the police database. She died from multiple injuries due to being run over by several vehicles on the M57. Her mouth and nose had not been obstructed by the plastic film wrapped around her. It seems that breathing holes had been inserted.'

'So, it's possible that the perpetrators may not have intended to kill this woman,' Murray suggested.

'There's no way we can prove that one, Alan,' said Tara.

'One interesting point,' Wilson continued, 'when the plastic film had been removed from the victims, particularly in the case of Olev Eesmaa, the pathologist suggested a possible MO. According to Doc Witney, the victim had been strung up, with hands above his head. There were marks on both wrists consistent with having been tied in some way. Several layers of plastic were wrapped around the body, legs and torso. Then the arms were placed by his sides and several more layers of film were applied around the head and binding the arms to the body. It's just his theory.'

'Certainly plausible,' said Tweedy. 'Tara, have you made any progress?'

'It's slow-going, sir. Residents of Treadwater, as Alan said, for some reason are reluctant to discuss either of the first two incidents.'

'Very strange,' said Tweedy, 'although someone anonymously gave us the initial information on Mandy Wright. Perhaps there are people on the estate who are prepared to talk. It might be worth keeping an eye on this community choir.'

'One more thing, sir,' said Tara. 'A chap I've befriended… well not so much a chap… he's transgender. Calls herself Katrina. She gets harassed by a youth on the estate. She issued a sort of threat yesterday to this lad. His name is Justin Boyle. Katrina told him that he needed to be careful on the estate. When I questioned her about it, she said it was just words, an empty threat.'

Tweedy nodded slowly, indicating that he was thinking the same thought as Tara was about to express.

'I'm wondering,' she said, 'if there is some kind of vigilante group operating on Treadwater.'

'A neighbourhood watch gone off-piste,' Murray quipped.

'The bodies are piling up,' said Wilson.

CHAPTER 52

Tara

Tara availed of the opportunity of being in the city to see Kate and Adele. Alone in that damned flat in Treadwater, she missed them terribly. By her reckoning, Kate should be on night shifts and might therefore be at home when she called.

'Hiya!' Tara said cheerfully when she opened the door and stepped inside.

'Tara, love! I'm so glad to see you home,' said Kate.

'It's not for long, unfortunately. I've got to go back. With those bodies being found yesterday it's even more important that I stay undercover.'

'Tara, Tara, play with me,' Adele shouted from across the room. She came running and Tara gathered her into her arms and swung her in the air.

'Hello, darling. Have you missed me?'

'Yes. Look.' She pointed to the sofa where a pink teddy bear sat.

'Wow! A new friend. She's beautiful. Has she got a name yet?'

'Pink Teddy.'

Tara laughed.

'That's a pretty name.' She lowered Adele to the floor and the child ran to fetch her new toy.

'A present from her father,' said Kate.

'So, how have you been?'

'Fine,' Kate replied. 'I've missed you. I'd just got used to having company again and then you cleared off.'

'Sorry about that. Hopefully, it won't be for too much longer. I've missed you too.'

'How's life in Treadwater?'

Tara groaned then slumped into her wonderfully comfortable sofa.

'Not a lifestyle I would recommend. There are a lot of lonely people in the world. People with problems, depression, no job, poor health, drink and drug habits. I've seen it all within a couple of days. But Treadwater seems to have something going on that is much worse.'

'What is that?'

'I'm not entirely sure yet, but life is far from normal in that place. It's as if the residents have drawn a collective sharp intake of breath. I need somebody to breathe out and reveal what is going on.'

'Coffee? Something stronger?' Kate suggested.

'Coffee is fine, but I'm going to have a shower first. That's something that I've missed more than anything.'

By four o'clock, Tara reluctantly entered her flat on Treadwater and immediately re-acclimatised to the grimy living room with its peculiar odours and poor light through filthy windows. All day, since leaving St Anne Street, she had pondered how best to progress the case. As Detective Inspector Tara Grogan, she could interview all those people who had beeped on her radar since coming here. Esther Dodds, Katrina, Justin Boyle, Raymond, Danni Pearce and her mother. She could ask them what they believed was happening on Treadwater. As Claire Brady, however, she would have to use more subtle methods.

One idea she had, was to persist with her inquiries about Mandy. She was posing as Mandy's friend, and it might cause someone to reveal more than they should, or it might incur the wrath of men like Raymond.

There was a heavy knock on her door but, before answering, she glanced around the room checking that nothing incriminating, such as her notebook, was lying around.

'Hiya, love,' said Katrina, 'thought we might return the favour.'

She held aloft a bottle of gin and a four-pack of lager. Katrina had her face on and stood tall in strappy heels, tight jeans and a baggy T-shirt with a printed slogan across the chest that read, 'it's not me it's you'. Beth attempted a smile as Tara opened the door wide.

'Just what I need,' Tara said. 'Helluva day.'

'What's up?' Katrina asked as she helped herself to glasses from the sparse selection in a cupboard.

'My probation officer asked me if I had found a job yet.'

Tara noticed Beth watching her. She sat in an armchair in the corner of the room.

'Tell her you're depressed,' said Katrina. 'That's what our Beth did. Isn't that right, love?'

'Or you could tell her to find you one, if you're keen to work,' said Beth.

Tara sat on the arm of the sofa and clicked open a can of lager. She handed another to Beth who also accepted a glass of gin from Katrina.

'For now,' said Tara, 'I want to find out what's happened to my friend Mandy.' She directed the comment at Katrina, knowing that Beth had little interest in the goings-on in the estate.

Katrina took a hefty drink from her gin then gasped satisfaction.

'God, I needed that one.'

Tara decided that Katrina was stalling.

'She's done this before,' Katrina said at last. 'Cleared off without a word.'

'I'm just worried about her,' said Tara. 'I even thought she might have been one of the bodies found on the football pitch.'

Katrina took another drink.

'Why think that?' The cheerfulness had vanished from Katrina's voice.

'I don't know,' Tara replied. 'Like I said, I'm just worried about her.'

'I thought you hadn't seen her in years?' Beth put in.

'I haven't, but we were close once.'

'I suppose you were close,' said Katrina, 'both on the game, and having to look out for each other.'

'Was Mandy still on the game here, in Treadwater?' Tara quickly grasped the news that Mandy was a prostitute and noted the suggestion that she was too.

'She certainly was,' said Katrina. 'Ran a nice little earner, right from her house.'

'You could do the same,' said Beth, a playful grin on her face. 'Then you could tell your probation bitch that you have a job.'

Katrina laughed heartily and poured herself another gin.

'I'm not that desperate yet, thanks, Beth,' said Tara.

She noted the sarcastic smile returned by Beth. Tara sipped her beer and, while Katrina prattled on about prostitutes, she attempted to keep the subject of Mandy to the fore.

'Do you think one of her clients may have snatched her?'

'Nope,' said Beth. 'Time to shut up about Mandy and talk about something else, while I get trashed.'

Tara knew she wasn't finished with Mandy Wright by a long way. The subject, however, seemed to get under the skin of everyone she questioned.

'Who do you think was dug up yesterday?' Tara asked.

CHAPTER 53

Justin

Justin couldn't afford any decent shit. He spent the night unable to sleep, having dosed himself with vodka, a few uppers and high energy drinks. His neck was stiff from lying on the sofa, his throat was dry, and his eyes were on stalks. It was hardly what he would call a good trip. Crumpled beneath him, was the letter causing him troubled thoughts. As matters stood, he was in the clear. No one, except for Raj, knew he had it. Unless he acted on it, he was safe. But the prospect of making a few quid, maybe even a grand or two, was ample inducement to crawl from his stinking flat into a morning filled with heavy cloud and a biting wind. By the time he stood outside the house on Ince Road, rain was lashing down.

The property looked no different from how he remembered it. The curtains were open, there were no cars in the drive and apparently no one within the house. Justin marched up to the postbox. He slipped a folded piece of paper through the slot. He noticed that there were no letters inside the box. Briefly, he looked around for the junk mail that he had discarded on his previous visit. There were no signs of it, not even an envelope soaked by rain and blown into a corner. Someone had been to the house since his visit, and they had cleared away his mess. He now felt confident that Dr Hazzard would find his note in the postbox. With that thought, he trotted off down Ince Road. Soon, he would receive a phone call and, hopefully, a chance of making some dosh. His words written on the note played through his mind on his journey home.

I have your letter. If you want it back, call this number. 07884129792. If you don't, I will give it to the bizzies.

CHAPTER 54

Tara

Friday was the day that Raymond and Mary went to the library to stock up on books for the week. Mary was unashamedly a reader of light romance, Cookson, Mills & Boon and Maeve Binchy. Raymond usually borrowed one or two books on military history or gardening. He wasn't such a voracious reader as Mary and would merely browse and look at the photographs. Whilst in the library, he also browsed the internet to brush up on current affairs.

The couple held hands as they walked, but they came to a halt when they reached the junction of Severn Way with Trent Lane. Forty yards from where they stood, was the scene of the police activity the previous day. An incident tent remained over the trench that formed the mass grave where the bodies of four men had been recovered. Forensics personnel were still examining the site. A TV news crew were recording a report, a reporter, camera and sound man stood on the grass a little way off the scene behind the cordon. Several other residents passing by had stopped to watch and to gossip. Although Mary and Raymond had viewed the scene yesterday, the shock still piqued Mary's emotions, and tears welled in her eyes. She squeezed Raymond's hand. He stared seemingly unmoved at the scene. He wasn't for lingering.

Tara, on her way back from the mini-market, with bread, milk and newspaper, had spied them. She hurried across the road.

'Hi there. Raymond and Mary, isn't it?'

'That's right, love,' Mary replied, but Raymond maintained a distant gaze as if Tara were not there. 'Coming back to choir next week?'

'Yes, I hope to. If you don't mind, I'd like to ask you both a couple of questions.'

'What sort of questions?' said Mary.

'About my friend Mandy Wright.'

Raymond frowned then glared coldly at Tara.

'I told you we don't talk about her kind round here anymore,' he snapped. 'The subject is closed.'

'For you maybe, but not for me. Mandy is my friend, and I want to find out what's happened to her.' Tara glanced from Raymond to Mary. The wife looked anxious and eager to be on her way. Neither one seemed willing to say anything more. 'Is it because she was a prostitute?' Tara continued. 'You don't approve, is that why you won't even discuss her? Or maybe she has been run off this estate by folk who don't approve of sex workers?'

Tara studied their eyes for a sign that maybe she had struck a nerve.

'Mandy was a lovely girl. We all liked her,' said Mary as Raymond winced.

'You liked her until you found out what she did for a living? Then someone decided that her kind weren't welcome round here.'

Mary was speechless. Raymond fumed, his face reddened, and Tara knew she had riled him.

'Listen, love,' he began, 'I don't even remember your name, but if you are a friend of Mandy's then I'm guessing that you do the same job as her. So, here's some advice for you. This is a quiet estate nowadays. We don't have trouble like we used to. We have a real community spirit going on. The likes of you coming here accusing us of all sorts will not make you any friends. If you are in the same business as Mandy, I suggest you take yourself elsewhere and leave us in peace.'

'Doesn't seem such a quiet place to me,' said Tara. 'Four bodies dug up yesterday and another one found in a sewer. And then there's Mandy, vanished. Not what I would call trouble-free.'

As Tara left them and returned to the other side of the road, she spied Danni Pearce walking through the park. She had a child at each hand. Tara wondered what Wilson thought of taking on a woman with a ready-made family. But it was none of her business. She crossed the road once again. A quick chat with Danni wouldn't go amiss. She noticed Raymond and Mary watching her, as they continued towards the library. Tara realised she had caused a stir with the couple but had the feeling also that she wasn't far from the truth as to why Mandy Wright had left Treadwater.

In the play park, Bradley and Mikaela had rushed to play on the see-saw, while their mother sat on a bench and smoked a cigarette. Tara entered the play park, and Danni watched her approach.

'Hiya,' said Tara. 'I'm Claire. I'm new round here. You're Danni, isn't that right? I didn't get to meet you at choir practice last week.'

She joined Danni on the bench. The strong wind of the early morning persisted, but the rain had cleared. It still felt miserable to be seated on a park bench.

Danni blew smoke in the air before saying anything.

'Yeah, I'm Danni.'

'Both yours?' Tara looked towards the children.

'Yeah.'

'I think I met your mum at choir. Valerie, isn't it?'

'Yeah.'

'She was all talk about you going on a date rather than coming to practice.'

Danni was now glaring at her as she took another drag on her cigarette.

'Enjoy singing, do ya?' she asked dryly.

'It's something to do. A way of making friends, I hope.' Tara smiled at the woman with pink hair and couldn't help picturing her with John Wilson. It seemed a bizarre pairing. Suddenly, Danni was examining her closely.

'Do I know you from somewhere? You seem familiar.'

Tara recalled the briefest of interviews on the landing outside Danni's flat, when they'd been doing the door-to-door inquiries. Surely Danni did not recall her from that one meeting. Since then, Tara had shaved her head and stopped wearing make-up. Of course, the lack of hair made no difference when she was wearing a baseball cap. Quickly, she removed it to reveal her bald pate.

'Maybe not,' said Danni, grinning at the absence of hair.

Tara breathed a sigh of relief. This was not the time to have your cover blown. She was feeling that she might be getting somewhere.

CHAPTER 55

Danni

'Don't know nothing about Mandy,' Danni said in reply to this woman Claire's question.

'But you knew her from choir?' Tara asked.

'Not very well.'

'I just find it amazing that nobody seems bothered that she's disappeared.'

Danni really didn't want to comment on that. For one thing, who the hell was this woman? Says she's a mate of Mandy's, but how could she be sure. She didn't feel like she could trust her. Didn't even like the look of her. Hard-looking. Just out of prison, she'd heard. She could be after Mandy for something.

'What do you reckon is happening here then?' Tara asked.

She'd changed the subject at least. Danni glanced over to the crime scene then shrugged.

'No idea.'

'Didn't think I would have all this going on when I moved in.'

'Why'd you come here?'

'Random choice. Had to go somewhere.'

'Where were you before?'

'Did some time, down south. I was caught in possession, and did a spot of dealing, to be honest.'

Danni suddenly felt she knew the reason why this woman was here. She was going to start dealing. Her unease increased. She didn't like this Claire. She was going to be trouble.

'The lad they found in the sewer,' said Tara, 'did you know him?'

'Not really.'

'But you saw him around the estate?'

Danni cursed inwardly. She should have answered with a straight no.

'Saw him selling drugs to kids coming out of school. Can't say that he'll be missed round here.' She fired Tara a disapproving look.

'Is that why he was murdered?'

'How the fuck would I know?' Danni stood and beckoned to her children. It was time to go.

'I just wondered if that's how they deal with people who step out of line around here,' Tara said.

Danni wanted to let the comment pass. She had no time for nosey bitches who didn't know what the fuck they were talking about. Instead, she grew increasingly defensive.

'Treadwater's no different from any other estate,' she said. 'There're good people living here and then there's those that want to cause trouble, beating up old people, stealing their pensions, giving drugs to school kids and racing cars through the streets. If you ask me, they get what they deserve.'

Mikaela and Bradley were ignoring Danni's attempts to call them, so she marched over to the swings, caught them by the hands and walked away without another word to this Claire woman. Danni hoped that she wasn't going to cause trouble. She did not like her one bit. Maybe she could get John Wilson to check her out. One thing was certain, if Claire caused any trouble she wouldn't be living here for long. Her friend, Mandy, hadn't lasted long once it was known what she got up to.

CHAPTER 56

Tara

It seemed that Tara's morning work amounted to pissing off three residents of the estate who also happened to be members of the Treadwater Community Choir. They had all gone on the defensive when she posed questions about Mandy and why people had been murdered. Now, Tara thought, it was time to speak with the woman who had quarrelled with Mandy Wright. Tara could not dismiss the notion that whoever was responsible for Mandy's disappearance was also connected to the murder of six people.

She called at the flat to collect the music for the songs she was supposed to be learning for the choir's performance at the leisure centre. It was an excellent way in, she hoped, to the confidence of Esther Dodds.

'Hello, Esther. Sorry for disturbing you, but I was wondering if you had the time to run through these songs with me?'

Esther stood by her door, for a moment, looking doubtful about her caller. It took a second for recognition to kick in.

'Claire! Yes, sorry I wasn't thinking straight. Come in.'

Tara, having changed into something more respectable-looking, a white blouse and dark jeans, stepped into the hallway. She was struck immediately by pleasant aromas of burning candles and impressed by the cosy surroundings. Esther, too, looked immaculate in green trousers and cream top.

'Please, Claire, make yourself comfortable, and I'll put the kettle on. Tea or coffee?'

'Coffee is great, thanks.'

Tara gazed around the living room. It was neat and tidy with plump cushions, a display of porcelain, and several photographs on the walls and set upon occasional tables. Although she hadn't been expected at the house, Esther's electronic piano was set up by the window ready to be played.

'I'm sorry I didn't get time to speak with you last week,' Esther called from her kitchen. 'What did you think of us?'

'Great,' said Tara. 'I really enjoyed myself.'

'That's good. Have you much experience of singing?'

'School choir mainly. Nothing too exciting.'

'Well, if you can learn the words of these songs, I see no reason why you can't be a part of the concert. It's a big deal for us. Up until now, we've been restricted to the community centre and a few church halls, but this performance is to be staged at the leisure centre and it's ticketed. Next year, I hope to enter us in a few competitions at music festivals. I think everyone will enjoy the opportunity to travel and to meet with other choirs.

Sorry, I do go on a bit when it comes to the choir. It's just that I'm so excited about our success. To tell you the truth, it's taken over my life.'

Tara smiled her understanding as Esther set a tray with coffee pot, mugs and a plate of buttered fruit scones on her coffee table. The conversation remained on all things choral as Tara enjoyed the refreshments. Esther had a wealth of musical experiences that she related to her guest. Tara listened as Esther spoke of teaching and performing since she was a teenager and even singing in an eighties pop band.

'We entered *A Song for Europe* once,' she said, 'but that was the year that Bucks Fizz won the whole thing, so we were quickly forgotten.'

'Did you carry on after that?'

'Oh yes, we kept going for a few years. We managed to tour with Orchestral Manoeuvres in the Dark, but one by one we left to get married and have kids. We lost contact after that.'

When they'd finished their coffee, Esther wasted no time in getting down to the music. One after another, she played through *Lifted, Good Day Sunshine, Penny Lane* and the other songs intended for the performance. As a soprano, Tara had no harmonies to sing, but Esther was nonetheless keen to get the tuning correct and to advise on phrasing and breathing. She was, however, impressed by Tara's efforts.

'Are you sure you haven't done more singing? You have a sweet voice and great tone.'

All that Tara could think of was her screaming along in the car to Freddie Mercury or the Foo Fighters.

'Mandy Wright and I used to sing karaoke when we lived down south,' Tara lied, but it was her way onto the subject of Mandy.

'You and Mandy were friends?'

'Oh yes, from way back.'

'Mandy had a wonderful voice,' said Esther. 'Such a shame she wasted it.'

'I was hoping to hook up with her again when I came to Treadwater, but it seems she's taken off somewhere.'

Esther made no reply and instead she leafed through her music in search of the next song to play. Tara wasn't about to let the subject drop.

'I heard that you and Mandy quarrelled, and that she left the choir and the estate shortly afterwards.'

For the first time, Tara felt Esther's cheery disposition vanish from the room. Her face was suddenly vexed, her eyes losing contact with her visitor.

'Let's try this one,' she said as if Tara had not posed the question.

She began playing *Rehab*, and Tara felt compelled to join in.

When the song was over, the cheerful Esther had not returned.

'Mm, I think we need a bit more work on that one, Claire. We'll leave it there for today, and I'll see you at practice on Wednesday.'

'Thanks very much for your help, Esther.'

'You're welcome, love.' She managed a smile as she tidied up the sheets of music.

'I'm sorry about earlier,' said Tara. 'I didn't mean to pry. It's just that Mandy is my friend, and I'm worried about her going off like that. Every time I ask someone about her, they get very annoyed.'

Esther looked worryingly at Tara as if she were trying to size her up, in a quandary over whether she could trust her.

'Mandy was very outspoken, Claire. She thought she knew better than me what was right for the choir. She hadn't built it from scratch; she hadn't noticed the change it brought to people's lives round here. She just wanted to get her way.'

'Is that the reason why she was forced out of the estate?'

'Of course not!' Esther sounded incredulous at Tara's insinuation. 'Our disagreement was between the two of us. No one else got involved.'

'Do you think she was threatened by someone because she was a sex worker?'

'Listen, Claire love. There are things going on around here, and it's best not to stir up trouble.'

'What sort of things?'

'All I can tell you is that Treadwater is a better place to live now than three years ago, before the choir was formed.'

'Are these murders connected to the choir?'

'Claire! That's a terrible thing to suggest. Take it from me, the choir is not involved in any murders. My God, how could you even think that? I think you should leave now.'

Esther went to her hallway and Tara was obliged to follow.

'I didn't mean to upset you, Esther. I'm just looking for the truth about Mandy. I don't know if she's alive or dead.'

'For your own good, Claire, just let it go.'

CHAPTER 57

Murray and Wilson

'All four of them died the same way – suffocation,' Murray explained.

'Any ID?' Tweedy asked. He sat at his desk, a sad yet eager expression on his lined face. At times it seemed that he was reliving the same horrid experience over and over.

A murder followed by a post-mortem, followed by a discussion, followed by investigation.

'Two have been identified so far from DNA matches to criminal records,' Murray explained. 'Linus Jones, his age now would be twenty-two, was of mixed race and from Treadwater. He had convictions for car theft, driving without a licence or insurance, and one conviction for assault. The second one is Dale Wycliffe. He would now be twenty-four years old and of no fixed abode. There were convictions for theft, burglary and possession of class A. No information so far on the other two.'

'OK, let's see if we can find someone who knew either man. The best place to start is back on Treadwater. Do we have an address for Linus Jones?'

'Yes, sir,' Murray replied. 'I'm thinking, though, that unless he had family at the address, there may be new occupants of the property.'

'Check it anyway. Anything else from the post-mortems?'

'The MO is the same as for Olev Eesmaa. Hands were secured at the wrists and probably raised above the head until the victim had been wrapped in the plastic. Then they were lowered and fixed by his sides. Finally, the head was wrapped until the victim suffocated. These victims, however, also displayed evidence of head and body injuries, consistent with beating and kicking.'

'It's clear that there is a systematic method of killing and perhaps a similar motive for each,' said Tweedy. 'Tara's theory of vigilantes dishing out justice may not be too far-fetched. Can you update her on the news?'

'Yes, sir. John and I will get over there ASAP to check out the address for Linus Jones.'

Wilson volunteered to drive, which gave Murray an opportunity to send a text to Tara.

'How are things going with the new woman?' he asked Wilson as he typed on his phone.

'Not bad. We've been out twice now,' Wilson replied.

'And?'

'And what?'

'C'mon, you know, have you consummated this new relationship?'

'Might have.'

'That's a yes then,' laughed Murray.

Wilson chuckled but said nothing more.

They drove past the flat where Tara was living.

'She's out,' said Murray. 'She's just replied to my text. Says she will speak later.'

Wilson had no trouble in locating the house where Linus Jones had lived. Before leaving the station, he had checked with the council housing department whether Jones had been the registered tenant of the house. It transpired that the current residents had lived at the address for two and a half years. Prior to this, the tenant had been a woman named Farley.

The marked police Ford stopped in the parking area to the rear of the house at twenty-three Cherwell Avenue. Murray and Wilson got out and walked down an alleyway leading to the front of the terraced houses. Number twenty-three looked reasonably tidy and well maintained. On Treadwater, well maintained meant that there were no discarded items of interior furniture in the garden, or weeds populating the flower beds. The front door also appeared intact and had a working doorbell. An attractive young woman with a baby in her arms answered the door. She didn't look much beyond a teenager, with a slight build, short brown hair and a clear complexion.

'Hiya,' she said, chirpily. 'Hope you two aren't Jehovah's or Mormons?'

Murray smiled his best and introduced himself and Wilson, whose smile outshone that of his colleague.

'We're following up on the finding of human remains on the football pitch a couple of days ago,' said Murray. The woman's expression altered instantly as she rocked on her feet to nurse her baby. Wilson reached her a photograph.

'Do you know this man?' he asked.

The woman examined the photo of Linus Jones that had been taken from police records. She shook her head.

'No. Was he one of the guys you found?'

'His name is Linus Jones, does that name mean anything to you?' Murray asked.

Again, the young mother shook her head.

'He was listed as living at this address three years ago,' Murray continued. 'The rent payer was a woman named Farley.'

'No, sorry. We've been here just over two years. We came from Walton. The house was empty when we got it. There was a terrible mess inside, too. We had to have a new kitchen, bathroom and heating installed. The place had been stripped bare. Maybe the neighbours can help you. Some of them have been here for years.'

Both detectives thanked the young mother for her help, leaving her to soothe her now crying baby. They walked immediately to the adjoining house, number twenty-five. It was another well-kept property with a working doorbell. This time the door was answered by a woman in her late thirties, attractive but wearing a serious expression. Her name was Dinah Sandford.

CHAPTER 58

Dinah

Dinah had been expecting this for the past three years – bizzies coming to her door to ask about Linus Jones. Not that he was missed. Treadwater was a better place without his kind. She was in the middle of preparing tea. She'd lifted the pan with sausages off the cooker when she heard the doorbell.

The two detectives smiled pleasantly and introduced themselves. Dinah wasn't the least intimidated by the two burly men in suits. She had an answer to their question ready and waiting.

'Yes,' she said, gazing at the photograph. 'Is he one of the guys you found buried in the park?'

She noticed how careful they were in not revealing information that they did not need to.

'His name is Linus Jones,' said Murray. 'I believe that he used to live next door at number twenty-three.'

'Yes, I remember Linus. He lived with his aunt, Joyce Farley. He didn't stay long, though. I think he was supposed to look after Joyce on behalf of the family. She had cancer. But he left before she died. That was years ago.' Dinah hoped she had said enough to satisfy this pair, enough to get them off her doorstep.

'What did you know about Linus?' Murray asked.

'Not much. A friendly lad, I suppose. He asked my Sheena out, but she was too young, only fourteen at the time, and he was an adult. I didn't allow it.'

'Did he cause any trouble around here?'

Dinah shook her head.

'Not that I know of.' She stared at the detectives, hoping to end the conversation.

And that would have been an end to it but for Marcus and Sheena walking up the path to home.

'Hi there,' said both officers.

The teenagers were intent on going directly inside, but Dinah felt obliged to introduce them.

'My kids, Marcus and Sheena.'

'Can we ask you some questions?' Murray asked.

'Police. They're asking about Linus,' Dinah explained.

Both kids suddenly stood like pillars of salt, stock-still and blank-faced.

'Can you tell us anything about Linus?' Wilson asked.

Sheena looked nervously towards her mother. Dinah remained poker-faced. Marcus shrugged indifference. The silence was awkward.

'Anything at all,' said Murray. 'Doesn't matter how trivial it may seem; it might be important.'

'I thought I saw him recently,' said Sheena.

'Oh, when was that?' Murray asked.

'Couple of months ago.'

'Where did you see him?'

'Liverpool One. Just a glimpse, can't be certain it was him.'

Murray examined the face of the teenager who stared intently right back at him.

'Had you seen him around the estate since then?'

'No, don't think so,' Sheena replied. 'Guys like Linus come and go from here all the time.'

Murray grinned as Sheena smiled dismissively. It signalled an end to the questions. The detectives thanked the teenagers who quickly disappeared indoors. Murray, however, had one more question for their mother.

'Did you know this man?' Wilson showed her a picture of Dale Wycliffe.

She felt her face grow warm as she stared at the image.

'No,' she said, then sounding flustered added, 'I'm sorry, but I have tea to get ready, a pot on the cooker. I can't tell you any more.'

She closed the door as Murray offered his thanks. Wilson shrugged at his colleague and they turned away from the house.

Dinah served the sausages, chips and beans and joined her children at the table. Marcus tucked right in, without a word. He had things to do this evening. There was always music to practice for choir and for the concert.

Sheena looked the most cheerful.

Dinah was glad the ordeal with the police was over. It had been easy talking about that little shit Linus, after what he had done to his Aunt Joyce, selling off her belongings when the woman was gravely ill. Dinah reckoned that she had played it exactly right, telling them little. And Sheena helped muddy the waters with her claim to have seen Linus in town. The rocky part came when the bizzies asked about Dale Wycliffe.

CHAPTER 59

Tara

Despite her experience as a police detective, the scrapes, traumas and tragedy, none of it seemed to help Tara deal with her present circumstances. Perhaps she wasn't cut out to be an undercover cop. A whole day of asking questions of people and mostly what she'd accomplished was to create a poor impression. The intention had been to wheedle her way into their confidence, to gain their trust and to get information. Instead, she had been told to drop the subject by more than one resident and essentially threatened by another who assumed she was a prostitute like Mandy Wright.

It didn't seem wise to go looking for a fight with another soul from the estate. When she got back to the flat, she called the station and spoke with Tweedy. He told her that no client lists or appointment books were found in the home of Mandy Wright. Unless Mandy was alive, living elsewhere and they could trace her, that lead had reached a dead end. Next she sent a text to John Wilson, suggesting that if he was still seeing Danni Pearce, he might want to bring up the victims' names in conversation. Following their meeting in the play park, Danni was unlikely to share anything with her. Since her visit to

Esther Dodds, Tara believed that there was more to be had from members of the community choir.

To maintain the persona of an ex-con settling into a new life, Tara decided to pay another visit to Beth. There had been no contact since they had watched the events on the football pitch. Although Beth was new to the estate and seemed to know little of what was going on, it would do no harm to raise the subject of the murders with her. Beth might offer a useful insight, and being friendly with Katrina, she may be able to extract something there.

As Tara had done previously, she knocked on Beth's door and when it opened brandished a six-pack of lager in the air.

'I'm dying for a drink,' said Beth, looking dishevelled as though she'd just crawled from bed at six in the evening. Her hair looked greasy, and her missing front tooth dominated what otherwise was an attractive face.

When Tara entered the flat, the stench of cigarette smoke was suffocating. Tara felt she would have to wash as soon as she got back to her flat.

'Have you spoken to Katrina today?' she asked Beth.

Her host snatched the lager from Tara's hands and clicked open a can. She took a long, slow drink before acknowledging that anyone was even in the room with her.

'Nope, why?'

Tara, too, was glad of the beer. It stopped her from gagging on the foul air.

'I wanted to ask her some questions.'

'Not more fucking questions. Do you people never stop?' Beth threw herself onto her sofa, beer spilling from the can and over her legs. She wasn't bothered.

'I was out today, asking questions about Mandy. Now I've pissed off half of the estate. They think I'm the same as Mandy.'

'What do you mean?'

'On the game,' said Tara.

Beth looked unmoved by Tara's problem. She was too busy pouring beer down her throat. She reached for a second can. Tara watched as Beth's hands trembled in trying to open the lager.

'Are you having a bad day?'

'Fuck. You could say that,' said Beth. 'My stomach feels like shit. I ate a meat pie from the food bank. It must have been off.'

'I can fetch a doctor or get you something from the chemist.'

'No doctor, they don't know shit.'

'I'll get something from the chemist to help settle your tummy.'

Beth didn't protest as Tara left her.

She bought some Gaviscon from the mini-market. It saved her a trip to a chemist. When she got back to Beth's flat, the beer was finished, and Beth looked drowsy. Tara gave her the medicine and waited to be sure that Beth had taken some. She fetched more beer from her flat and left it in with Beth before heading out again. Tara had decided that it was worth calling with Katrina to ask questions about Linus Jones and Dale Wycliffe.

It wasn't far from Deeside Crescent to Clyde Lane, both streets similar in layout. Katrina occupied a ground-floor flat exactly like Beth's. There was, however, a more pleasant atmosphere, a perfumed aroma greeting Tara, as Katrina ushered her inside.

'Party time, girls,' said Katrina, cheerfully. 'Claire, this is my friend, Sheena. I don't know if you've already met.'

The presence of another stranger, ensconced in an armchair, feet up, shoes off, was not the situation Tara had envisaged. But perhaps Sheena would have something useful to say.

CHAPTER 60

Justin

Justin shivered. His living room was cold and had no source of heating in a working condition. But Justin was not shivering from just feeling cold. He hadn't had anything for three days, and boy was he suffering. No weed, blow, crack or pills, nothing. He was skint. The worse he felt the harder it was to prowl the streets, to raid postboxes for cash. With the shakes came blinding headaches and nausea. He'd hardly eaten for two days. He hadn't washed or done a shite in nearly a week. It may have been longer, but he'd lost all sense of time. Barefoot, wearing jeans and a sweatshirt, he lay curled up on the floor of his living room with a blanket around his shoulders. The only thing that smelled worse than him was the filthy carpet, rich in beer stains, vomit and urine. He didn't care. He knew that one day he would lie on this floor for one last time, and it would be months before anyone found him. By then his decomposing body would have seeped into the damn carpet. He heard his phone ringing, death metal, such an appropriate ringtone.

He raised himself wearily from the floor and searched for the mobile. He found it squeezed between the cushions of the sofa. It was still ringing as he tried to focus on the display. The number was withheld. He swiped the screen to answer the call.

'I got your message,' said a male voice. It sounded blunt and lacked emotion. It took Justin several seconds to realise exactly who was calling him. 'You do know what I'm talking about?' said the man.

'Yeah,' Justin replied. Adrenalin suddenly coursed through his dilapidated body. It was a high of sorts. 'If you want it back, it'll cost ya.'

'Listen to me,' said the voice. 'You don't know who you're dealing with.'

'Don't give a fuck either,' said Justin. 'If you want it back, then I need a grand.'

'OK. I'll meet you.'

'At the house?'

'What house?'

'Where I found the letter,' said Justin.

'No, not there. The car park at the lake in Crosby. Do you know it?'

'How the fuck do I get out there?'

'Your problem. Eight o'clock, be there. I won't wait long.'

The call ended. Justin raised a smile, his first real smile in weeks. Now he was at last on the up. It was close to five o'clock, and he had three hours to get sorted and make his way to Crosby. He left out some food for the dog, but it would have to wait for a walk until he got back.

He caught a bus on the Northern Perimeter Road and got off on Bramhall Road. From there, it was only a half-mile walk to the lake car park. His eagerness got him there with ninety minutes to wait for his meeting with Dr Hazzard, if that was his real name.

Justin sat on a low wall and shivered. His body tingled with nerves, but he wasn't frightened. He felt confident that soon he would have enough money to buy some good gear. All he had to do was get the cash, hand over the letter and clear off. As he waited, studying every car that drove into the car park, he began wondering just how much this guy would really pay to have his letter returned. Maybe a grand was pittance. He should have asked for more.

What Justin had not factored into his clandestine business deal was that at eight o'clock it was dark.

Suddenly, he felt vulnerable, alone in a car park except for several vehicles, some with couples doing what couples do, and a group of young lads in souped-up Peugeots parked window to window eating chips and sharing a chat. Nervously, he kept checking his phone, expecting another call or a text, but nothing came.

At one minute after eight, a flash-looking Mercedes entered the car park, circled once, then rolled to a halt twenty yards from Justin. This was it. He squinted into the glare from the headlights. Then the lights flashed. He rose from the wall and approached the driver's side of the car. The window was already down.

'Get in,' said a man. From the brief glimpse, Justin saw that he was well-groomed and around forty. 'We can't talk here, get in.'

Justin did as he was instructed. He climbed into the passenger seat, and the car immediately roared away.

CHAPTER 61

Barry

Barry didn't do much other than eat, smoke, drink, watch TV, and go to the match when Everton played at home. He did do one more thing, but usually it was confined to his lurid and rather disturbed imagination. There were times, though, when he needed to vent his frustration. His partner, Valerie, worked in the daytime and she went out two or three nights a week. That allowed Barry plenty of time.

There weren't many pretty ones on this side of the estate, but there were at least a couple. His house was close to the entrance of the cul-de-sac, and he could watch from his living room window as they came and went. There was also Danni, Valerie's daughter. He would certainly love to have her. He conjured images of the pair of them together acting out things he'd watched on DVD, things he did to her, and things she did to him. Valerie would join in, and then his mind flashed to somebody else, a girl on TV or young Carrie strutting by the window. She was just the right age for him. In truth, he could take them at any age, but teenagers were just ripe, and some of them were really gagging for it. Carrie, for instance, had already gained something of a reputation. He'd spoken to her a couple of days ago when all the fun was happening at the park. He'd watched her sniffing around some bloke, old enough to be her father, so he knew she would be up for it.

Late in the afternoon, he'd spied her going past, dressed to the nines, short skirt, high heels, leather jacket and hair sailing in the breeze. After two hours of sitting by his window awaiting her return, his frustration had increased.

He pulled on a fleece jacket and ventured out. At first, he strayed no further than the end of his road. From there he had a view across the park towards the 'river roads', to the shops and community centre. He would be able to see her approaching. As time dragged on and there was no sign of Carrie, he wandered further, into the parkland and eventually all the way to the shops then right out of the estate. All he could think about was what he would do with this girl when he got his chance.

As the day faded to dusk then darkness, feeling disappointed, he ambled towards home. Maybe Carrie was not for returning until late into the night. He had no doubt that she was a busy young thing. Not once did it occur to him that she might be listening to music or watching TV at a friend's house nearby. As far as Barry was concerned, she had to be screwing some bloke. Why then couldn't he have his share?

Suddenly, at last, his heart raced. He had just exited the park and crossed the road when Carrie stepped from a house, laughing as she went. Another teenage girl stood on the doorstep sharing a cheerful goodnight with Carrie. Barry's pace was slow, perfect for following her.

Most people on the estate took shortcuts. They didn't walk the length of a street if they were able to cut through an alleyway, even if the route was no shorter. Barry hoped that Carrie would behave in the same manner. To his delight, she veered right and disappeared between the houses, and down an alley that led to a parking area at the rear. He knew then that she would cross the open space before entering another passageway. Barry didn't follow. Instead, he hurried past the first alley, along the street and into another where he could meet Carrie coming the other way.

He was already halfway down the passage when Carrie entered it. She didn't hesitate when she saw him. Treadwater was safe nowadays.

'Hiya, Carrie,' he said.

'Hiya,' she replied.

Barry stepped in front of her. She smiled curiously then went to walk around him. As if in confusion, Barry moved the same way. She smiled nervously.

'Are you heading home?' he asked her.

'Yes.'

'Where's my goodnight kiss then?'

She attempted to squeeze past his bulk, but he used his girth to block her way and pressed her against the wall.

'C'mon, Carrie love, where's the harm? You know me, don't you? Just a goodnight kiss.'

'Let me go!'

He squeezed his body against hers and attempted to kiss her. Carrie shook her head from side to side.

'No! Get off me!'

Barry couldn't stop himself. His hand moved to her skirt then slid between her legs. The girl broke into tears as she punched his chest.

'What the fuck?'

Barry saw her standing in the darkened alley, a child at each hand. Barry immediately stepped away, and Carrie hurried off in tears.

'You dirty bastard,' said Danni.

CHAPTER 62

Stan

He often thought of him. Alec was his older brother. Of course, at his age, Stan was prone to nostalgia, recalling those times way back when they were kids. He could see them both, kicking a football at a street corner in Bootle, goalposts painted on the gable wall, and not a care in the world. They shared a happy but tough childhood and then both had joined the army. They even served together for a while, in West Belfast, Germany then Londonderry. After that, Alec went off to be an instructor at an army training centre, while Stan remained with his regiment and eventually became a sergeant.

Alec retired first. He resettled in Bootle with his wife, Gladys, and his multiple sclerosis.

It was the disease that weakened him, otherwise he would have fought them off. One night a pair of drug-crazed youths tied him up and forced Gladys to hand over what little cash and valuables they had in their home. Then the bastards stabbed both Gladys and Alec until there was little blood left in them to drip on the floor.

Stan was the one who found them. He called every Sunday morning to bring them their papers and to collect their weekly shopping list. Hannah always did their shopping along with their own. In his life, Stan had seen blood spilled many times, but when it was one of his own, he was unable to deal with it. He knew afterwards that he took his anger out on Hannah. She was good for it anyway, the dull, silly woman.

Sometimes he pushed the images to the back of his mind and concentrated on the good times he and Alec had shared. Lately, though, that had been impossible. Hannah had annoyed him several times. She had sneaked out of the house the other day. God knows who she spoke to and what they discussed. The bitch couldn't be trusted.

His wife's behaviour, however, was not the source of his present trouble. It was another woman. The new one who had joined the choir – not her with the shaved head but the hard-looking one. He knew her. Oh yes, he remembered her from living on this estate years ago. Beth Chapman was her name. And now she was singing in his choir and making friends with Hannah. Beth didn't know anything about him. But he recognised her.

Beth and her boyfriend had murdered Alec and Gladys. She had done her time, and he'd heard that the bastard boyfriend had died in jail. Seventeen years was all that she served. That wasn't enough for him. Murder should mean the death penalty. He wouldn't rest until this Beth got what she deserved.

CHAPTER 63

Tara, Sheena and Katrina

Sheena seemed quite a shy girl as far as Tara could tell. She had a pretty face, although her eyes were set a little deep, and she could have smiled more.

Katrina handed Tara a generous pouring of vodka and offered Diet Coke to go with it. She replenished Sheena's gin, one of those brands with an exotic flavouring. Finally, Katrina topped up her own glass with neat gin and slumped into the sofa beside Tara. The living room was tidy with a three-piece suite, coffee table, a television mounted on the wall, uplighters in two corners and laminate flooring.

'Now, what are we girls going to talk about?' Katrina asked.

Tara smiled at the question, but Sheena offered nothing. There was rap music playing in the background. It didn't appeal to Tara, but at least it made the lack of chat less ominous. Suddenly, she went for it.

'I heard they identified two of the bodies that were dug up.'

Sheena eyed Tara suspiciously, while Katrina gulped her drink.

'A Dale something and the other was Linus Jones,' Tara added. 'Can't say I ever heard of them.'

'Why would you, Claire love?' said Katrina. 'You don't come from round here.'

'Did either of you know them?' Tara asked.

Sheena adjusted herself in the armchair but didn't reply. It was Katrina who offered something, although Tara was not inclined to believe her.

'I don't think they came from round here.'

'There used to be a lot of gangs on the estate,' said Sheena. 'They most likely came from one of them. My mum told me that when I was a kid there used to be fighting every night on the football pitch. It all stopped after the gangs got broken up.'

'The thing is,' said Tara, 'I don't think those guys have been dead that long.'

'Where did you hear that?' Katrina asked.

'On the news, this morning.'

Katrina shook her head which, this evening, was adorned in a black bob wig. Stubble showed through her make-up and, without lipstick, the fact that Katrina was still physically male was very apparent.

'I didn't hear it,' she said bluntly.

Tara sensed the defensiveness in the comment. She was going too far, asking too many questions. It seemed that even the younger people of Treadwater were easily irritated by the subject of the murders.

'Maybe it was last night I heard it,' said Tara. 'Anyway, that's enough morbid talk. Any chance you've got some Foo Fighters to listen to?'

'That's my girl,' said Katrina. She jumped from the sofa and went to the iPod. 'Sorry Sheena, you're outvoted, love.' She changed the music and soon the room was filled with the sound of *The Pretender* by the Foo Fighters. Katrina attempted a crude dance, with her glass of gin in her hand. 'Did you know that George Harrison said that rap music was spelt with a silent c?' she said.

As the night wore on, Tara found Sheena to be a cheerful girl, full of witty remarks and with an endearing giggle. Such was the power of alcohol to lower barriers. For a couple of hours, Tara felt like she was one of them. They discussed music, night clubs, clothes and make-up.

She refrained from asking any more probing questions, and there were no more awkward silences. They simply got drunk and had a blast.

After midnight, Tara made her way back to her temporary home. Sheena accompanied her part of the way then headed to her house in Cherwell Avenue. At times, Tara saw the pavement rising to meet her. Then she would stagger, regain her footing and hobble on. When she reached her block, she found her key and, at the third attempt, opened the door and rolled inside. By her sink, she filled a pint glass with water and drank as much as her stomach could take. A hangover in the morning was the last thing she wanted. She checked the time. It was just gone half past one. Her drunkenness made the decision for her. It wasn't too late to call Murray.

'Helloo, Alan love.'

'Tara! Is everything all right? It's nearly two in the morning.'

'I'm fine and dandy, how are you, sweetheart?'

'What's up, you sound like you've been on the razzle?'

'Hazard of the job. Might have had a couple. Listen, I need you to do something for me.'

'Why don't we talk in the morning, Tara? It's late, try to get some sleep.'

'It's ma'am to you, DS Murray and don't you f–for–forget it. I don't want to sleep. Just listen. Will you listen, for fuck's sake?'

'OK, OK, what do you have to tell me?'

'I want you to check…' At that point Tara hiccupped and felt rather nauseous. 'I want you… have to go!' She dropped her phone and scurried to the bathroom.

Murray waited for a few minutes, decided his boss was not about to resume her conversation and ended the call.

CHAPTER 64

The committee

'Has anyone seen Justin Boyle lately?' the chairperson asked.

There was no response.

'Has the second warning been delivered?'

'Yes,' the secretary replied.

'And has he responded?'

'Nope.'

'In that case I suggest we move to the next stage with young Justin,' said the chairperson. 'All those in favour?'

Six hands were raised in addition to that of the chairperson. The vote was unanimous.

'Right, carried. Justin Boyle is to be forcibly removed from the estate. A date needs to be set for that.'

'We have to find him first,' said the treasurer, chuckling.

'Fine! The date of removal to be set once Justin has returned home,' said the chairperson.

It was hardly a satisfactory conclusion to the issue. The committee had become used to absolutes. Usually, a date was set, and the sentence was carried out. That was how they operated. An offender who was difficult to apprehend might lead to problems later.

'Next item is Stan Oldfield,' said the chairperson. 'Any more thoughts about him?'

'Nothing to add from my proposal,' said one member.

'Do we issue a first warning, or do we wait for further evidence?' the chairperson asked.

'We need more,' said one. 'We're not bullies, our only aim is to keep Treadwater safe.'

'I agree,' said another.

'So, we defer until such time as there is more information? All those in favour?'

The vote was again unanimous, although the proposer of Stan Oldfield did not look happy.

The meeting was then paused for tea and biscuits. Conversation was muted. These were the most difficult times since the formation of the Treadwater Residents' Committee. Past decisions and executions were under police investigation because they had been reckless in disposing of offenders. The chairperson, however, was determined that their good work should not be undone. For the decent people of Treadwater, it was vital that they carried on.

The chairperson called the meeting to order once again as members set down their teacups.

'I hope that tonight there are no further names, but we are obliged to consider all proposals. That is how we have been successful in improving life on the estate.'

Immediately, four pieces of paper were placed face down on the coffee table.

'My God,' said the chairperson. 'What is going on?'

There was a ripple of nervous laughter. The submission of names did not mean that action would have to be taken. All cases would be discussed and considered very carefully before moving to the next stage. Still, it was unprecedented for four papers to be submitted on the same night.

The chairperson lifted one paper from the table.

'We have a Barry Sugden. I don't know of him. What's the charge?'

'Pervert!' a member blurted.

'We're going to need more than that,' said the chairperson.

There were chuckles from the others.

'He has been trying it on with young teenage girls,' a member explained. 'One girl was assaulted, the night before last.'

'Who was it?' another member asked.

The chairperson interjected.

'We don't have to know that. All we need is genuine information regarding Barry Sugden. Does anyone have anything to add regarding his character?'

'He always seemed that way to me,' said another member. 'I wouldn't trust him around young girls. I've seen him several times hanging around the park.'

'OK, we'll take it in hand,' said the chairperson. The second slip of paper was turned over. 'Next, we have Beth Chapman. What's the charge?'

'She's an ex-offender, only moved here a few weeks ago,' the secretary explained. 'Best that she moves out again.'

There was sniggering from the others.

'Hardly enough to go on,' said the chairperson. 'Is there any evidence that she's up to no good?'

There were no replies.

'Right then, we'll set her to the side.' Another slip of paper was turned over. 'Claire Brady.'

'Also new here, and she is also an ex-offender,' said the proposer.

'Again, not enough to warrant action,' said the chairperson.

Serious looks were exchanged between the proposer and the chairperson.

'She's been asking a hell of a lot of questions about Mandy,' the proposer responded. 'They are friends.'

'Still not enough for action,' the chairperson declared. 'But she may be worth watching.'

The fourth and final piece of paper was turned over on the coffee table, all eyes upon it. For the second meeting in succession, there were gasps all around. Except for one man, who sat ashen-faced, gazing from the slip of paper to the faces of each colleague. It was his name written on the paper.

'Well, Ian,' said the chairperson, 'have you anything to say?'

CHAPTER 65

Tara

A rather sheepish Detective Inspector Grogan climbed into the unmarked police car. She'd walked over a mile beyond Treadwater to meet Murray in a lay-by close to the junction with the M57. Two days had passed since her drunken phone call in the middle of the night to her DS. She did not remember what she had said, only that she woke him around two in the morning then had to call later that day to apologise and to request that he check the crime statistics for the Treadwater Estate over the last five years.

'Morning, ma'am, how are we today?'

Tara realised that he'd draped the question in his facetious wit, but what could she say? She'd been drunk and made a fool of herself.

'I'm fine, Alan, thanks for asking. And how about you?' she replied in a faux-business-like manner.

'Not bad, although I haven't had a good night's sleep for the past couple of nights – late night pranksters on the phone.'

'OK, OK, is that it, are you finished now? What have you got for me?'

'Well, ma'am, it is as you thought. There's been a marked reduction in moderate to serious crime in Treadwater over the last two and half years. I'm excluding, of course, the ongoing murder inquiries. Gun and drug-related crime are nil for the period.'

'The community choir started almost three years ago, so that would tie in with the reduced crime rate.'

'The only serious incidents have been the findings of the bodies. Gang trouble has virtually disappeared. As for petty crime, if there is any occurring, it is not being reported to us.'

'What's really getting me, Alan, is that not one person on that estate wants to discuss anything to do with crime or missing people. I haven't even found someone who might be a suspect. It's bizarre.'

'What about this choir?'

'Most of the people I've had contact with so far are members. They're all quite affable, except for one man who told me to drop the subject of Mandy Wright. I had a row with him the day after the bodies were found on the playing fields. He accused me of being a prostitute and suggested I leave the estate.'

'Raymond Glover?'

'That's him.'

'We've run a check on him,' said Murray. 'He's clean as a whistle. Never even had a parking ticket.'

'Why does that not surprise me? I tried to get something out of the choir's leader, Esther Dodds. She was very defensive, but also proud that the choir has improved the lives of so many people on the estate. She was horrified by the suggestion that a vigilante group is operating on the estate and may consist of choir members.'

'Tweedy is considering calling you back in,' said Murray. 'He thinks that it might be better to tackle this from the crime scene evidence.'

'Which amounts to zilch. No, tell him that I want to keep at it for a while longer. Maybe getting under the skin of a man like Raymond Glover will cause these vigilantes, if they do exist, to reveal themselves.'

'You mean, you're going to have them come after you?' said Murray. 'Too dangerous, ma'am.'

'We'll soon see.'

CHAPTER 66

The choir

'That was a terrible start! Let's try it again.'

Esther observed the faces in the room. Not one of them looked enthusiastic.

'Marcus, play the introduction. Listen up, sopranos, and be ready to come in.'

The music began and the voices joined in. The choir already knew the song well. Esther couldn't understand it. Two weeks until their big night and not one person looked as though they cared to be here. Ian Bankhead had his head down, singing into his lap. Stan was hardly making a sound at all. Valerie wasn't concentrating, and she was singing flat. Danni, for the second week in a row, had not even turned up. Carrie seemed on the verge of tears. She kept blowing her nose then dabbing at her eyes with a tissue.

As the evening wore on, Esther's confidence that they would be ready to perform in two weeks' time was floundering. Worryingly, she knew the reason behind their lethargy. Bad things were happening on this estate. That new girl, Claire, had her wondering. If only she hadn't quarrelled with Mandy Wright.

When practice had finished, Esther immediately sought out Dinah. If she had a friend in this choir, it was Dinah.

'Did you feel it tonight?'

'What do you mean?' Dinah asked.

'Something's not right, Dinah. I feel that there's something going on that I should know about.'

'I don't think so, Esther. Everyone is nervous; the concert is only a fortnight away.'

'That's what I'm worried about.'

Dinah threw her arms around Esther.

'Everything will be fine, love,' Dinah said. 'You've put your heart and soul into this choir. We won't let you down, I promise. Now go home, pour yourself a G&T then get a good night's sleep. I'll come and see you tomorrow and we can talk more.'

Dinah gave her another hug. Esther couldn't hold back her tears but took solace from Dinah's encouragement.

Tara, aka Claire, found herself in a huddle of women when practice had ended.

'Danni out with her new beau again?' Katrina asked Valerie.

Valerie's expression didn't seem to welcome the question.

'No idea,' she replied. 'She just rang me and said that she wasn't bringing the kids over.'

'It must be love then,' said Katrina, pushing the brown hair of her long wig behind her shoulders. Yet again, she was dressed to thrill, a black vinyl miniskirt with silver buckles, fake tanned legs and black stilettos.

Smiling sweetly next to Tara was Hannah, a woman who only ever seemed on the periphery of conversations.

'Hello, love,' Tara said. 'How are you keeping?'

'I'm fine, thank you. Just the usual aches and pains for a woman my age.'

'You're not that old surely?'

'Eighty-two next birthday, if I make it that far.'

'Have you met Beth?' Tara asked.

Beth smiled, her missing tooth causing it to look more of a sneer.

'Hiya, love,' said Beth. 'I think we've already met.'

'I know, dear. Are you both enjoying the choir?'

'It's great,' Beth replied.

Tara noticed that Katrina seemed to be taking an interest in their conversation, her gaze was fixed on Hannah.

'You're looking lovely this evening, Nathan love,' said Hannah. 'How on earth can you walk in those heels?'

'Practice and blisters, love.' Katrina seemed amused by her being called Nathan. Tonight, she looked convincing as a woman.

'Hannah!'

Stan was suddenly standing over them. His face looked angry, Tara thought.

'Time to go,' he said.

Hannah rose immediately from her chair. Her warm smile had vanished with her husband's appearance. She didn't utter another word as she walked away.

'You take good care of our Hannah, Stanley!' Katrina called out.

Stan turned and glared, his face glowing red, his green eyes firmly set on Katrina.

Katrina ignored his stare and called to Hannah.

'Bye, Hannah love. See you next week. Mind how you go.'

Stan took Hannah firmly by the arm and marched her from the room. His actions didn't go unnoticed by the others.

'They seem a bit like chalk and cheese, those two,' said Tara.

'Darby and Joan, they are not,' said Valerie. 'The poor woman, having to live with that.'

'Do you think he rules the roost?' Tara persisted.

'Definitely,' Katrina replied, looking towards the door from where the couple had just departed. 'I would say he's a right bastard, and it wouldn't surprise me if he keeps Hannah under lock and key.'

CHAPTER 67

Ian and Carrie

Ian stopped his car in Sefton Mill Lane, at the dead end beside the church. It was dark and deserted, save for one ornate street light casting shadows within the car. Carrie immediately climbed from her seat and attempted to sit on his lap, but he pushed her back.

'Not now, Carrie, we need to talk.'

'Kiss me first.'

'Listen, please, this is important.'

'Kiss me first!'

Caving into her request, he leaned across and kissed her once on the lips. She smiled lovingly.

'That's better. Now, what do you want to talk about?' she said.

Carrie had a broad smile, she felt completely at ease with Ian. She loved him so much. Being with him, she could almost forget what that pervert Barry Sugden had tried to do. But she knew that Sugden would get what he deserved. When Ian had finished what he had to say, she would tell him about Barry. She knew that he would sort out the creepy git.

'We have to stop this, Carrie.'

'Stop what?' She laughed nervously.

'Seeing each other. At least for a while, until you're sixteen and maybe longer.'

'But we love each other. You're not worried about other people again, are you?'

'Yes I am. I've been handed a warning, Carrie.'

'Warning? Who from? My mum and dad don't know about us.'

'From the people on the estate.'

'What people? You're not making any sense, Ian. I'll be sixteen in a few months, so tell them to go and fuck themselves.'

Ian took hold of Carrie by the arms and looked into her eyes. She was so beautiful and pure, and he knew that she loved him. This damn committee was spoiling everything for him.

'It doesn't work like that, Carrie. These people, they control everything that happens on Treadwater. They keep us all safe. They get rid of anyone who dares to cause trouble.'

Carrie's face was filled with confusion. Ian wasn't talking sense.

'What people, Ian? Do you even know who they are?'

'Yes, I do. We just have to cool things until you turn sixteen. Then it won't even matter if your parents know about us.'

'But I don't want to. I can't be without you, Ian. I love you so much and…'

'What?'

'I think I'm pregnant.'

'You think?'

'I'm five days late.'

'God!'

Carrie broke into tears.

'It's all right, Carrie. We can get rid of it.'

It was the wrong thing to say to a girl so hopelessly in love with him and until that moment a girl who had been so joyous. Now what was he to do? How would the others on the committee judge him?

When Carrie had stopped crying, he touched her face, gently wiping away the tears running with mascara. He smiled, but she couldn't match him.

'Maybe we could go away,' he suggested.

'Do you mean it?'

'Yes, of course I do. You want to be with me, don't you?'

'More than anything.'

He kissed her and she snuggled into his chest. Her hand moved to his fly and he knew she would be all right. What the future held, he had no clue.

CHAPTER 68

Stan and Hannah

Stan had barely closed the front door behind them when he struck out with his hand, catching her on the side of the face with his knuckles. Hannah fell backwards, crying out as she landed on the stairs.

'What have I told you? Don't talk to anyone without me.'

'But, Stan, the women spoke to me first. It would have been rude not to answer them.'

'I don't care if it's rude. You don't speak to people when I'm not there to hear you. Get up!'

He grasped her wrists and hauled her towards him. Holding her firmly in front of him, he pushed his face close to hers.

'What did you tell them?'

'Nothing. It was just a casual chat about the choir.'

'I don't believe you. You told them about me, didn't you? How I treat you.' He shook her hard to get her answer.

'No, Stan, honestly. I didn't.'

'Liar! Why would that queer tell me to look after you if he didn't know anything? You told him, didn't you?'

'No. Please, Stan. I didn't.'

He dragged her upstairs, her feet barely landing on each step. Then he thrust open the door of her room, pulled her inside and threw her down on the bed.

'You will stay there until you tell me the truth, bitch!'

The door slammed behind him as Hannah sobbed into her pillow.

Stan continued to fume as he settled into his own bed. He was certain that people were talking about him. That queer's comment convinced him. But he was more irritated that Hannah had been talking to that murdering bitch Beth Chapman.

CHAPTER 69

Dinah

Dinah rose from her knees by the table she used as her prayer corner. She closed her *Book of Common Prayer*, still using it daily even though she was a member of the local Baptist church and not Church of England. After making coffee and a slice of toast, she sat in her living room with her Bible resting on her lap. This was her quiet time, seven in the morning, before her kids had crawled from their beds, and before it was time for her to go to work.

Lately, Dinah had found that she needed her quiet time more than ever. Not since her partner, Gerry, had flitted back to Ireland, had she felt her burden so heavy. She sought reassurance from God's word that she was following a righteous path.

This morning, she read from the Psalms. There were three in a row: 138, 139 and 140 that formed her prayers and lightened her heart.

From 138 she read:

The Lord will fulfil his purpose for me; your steadfast love, O Lord, endures forever.

From 139:

Search me, O God, and know my heart! Try me and know my thoughts!

And from 140:

Guard me, O Lord, from the hands of the wicked; preserve me from violent men, who have planned to trip up my feet. [...] I know that the Lord will maintain the cause of the afflicted and will execute justice for the needy. Surely the righteous shall give thanks to your name; the upright shall dwell in your presence.

Sheena padded into the living room in her pyjamas, yawning and running fingers through her hair.

'Morning.'

'Morning, Mum. Have we any Shredded Wheat left?'

'I don't know, darling. Have a look, but save some milk for Marcus, there isn't much left.'

Dinah took a final glance at the Psalms then closed her Bible. More than ever, she needed those words to be true, not just for her but for her children. Sheena had grown into the woman she had wished her to be, strong-willed, tenacious and, above all, with a view of what is right and wrong in the world.

When Marcus and Sheena finished breakfast and got dressed, all three were out of the house and on their way to work or college.

In mid-afternoon when Dinah had finished work, she called with Esther as she had promised the night before.

She was pleased to find her closest friend back to her jovial and busy self. Esther had made tea and had baked scones, serving them with cream and strawberry jam.

'I'm glad to see you looking better,' said Dinah.

Esther looked as though she was about to hit town on a shopping trip. She had freshly washed hair and wore a satin blouse with a short leather skirt that only she could get away with. Dinah never had the confidence to dress like that.

'We all have to keep going, don't we?' said Esther with a sigh. 'I've been looking forward to a nice cuppa with you. I've been out all morning. I was meeting with the manager of the leisure centre, sorting out the arrangements for the concert.'

She sat down opposite her friend and poured the tea into china cups.

'How did it go?' asked Dinah.

'Very well, I think. Mary should be here any minute. She's agreed to help with refreshments, flowers and typing up the programme for the big night.'

It was then that Dinah noticed a third teacup and side-plate sitting on the tray. Esther's despondency from last night had evaporated and Dinah was happy to see it.

'Ah, here she is now.' Esther went to open the front door for Mary. When she came into the living room, Dinah rose from her seat and hugged her.

'This is lovely,' said Mary. 'All the girls together. I'm so glad to get out of the house. Raymond is like a bear with a sore head today. He's moaning about everything and sniping at me. It's not my fault it's rained all day, and he can't get out to his plants.'

Mary removed her coat and sat next to Dinah on the sofa, while Esther poured some tea for her.

'They say that bad weather is enough to put anyone in a foul mood,' said Esther, handing a plate with a scone to Mary.

'I don't think that's our Raymond's problem. He's been down for days now, ever since he had the row with that new girl, Claire.'

'He had a row?' asked Dinah.

'Yes, she came up to us in the street one day and started asking questions about Mandy. She told us that she was a friend of hers. Raymond gave her short shrift, although he went a bit too far.'

'How do you mean?' Dinah again raised the question.

Esther sat tight-lipped and rather po-faced.

'Well, he told her that if she was Mandy's friend then more than likely she was also a prostitute, and if she was intending to do that kind of thing, she should get out of Treadwater.'

'Poor girl,' said Dinah.

'She came round here,' said Esther. 'We were going through the songs for the concert, but then she started asking about Mandy.'

'What did you tell her?' Dinah asked, her expression looking increasingly concerned.

'She knew that Mandy and I had argued, but she suggested that was the reason why Mandy had left. I told her she was wrong about that. We only quarrelled about song choices for the choir, hardly enough to have her disappear.

'Claire also suggested that Mandy was forced off the estate,' Esther continued. 'Then she had the nerve to suggest that the murders were connected to the choir.'

Esther, in surprise at the lack of response, examined the faces of Dinah and Mary.

'What do you think about that?' Esther asked.

'I daren't tell my Raymond that one,' Mary said. 'He'd go spare. He didn't like the girl from the start.'

CHAPTER 70

Tara

It was an ominous development, but things were moving faster than she had even hoped. Standing barefoot in pyjamas by the door of her flat, Tara read the letter for a second time.

It has come to our attention that your presence on this estate is causing upset among residents. Your behaviour is not conducive to peaceful community living. Kindly desist from your current activities. If you do not, we request that you arrange to quit this estate at the earliest date possible. Failure to do so will result in an upscale in consequences for you.

The envelope was addressed to the occupier. The letter had been typed, printed and signed Treadwater Residents' Committee. Tara was amazed and confounded by the audacity of whoever had sent it. Nevertheless, here was confirmation that a vigilante group was operational on the estate. With the reduction in crime in the area, it seemed that residents of Treadwater were dedicated to taking the law into their own hands.

As she prepared some coffee and sat at her Formica-topped table with uneven legs that rocked on the floor, she wondered just what behaviour had been referred to in the letter. Was it simply her asking questions of everyone she met? Perhaps, they did not like the idea of her being a friend of Mandy Wright's. Or was it down to the belief, expressed by Raymond Glover, that she was a working prostitute? No matter which was correct, it gave her the scope to escalate the dispute.

Drifting off on her plans, she was startled by a loud knocking on the door. Suddenly, she was fearful of being confronted by vigilantes.

'Who's there?' she asked, standing well back from the door.

'It's Beth.'

Tara swung the door open to find Beth holding a letter in her hand.

'Take a look at this,' Beth said, sounding irritated. She barged in and thrust the letter at Tara.

Tara examined a duplicate of the letter she had received.

'I got one, too,' she said, handing it back.

'Bloody hell, Claire, what have we done to deserve this? And who the fuck do these assholes think they are?'

Tara was more surprised and puzzled as to why Beth had been issued with the same threat. As far as she knew, Beth had kept her head down. Aside from joining the choir and befriending Katrina, she had not associated with anyone.

She offered Beth some coffee and the pair sat down at the wonky table.

'I know I've upset people by asking questions about Mandy,' said Tara. 'Because of that they also think I'm on the game. But what have you done to cross them?'

'No fucking idea. I might have cheeked the sarky cow at the library.'

'Hardly enough, surely.'

'Maybe they found out that I've done time.'

'You too?' said Tara. 'It might be that. Have you told anyone round here?'

Beth thought for a moment, then slowly shook her head.

'I don't think I have. I've really only spoken to you and Katrina.'

'Well, you hadn't told me that you've done time. What were you inside for?'

'Murder.'

'Maybe they found out,' Tara suggested.

'Who the fuck are *they*, Claire?'

'I don't know, but I'm wondering if they are responsible for the murders on the estate. I don't mind telling you, Beth, that I'm shit scared.'

* * *

When Beth had gone back to her own flat, Tara called Murray. If she wished to force these people to increase the threat level, she would have to make a more public showing of her undesirable behaviour.

'What's up, ma'am?' asked Murray.

Tara told Murray about the letters and explained her plans.

'I need to create the impression that I'm a sex worker.' As soon as she said it, she could visualise the smirk on Murray's face. Give it a minute and the jokes would be bouncing around the operations room. 'I need several fake clients to call at the flat. Just make sure they won't be recognised on the estate. They must make their presence obvious. Get them to ask for directions, or something. Word needs to get about the estate that they are calling at my flat and that I'm a prostitute.'

'How much will you be charging for this service, ma'am?'

'Don't be smart, Alan. It's clear from those letters that someone in Treadwater is dishing out street justice. I want to provoke them, to get another reaction from them. Please explain all of this to Tweedy.'

'Yes, ma'am, will do. I'll let you know when I have your clients set up.'

'Thank you. I'll make them a cup of tea for their trouble.'

'Take care, ma'am.'

'Yes, Alan, I will. Thank you.'

Tara got dressed and hurried from the flat. She caught a bus from the terminus beside the shops and travelled to the outskirts of the city. In and around Bold Street, she browsed several charity shops for tarty-looking clothes that would make her look like a sex worker. An hour later, she made her way home to Wapping Dock. She could do with some proper company for a while. Kate and Adele were both overjoyed to see her. She asked Kate to wash her nearly new clothes, while she lingered in a warm shower. It was the thing she missed the most while she'd been skulking in the Treadwater flat.

They enjoyed lunch together, and Tara related her experience of life on the council estate.

'Promise me you'll take care of yourself,' said Kate. 'And I don't want you moving there permanently, understand. Adele and I need you here.'

'I'll be fine. If things go to plan it should all be over in a couple of weeks. If it's not, then you can both come to hear me singing in the community choir.'

'Definitely.'

It was dark and quite late when Kate dropped her off close to the estate entrance. They had spent the evening trying on the clothes Tara had bought, and together with a long black wig, Kate had transformed her to the persona of a working prostitute.

Tara strutted through the estate, dressed in her new working clothes, although her progress was difficult in a pair of stiletto boots. When she reached her building on Deeside Crescent, it was clear that matters had already escalated.

There was a large hole in Beth's living room window.

CHAPTER 71

Tara

Tara was awakened by a call from Murray.

'What time is it?' she asked.

'Just after nine, ma'am.'

She sat upright in bed. Not that she had a tight schedule for the day, but she had overslept.

'What do you want?'

'And good morning to you, ma'am. I have some news for you.'

'I'm all ears.'

'The woman found on the M57; we may have an ID.'

'How so?'

'We were contacted by Greater Manchester Police. They were interested in Olev Eesmaa. They are looking for his girlfriend, Elsa Remmel. She's only nineteen and came to the UK looking for Olev. Her parents have been unable to contact her. It seems that Olev came to England looking for work and ended up dealing drugs. He was supposed to return home six months ago. When he didn't show, Elsa came looking for him. She was staying in Manchester when her family last heard from her.'

'It seems likely then.'

'We're waiting on a DNA profile from Estonia, via Manchester, to check against our victim.'

'Good. Thanks, Alan. I'll speak to you later. I've another matter to deal with this morning. My neighbour, Beth, has a broken window. I'm going to check if it was a deliberate attack.'

Tara ended the call, slipped from her bed and quickly dressed. She went downstairs and knocked on Beth's door. It was opened immediately.

'I was just coming to call with you,' said Beth. 'Some bastard put a brick through my window last night.'

Beth walked back inside, and Tara followed, the stench of cigarette smoke ripe in the air.

'I saw it,' said Tara. 'It was late when I got back, and I didn't want to wake you.'

'I didn't sleep a wink.'

Tara examined the broken window.

'What happened?'

'Luckily, I was in the kitchen when I heard the crash,' said Beth. 'That bloody great brick was lying on the floor.' Beth pointed to a piece of paving slab on the windowsill. Splinters of glass were scattered around the floor. 'And there was a note wrapped around the sodding thing.' Beth lifted a crumpled paper from the sofa and showed it to

Tara. She continued talking as Tara read the message. 'They didn't give us much time from the first one, did they? Bastards.'

Get out of Treadwater. I know who you are.

'I rushed outside, but it was dark,' said Beth. 'I didn't see a soul.'

Tara read the note again.

'I don't think this note came from the same source.' Tara was suddenly conscious of sounding like a police officer, and quickly altered her tone. 'Somebody else did this.'

'Don't fucking matter, does it?' snapped Beth. 'Amounts to the same thing. Bastards!'

'We should call the police,' said Tara.

'Bizzies? What the hell will they do about it? They can't manage to catch murderers round here, why would they even bother about the likes of us?'

'These letters and the brick through your window might be connected to the murders. Maybe the people that were killed were threatened first and told to leave the estate.'

'Fucking great! So, if we don't clear out, they're going to kill us?' Beth searched for her rolling tobacco and cigarette papers. 'Fuck me, Claire. I can't take much more of this hassle.'

'You sit down and have a smoke,' said Tara. 'I'll make some tea.'

Beth did as Tara suggested. In the kitchen Tara found some tea bags on the bench and milk in the small fridge. She filled the kettle and switched it on. While she waited, she washed out two mugs and thought about the latest note. It was handwritten with a pen and was a terse statement, unlike the first two letters which had been business-like in tone, typed and posted through the letter box. And why send this one only to Beth?

CHAPTER 72

Danni

Danni awoke from one hell of a bad night. Mikaela and Bradley hardly slept. They were up before five and playing riotously in their room. The dog next door had barked continuously. Her head throbbed. It was a tension headache, and she knew it would not go away easily. Her throat was parched, a sign that she'd snored during what fitful sleep she did have. Traipsing into the living room after nine o'clock, she found the kids on the sofa watching TV, a documentary about lions and big cats. At least they were now quiet. She smiled at Mikaela who was munching on dry Coco Pops, her eyes on the TV and not on the crumbs falling around her. Bradley, just as interested in the lions, had both hands set on a half-built LEGO model.

Neither child acknowledged their mother's presence. The dog next door was still barking. She was thinking that Justin should be reported to the council for not looking after the vicious mutt properly, when she heard more noise from outside. There were feet shuffling on the stairs. Then she heard shouting and banging on a door.

Still in her pyjamas, she stepped onto the landing. A man in a high-vis jacket was banging his fist on the door of Justin's flat. Danni saw that his jacket had RSPCA printed on the back. Inside, the dog was going frantic, barking and scratching on the door. Also present, were two elderly women Danni recognised as neighbours from the house adjoining the four flats. They were twin sisters, both dressed in floral dressing gowns and fluffy slippers. One of them wore curlers in her silver hair. The RSPCA man ceased his hammering on the door and turned to Danni.

'Do you know if there's anyone in, love?'

Danni hadn't really considered the idea of Justin not being there. She assumed he was on another bender and had passed out. The dog barking would go unnoticed.

'I'm not sure,' Danni replied, 'I haven't seen him for a while.'

'Can't you break down the door?' asked the woman wearing curlers.

'I can only do that if I'm convinced the dog's well-being is at risk,' the man replied.

'But it's been barking like that all night and most of yesterday,' said the other twin.

'Justin might be in there,' said Danni. 'He's an addict.'

'Then we should call the police,' said the man.

Twenty minutes later, two uniforms bounded up the concrete stairs and joined the RSPCA officer and Danni on the landing. The twins had returned to their house.

'I can't be sure there's anyone inside,' the RSPCA officer explained.

'Who lives here?' a female constable asked Danni.

'Justin Boyle,' she answered.

The constable banged on the door.

'Mr Boyle? Police. Can you open the door please?'

Danni smirked when the RSPCA man gazed at her, rolling his eyes. As if he hadn't already tried that.

'Nothing but the dog barking,' said the RSPCA man. 'If the lad is in there he might be in trouble, passed out or something.'

The male uniform took his cue from his colleague.

'Stand back. I'll have to force it.'

He snap-kicked his foot close to the lock but without success. A second more forceful kick sent the door swinging inward and a barking dog rushing out. The RSPCA man swiftly gathered the dog and managed to get a chain lead around its neck. He led it downstairs and outside.

Danni waited as the two uniforms entered the flat, calling out for Justin Boyle. There was no reply. She was convinced the bizzies would find Justin's lifeless body and steeled herself for the news.

'Clear!' said the female constable.

CHAPTER 73

Ian and Carrie

'Did you do the test?'

Carrie wasn't fully inside the car as Ian blurted his question. He was a man on edge. Trouble was coming at him from every direction. His eldest was hoping to go to university in September and Ian would have to help him financially. His ex-wife was giving him grief, asking for more cash for the other two children, both with school trips coming up. Now he had the committee on his back. Someone had found out about Carrie and squealed to them. Rather than sitting in judgement of others, he was now a subject of their scrutiny. He had tried to explain that there was nothing for the committee to worry about. It was not a sexual relationship, merely a friendship, like father to daughter. Not one of them had looked convinced by his lies. At least they afforded him some respect and had not issued a warning letter.

If Carrie were pregnant, he would be exposed. He thought she had been careful and that she had always taken her pill. He had used condoms, but lately there had been one or two spontaneous moments.

Carrie couldn't help smiling. It unnerved him further.

'Well?' he asked.

Her smile remained, but it only increased his irritation.

'Carrie! It's not funny. I need to know. Are you fucking pregnant or not?'

She was instantly transformed from a beaming teenager to a scolded child. But her tears were not going to help either of them.

'Tell me, Carrie, for fuck's sake!'

She nodded but failed to speak.

Ian saw his world crashing down around him. What would her parents say? He realised then that Carrie was incapable of secrets; she would blurt everything. The police would be involved. A couple in love they may well be, but in the eyes of the law he was the rapist of a child. For a moment, he thought the committee might be more of a saviour. Surely, they would give him an opportunity to get away. But Carrie's thoughts of eloping were pure fantasy. As he drove them to a private spot where they could discuss the issue, his mind raced with options.

Carrie remained tearful for the whole journey to Formby, where Ian stopped the car by the side of a quiet road and under a canopy of trees. By this point, he had settled on one of two options. He could flee, leaving Carrie behind, or he could stay and hope to keep a lid on things. He turned to face her. She was sniffing back tears.

'I think you should have an abortion.'

CHAPTER 74

The choir

Dinah went directly to Esther when she arrived at the community centre. She greeted her with an affectionate hug.

'It will be better this evening, Esther love. We're all behind you.'

'Thanks, Dinah. I'm feeling much better about things. It was probably just nerves getting the better of me the other day.'

Esther turned away to speak with Marcus. She had certain pieces to cover this evening, and she wanted him to play piano. Tonight was an extra practice as activities were ramped up for the concert at the leisure centre. Esther was hoping for a full turnout. Already, however, she noticed Stan arriving alone.

'Is Hannah not coming tonight, Stan?' Mary asked, as Stan took a seat next to Raymond.

'Not feeling well, upset tummy,' he answered.

'Best to take things easy for a day or two,' said Mary. 'Is there anything I can do to help?'

Stan ignored her question and began a conversation with Raymond.

Katrina, who came in with Tara and Beth, had overheard the exchange yet deliberately repeated Mary's question.

'Hannah not coming tonight, Stan?'

The old man glared in her direction but said nothing. He would never understand these weirdos, running the streets in women's clothes, pretending to be something they weren't.

Aside from her usual heavy make-up, as a transgender was compelled to wear to convincingly pass as female, Katrina was moderately dressed. She wore slim-fitting jeans, kitten-heeled shoes and a plain blouse. Tonight, it was Tara who was attracting attention. She wanted to advertise, to make it obvious to those people who resented her presence on Treadwater that her body was open for business. Half of them already believed she was a sex worker; she didn't want to disappoint them. Her skirt barely covered her bottom, she wore boots to her thighs, and her camisole top just about covered the essentials. She'd decided against the wig; thinking that hair, no matter the colour or style, might trigger the memory of one or two people who had met her as a police detective.

When Tara took her seat next to Valerie, she noticed that Danni was also present. That meant that she wasn't on a date with DC John Wilson. She overheard Valerie speaking quietly to her daughter.

'Who's looking after the kids?'

'John offered to do it.'

'You know that Barry doesn't mind.'

'I don't want Barry looking after them anymore.' Danni's voice had fallen to a whisper.

'Why ever not?'

Danni refused to answer, but Valerie persisted.

'Why not, Danni?'

'Just leave it, Mum.'

'No, I won't leave it. Why don't you want Barry to look after my grandchildren? What's he done?'

'Leave it, Mum. Please.'

'If you can't tell me then I'll ask Barry.'

Marcus began to play their intended opening song for the concert, *Good Day Sunshine*. Esther brought the choir in on cue and the hall filled with singing voices.

Ian sang heartily, he felt a little easier following his meeting with Carrie. He was sure that she would have an abortion. The girl would do anything for him. They could cool things for a few months until she was sixteen then all would be fine.

Carrie could scarcely get the words out. Her eyes watered at every note. She had more than just the news of her pregnancy to endure. She was still suffering from the terror of Barry Sugden with his hand up her skirt. With Ian being so angry at her, she hadn't told him about her ordeal. Danni looked in her direction. She knew what had happened, and had come to her rescue, but seeing her tonight wasn't helping. Carrie couldn't bear to look at Ian. She wanted to keep their baby. She loved him. It was the start of their life together. She would be sixteen soon and all this age nonsense would go away. Then she could tell her mum and dad all about Ian.

As Esther moved on to their next song on the programme, *Everybody Wants to Rule the World*, Beth's mind was stuck on the thought of who, within this happy bunch of people, knew of her past and wanted her off the estate. Who was mad enough to throw a brick through her window?

Sheena and her best mate, Katrina, sang heartily. Of all those present in the choir they appeared to have the least to worry about. Sheena's mother, Dinah, sang joyously. She sang always to praise her Lord.

Mary, at first, was tickled to notice Raymond glancing over as they sang. Then she realised that he was staring at one of the younger women. It may have been Sheena or Danni, but then she noticed Claire. The woman Raymond had accused of being a whore. Tonight, she was certainly dressed like one.

Stan felt no guilt that Hannah was missing from choir practice. He'd ordered her to stay at home. After the way she'd behaved last week, he didn't want her chatting to anyone. It was her punishment. She would have to learn that he meant what he said. Besides, how could he allow her to speak with that murdering bitch? It felt good to know that he may have put the fear of God into Beth. She might not be too afraid with just a brick through her window, but if she didn't clear off, next time it would be petrol and a lit match.

Tara couldn't help but enjoy singing. It was lively and uplifting. Esther had a remarkable talent in getting the absolute best out of her choir. Tara hoped also that tonight she had managed to turn a few heads. She didn't feel particularly comfortable in what she wore, but she did feel strangely empowered. And she noticed Raymond watching her closely. Devilishly, she considered offering him her services to see if he would bite. If not, then surely her behaviour would aggravate her situation and cause the vigilantes to act.

Esther felt proud. The singing was amazing. She had arranged these songs, taught the choir how to sing them, blended their voices and now they had a real community choir. She could hardly wait for the concert. It was all coming together so wonderfully well.

CHAPTER 75

Raymond and Mary

'I'll put the kettle on,' said Raymond as they stepped inside their home.

Mary removed her coat and hung it on one of the pegs beneath the stairs. Her mind was still in flux, wondering about Raymond. For months she had suspected that he had something secret going on. This evening, as she observed him ogling that Claire in her miniskirt and boots, she wondered what he got up to when he went out every Tuesday night. The pub with his old work mates, was all he ever told her, but several times she had followed him, and he hadn't gone near any pub. It was a house on the estate, a house she knew well, and the woman who lived there was supposed to be her friend. And then, the other day, he had threatened Claire, a woman he hardly knew when she asked him why no one was prepared to talk about Mandy. Of course, it was Mandy who was gone, and now she realised why Raymond was never willing to discuss the matter. He had been availing of her services. He had been paying her for sex. What a hypocrite, threatening Claire Brady and then tonight he sat lusting over her in those clothes. Was he intending to pay her for sex too?

Raymond entered the living room with two cups of tea. Mary was seated in her usual armchair. She watched his every movement as he placed a cup beside her on the table, lifting the TV remote and settling his body on the sofa. Did he have anything to say to her?

'Well?' she said, expectantly.

'Well, what?' He was reading the TV guide on the screen.

'Have you anything to say about tonight?'

'What about it?'

With each question, Mary felt her frustration surge. She had a headache and thought that her blood pressure was probably raised.

'That girl you had the row with the other day. Claire.'

'What about her?' He hadn't taken his eyes off the TV, and now had found a highlights programme on European Championship football.

'You didn't take your eyes off her all through practice.'

'It's not what you think.'

'Oh, and what do I think, Raymond love?'

He drank some of his tea and showed little interest in her question. Liverpool were on TV, away to Dortmund.

Although Mary didn't expect any more from her husband on the subject, she still had many questions requiring answers. Making them up in her head was not helping. Her Raymond had been troubled since Mandy had gone, but she wasn't entirely sure if that was the reason. If he refused to discuss his worries with her then she remained in turmoil. She would have to keep an eye on Raymond and on this young tart, Claire, who was cavorting around the estate.

CHAPTER 76

Tara

Tara had received four male visitors, two in the morning and two in the afternoon. She made a display of dressing in lingerie, standing by her bedroom window then closing the curtains as each 'client' arrived. Hopefully, someone would notice, and if they were not troubled by it, they may at least pass a comment to someone who was. Beth had noticed the arrival of client number two. She was about to call with Tara when the man took to the stairwell ahead of her. Beth and Tara's eyes met when her door was opened. A wistful smile was exchanged between them.

Mary Glover had witnessed the arrival of man number four. She had deliberately walked a route to the shop that would take her past Claire's flat. Pausing in the street, she saw a man of about forty get out of an Audi car and hurry indoors. Then she witnessed Claire's blatant performance when closing her curtains while wearing just a bra and panties. When she arrived at the mini-market, Mary met Dinah who was just coming out of the shop. Her observation on Deeside Crescent was swiftly reported to her fellow choir member.

For Tara and her caller, it was simply a matter of a nice cup of coffee and a chat over the latest from St Anne Street station. They shared a few personal stories to eke out the time to forty-five minutes. A couple of days more of this and Tara was confident that the right people on Treadwater would have learned of the activities. She fully expected to encounter the next stage in the vigilante process.

The first officer who called with her had brought news from Murray on developments in the murder investigations. The officer, a DC called Derek Courtley, a man in his twenties, fresh-faced with an athletic physique, sat opposite Tara in her kitchen. She didn't think he looked the type who would usually be seen entering the home of a working prostitute, but she decided Murray, in his facetious style, had run something of a lottery among colleagues for doing the job.

'Ma'am, the ID for the M57 victim has now been confirmed as Elsa Remmel,' said Courtley, reading from a notebook. 'She came to England in search of her boyfriend Olev Eesmaa.'

'And they both end up dead on or near this estate.'

'Yes, ma'am. DS Murray told me to tell you that they are now following leads to drug dealing activities in the North Liverpool area. Two of the victims recovered from the football pitch, Dale Wycliffe and Linus Jones, may have been connected to dealing.'

'Any ID for the other two?'

'Not yet. Nothing matches on DNA or on mispers.'

'You can tell DS Murray that I am confident that the truth lies on this estate, whether it be drug dealing or vigilante justice.'

'Yes, ma'am.'

'Can you find out if Elsa Remmel lived on Treadwater for any length of time, or did she merely wander in and upset some of the residents, enough to get her killed.'

Tara wondered just how these people arrived at their verdicts. How had she been judged so far? More crucially, she wondered, who was sitting in judgement.

CHAPTER 77

Danni and Valerie

Valerie didn't even wait until she'd stepped inside her daughter's flat.

'Barry's not friggin' saying anything. I want to know what's going on, Danni.'

This afternoon, Danni had more pills inside her than she cared to admit. Her kids were driving her nuts since she'd collected them from nursery. She felt as though she was hovering in the air high above her mother. But she heard Valerie's demand to know what was going on. At that moment, Valerie had the look of a daughter and Danni the downtrodden mother. She held a glass of neat vodka in her hand.

'Why the hell are you drinking at this time of the day?' Valerie snapped.

'It's water, Mum.'

'Don't lie to me, you're barely awake. What's John going to think if you're boozing all day?'

'Mum, please stop giving me a hard time.' Danni flopped into an armchair, the armrests faded and torn by the kids' playing.

'Tell me why you don't want Barry to mind the kids. What's he done? Has he touched them or something?'

'No, Mum. I don't trust him, that's all.'

'Why not, for goodness sake, Danni?' Valerie stood over her daughter. She wore heels as always. Suddenly, she snatched the glass from Danni's hand and threw it across the room. On hearing the smash of glass on the floor, Bradley and Mikaela came running into the living room.

'Back to your room, it's all right. Gran and I are just talking.'

'I'm not leaving here until you tell me what's going on,' said Valerie.

'Please, Mum, I don't want any more trouble.'

'If there's something up with Barry, so help me, I'll throw the bastard out. What has he done?'

'Don't you even notice? He's always trying to kiss me, and he's felt me up more than once. He's a dirty old man.'

'There's more, Danni, I bloody well know there is. Has he raped you?'

'No! He…'

'What?'

'I saw him the other night down one of the alleys, close to your house. He was trying it on with Carrie.'

'What do you mean, trying it on? Everybody knows that girl has already got herself a reputation.'

'Mum! He was groping her. He had her pinned against the wall. If I hadn't come along, he would have raped her.'

'Right, I'll see you later.'

Valerie bounded from the flat. Danni found a fresh glass and poured another drink. She hoped that was an end to fucking Barry.

CHAPTER 78

Wilson

DC John Wilson had his evening all planned. Finish work at St Anne Street station early, sprint home to shower and change, and then up to Treadwater for a night out with Danni. He had tickets for a Michael McIntyre show at the M&S Bank Arena followed by dinner at an Indian restaurant. Then, hopefully, it was his place or hers if the kids had been farmed out to their gran's. He, of course, was unaware of the afternoon endured by Danni and the fact that she'd consumed three-quarters of a bottle of vodka following her quarrel with Valerie. At the time he was about to leave the station, Danni had passed out on her sofa, oblivious to her children running amok in the flat with Mummy's make-up.

None of that became relevant because before he had the chance to depart the station, Wilson and Murray were summoned to a wooded area near Little Crosby. A man, still alive, had been discovered lying within the wood. Initial reports said that he had been severely beaten, was unconscious and possibly had been lying at that spot for several days.

Murray parked on a side road that skirted the patch of forest and meadow about half a mile from the village of Little Crosby. They had to scale a stone wall to reach the scene. A couple of uniforms had remained and were performing a search of the immediate area where the man had been discovered.

'Hi, guys, what's the story?' Murray asked. He flashed his warrant card to a female PC. She smiled.

'Sir, one male was discovered about an hour ago by two young lads on their way home from school. He was unconscious and looked savagely beaten. He's been taken to Aintree Hospital. No ID, but I would guess he was early twenties. The only thing found so far is this key.' She handed it to Murray.

'Looks like a house key, that's all you could say about it.'

'Sorry I can't be of more help, sir.' She smiled again.

'That's fine. I think we'll get over to the hospital and see how things are.'

On the way to Aintree, Wilson tried calling Danni. At best, he was going to be late, but her phone went immediately to voicemail. He left a message, full of apology, in case he didn't make it at all.

In Accident and Emergency, the pair of detectives had two hours to wait until they could even get a look at the victim. A doctor explained that the man had regained consciousness for a short time but then had been placed in an induced coma to aid recovery from the head injury incurred.

Wilson's planned evening was well and truly trashed. He sat on a plastic chair in the waiting area of A&E, drinking from a can of diet cola, and still he had no reply from Danni. He'd left five messages on her voicemail, but by this time he'd expected a call from her. The evening got a whole lot worse when they were at last permitted to see the victim. A nurse remained by the bed.

'He was awake for a short time,' she said. 'But he'll be asleep now for quite a while.'

'Did he say anything?' Murray asked.

'His name is Justin Boyle. Lives on the Treadwater Estate. That's all, I'm afraid.'

CHAPTER 79

The committee

It was the most raucous meeting they'd all experienced since the project first began. Accusations flew and arguments ensued until the chairperson lost patience.

'Enough! Please, enough of this. Let's settle down and address comments through the chair. Firstly, let's talk about Justin Boyle. Did anyone here sanction this beating?'

There was no response, only furtive glances from one to another.

'Good. Dishing out a beating is not our way to deal with problem people. Now, how far along had we got with Justin?'

'It was decided at the last meeting to move to stage three, removal from the estate,' said the secretary.

'But we haven't seen him since then,' said another. 'RSPCA were called out to rescue his dog. As far as I know Justin had not been at his flat for days.'

'Right, as long as we are sure there has been no involvement from us in this beating,' said the chairperson.

'The lad got up to all kinds of mischief. It could have been anyone who gave him a hiding,' said a member.

'Remember, we must be careful,' said the chairperson. 'The police will be here again asking questions. Heaven forbid, if we are ever to be exposed, I don't want us to go down for something that we haven't done. Our lives depend on us being careful. The work and secrecy of this committee must not be undermined.'

The chairperson continued with the agenda. 'Next is the broken window and threatening note at Beth Chapman's flat. Anyone wish to comment?'

'Beth Chapman and Claire Brady were issued with stage one letters, that's all,' said a member.

The secretary interjected.

'Hold on! For both cases there was no action sanctioned. There was no ruling that they should be issued with stage one letters. Who went ahead with this?'

Another argument ensued as the secretary's take on the matter was challenged. The chairperson was frustrated. They'd never had such chaos before. Firstly, they had an accidental death on the motorway, then the discovery of bodies, and now it appeared that committee members were acting without the proper authority.

'Is anyone here responsible for throwing a brick through Beth's window?' the chairperson asked, trying to restore order.

Heads shook and there were several mumbled replies of no.

'Does anyone know who did it?' Looks were exchanged but no one offered an explanation. 'Any response to our letters from either of these women?'

'There seems to have been some activity from the Brady woman,' said a member.

'What kind of activity?'

'Well, she was assumed to be a prostitute and that appears to be what is going on at her flat. I've heard that men have been calling during the day. She's been seen at her bedroom window dressed only in her underwear. And she's been walking around the estate dressed like a slut. You all must have noticed her at choir practice.'

'No need to use words like that, thank you,' said the chairperson. 'Some women have no choice other than to be sex workers. That's their business. Ours is only to make sure they don't operate within Treadwater. That's why we are here. Even though the letters should not have been issued in the first place, do I take it then that neither woman shows any sign of heeding our warning?'

Heads again were shaking no.

'Right then, we move to stage two for both – agreed?'

With the action against Claire and Beth agreed, the committee discussed the developments in the cases of other aggressors. Nothing was added to the record for Stan Oldfield or for Barry Sugden. Both names remained on hold. The chairperson repeated the warning about acting without a directive from the committee.

Thankfully, this evening there were no new reports of anti-social activity for the committee to consider. The chairperson, dreading the final item on the agenda, spoke quietly and tactfully.

'Ian, you were excused the formality of a warning letter. Can you advise the committee of your intentions in the matter for which you are accused?'

A doleful-looking Ian Bankhead had rehearsed his staring directly at the chairperson and no one else.

'The relationship is over,' he replied.

CHAPTER 80

Tara

Tara answered the knock on her door. It was not the person she had expected.

'Hiya, Claire love. Thought I'd call round, see how you are after getting that nasty letter.'

'Hi, Katrina, come in. I thought it was someone else at the door.'

'Expecting someone?'

'Yes, a client.'

Katrina followed Tara into the kitchen. Today, she wore a loose-fitting dress with pink flowers, pink platform trainers and a blue denim blazer. Tara couldn't help wondering how someone so dependent on benefits could afford the outfits.

'A client? Do tell.'

Tara was in her dressing gown, but she made a point of allowing it to fall open slightly to reveal black lace underwear. She was inclined to trust Katrina, but at the same time she realised that she didn't know any Treadwater resident well enough to confide in. If Katrina was not to be trusted, then Tara imagined that the details of this visit would meet the ears of those in power on the estate. She made some coffee and sat down with Katrina at her table.

'I need the money, Katrina. This is the easiest way of earning. Just a few clients so far, but if it pays here then I'm for staying put, to hell with a stupid letter. Who the fuck are these people, laying down the law? They should mind their own fucking business.'

'You go, girl!'

Tara watched as Katrina's eyes scanned the room, although there was little for her to see. Knickers airing over the radiator didn't indicate that a prostitute operated from this flat.

'You know, I could do your make-up,' said Katrina. 'I'm good. Look at me, for goodness sake. Have to be, don't I?'

'I'm fine, thanks. I don't wear too much; it ends up smeared over the punter.'

'So, you and Mandy, did you work together?'

'It's how we met. We looked out for each other. That's why I'm still worried about her. If she has gone for good, what about her house? Is all her stuff inside? You know, Katrina, I can't help thinking that these thugs, whoever they are, have done something to her. Did she get any threatening letters? Is that why she left? Or did she ignore them, and things got worse? Is she buried somewhere on this estate?'

Katrina's ever-present smile had gradually disappeared. Without it she looked more male than female. Her eyes were focused on her coffee mug. Tara could see that her rant was affecting her visitor. She continued.

'I heard they found a guy from the estate yesterday. He'd been beaten within an inch of his life. How the hell can so-called protectors of the community justify that?'

'It wasn't…'

'Wasn't what?'

Tara saw anger on Katrina's face. She looked on the verge of hitting out. Just as quickly, Katrina settled herself and spoke calmly.

'I was going to say that beating someone up doesn't sound like the kind of thing that people here would do.'

'Oh? Why not? They put bricks through windows; they wrap people in plastic and dump them in sewers. Why wouldn't they dish out a plain ordinary hiding?'

'It isn't their style.'

'Do you know these people, Katrina? You told Justin Boyle that he needed to be careful. And now he's in hospital.'

'Of course, I don't know them. Nobody does. I hope you're not accusing me of arranging a beating for Justin?'

'So, all of this summary justice happens like Santa coming at Christmas?'

Katrina suddenly got to her feet. She was taller than Tara, and she looked down at her with a serious expression. With a slight tremor in her voice, she said quietly, 'You need to be careful, Claire. I wouldn't want to see anything bad happen to you.'

'Is that a threat, Katrina?'

'Of course not! I've seen what can happen round here, especially to those who go shooting their mouth off. I'll go now, and let you get ready for your *client*. Please, Claire, don't antagonise these people.'

CHAPTER 81

The choir

There was growing excitement for the forthcoming choir performance. Tonight was the usual choir practice evening, although Esther had several extra practices scheduled in the run-up to their concert. All members were present, and the room was filled with chat and laughter. Esther was deep in conversation with Marcus about the order of music for the practice. He played through several intros for songs and Esther mulled over the best arrangement, tweaking pieces here and there.

This evening, they intended to rehearse all the solo pieces with and without the other voices joining in. It meant also that seating arrangements were altered. Each member was now seated next to the person they would stand alongside during the concert. Tara had Katrina to her right and Hannah to her left. She wondered if she would still be working undercover by the night of the performance. It would be a pity to miss it. She promised herself that she would carry on singing somewhere when this case was over.

Heads turned again to examine her appearance. Tonight, she had decided to risk the long black wig and bold make-up. A pair of heels and another short skirt had the men stealing glances at her. She noted also the scowls from certain women. Mary was no real surprise. Perhaps she and husband Raymond were of one voice in their attitude to sex workers. Esther had smiled and seemed quite impressed by Tara's hair.

Dinah was a woman with whom she'd had little interaction. By now, Tara had learned names and could recognise each choir member. There were some who stood out from the others.

Sheena and Dinah were seated together in the front row. Both had excellent voices and had solo parts to sing. Before practice commenced, Sheena turned around, smiled and called a hello to Katrina. Her smile weakened when she made eye contact with Tara. To the teenager, Tara and Katrina must have looked a right pair of ladies. Katrina wore a mini-dress and platform sandals, and her make-up was more skilfully applied than Tara's.

When Sheena turned to face forwards, Tara noticed her whispering to her mother, who immediately spun around and glared right at her. The contemptuous look convinced Tara that Dinah did not approve of her appearance. If Dinah did not approve of her, then, presumably, she did not look favourably upon Katrina either.

Beth had surprised herself by continuing to attend practice. Although she would be loath to admit it, choir practice had quickly become the highlight of her week. She enjoyed singing and found that it lifted her spirits in a way that booze and drugs had never done. This was perhaps the only sober high she had ever experienced. Katrina was good company, too. Beth never imagined having friends when she moved into Treadwater. Since that toerag Bryn, she had never cared for or trusted anyone. Tara, she found, was a more complex woman. There was something going on with her.

Beth sat to Hannah's left. When she heard Katrina speak to the old woman her blood suddenly ran cold.

'Hello, Mrs Oldfield, allowed out tonight? Great to see you looking so well, love.'

'Thank you, dear,' Hannah replied with a broad smile. 'That's a beautiful dress you're wearing.'

'Thanks, love, you're so sweet.'

Beth's mind was suddenly visualising the living room of a house, more than eighteen years ago. A woman was bleeding to death on her sofa, her husband beaten with a hammer and forced to give what little cash he had to Bryn. Then Bryn passed it to her, while he finished off the old man with his knife. Beth could feel his warm blood spraying over her face as her boyfriend stabbed once, twice, three... she'd lost count. If she hadn't pulled him away, Bryn would have continued stabbing with the knife. They ran off with forty-eight quid, a cheque book and a bank card. The name of the account holder was Alec Oldfield. She'd served seventeen years for her part in the murder of the pensioners.

Now, she had just heard the name Oldfield uttered by Katrina. Were Hannah and Stan Oldfield related to Alec? Was Stan responsible for the brick crashing through her window? Was he out to get her?

CHAPTER 82

Tara

We informed you in our previous letter that owing to your anti-social behaviour you are not welcome on the Treadwater Estate. You have not ceased your activities. If you persist, you will be forcibly removed from the estate. This is the second and final time of asking.

Tara had to smile at their arrogance. She wondered how many times their process of intimidation had been successful. Those who resisted seemed to end up bound in plastic film and dumped on a motorway or in a sewer. She thought also of Mandy Wright; was she dead or had she fled the estate and was alive, well and living elsewhere?

Justin Boyle, though, had been treated in a different manner. A severe beating did not fit with the usual MO for this secret organisation. The latest she had heard from St Anne Street was that Boyle remained in a coma, his condition stable.

Outside, she found Beth looking on as council workers replaced her broken window. Tara didn't think that Beth looked well, not that she had ever appeared healthy. Her hair was matted, her sweatshirt dirty, her face was pale, and she was finding it difficult to stand still. She paced nervously back and forth along the path to the front door, a roll-up smouldering in her hand. Tara noticed that Beth was barefoot, and this morning it was freezing cold.

'You all right, Beth?' Tara asked.

'Fine and fucking dandy.'

'Did you get another letter?'

'Yep. Bastards! Don't know what I've done other than have a murder conviction. Some people are easily annoyed. I'm not surprised about you, though. You've deliberately rubbed their face in it.'

'Whoever they are,' said Tara, 'they don't frighten me. I've dealt with worse.'

Beth stared curiously at Tara then took a long drag on the remainder of her roll-up.

'I have a good idea who's behind it,' said Beth, blowing smoke into the air.

'You do?'

'Oldfield. I think he's the sod who put the brick through my window.'

'You mean, Stan Oldfield?'

'That's him. I only found out his surname last night at choir practice when Katrina spoke to Hannah.'

'But how does that make him the man who threatened you?' Tara asked.

'Oldfield was the name of the couple I got sent down for killing. I reckon Stan is family, a brother or something.

He probably remembers me from the trial or maybe from when I lived on Treadwater as a kid.'

'I don't think he's behind these letters,' said Tara. 'Throwing a brick through a window doesn't seem like the style for whoever wrote the letters.'

'I don't give a shit. I'm going to have a word with our Stan anyway.'

'Do you think that's wise? He could turn nasty.'

'Nasty I can cope with. It's the sneaking around I can't fucking stand.'

Beth was suddenly aware that she was barefoot in the cold. She tiptoed inside, leaving Tara to ponder just how much crime goes unreported. If there are people like Stan and Beth all over the place, taking the law into their own hands, the number of incidents that never come to light must be enormous. The Treadwater vigilante group probably operated in the knowledge that most of what they do never flashes on any police radar.

CHAPTER 83

Barry

Neighbours had come to their doorsteps just to watch. Traumatic perhaps for the couple embroiled in the row, but to the onlooker this was free entertainment. Many were also happy to see Barry Sugden get what he deserved.

Wearing a sweatshirt and jogging trousers, he stood on a tiny patch of lawn oblivious to the gathering witnesses as he shouted abuse at Valerie. She could be seen periodically at their bedroom window. When she disappeared briefly, it was to fetch another item of Barry's belongings to be thrown outside. The hapless Barry attempted to catch the clothing as it fell, and this was the initial source of entertainment for neighbours. The laughter increased when a shoe hit him on the forehead and, as his hand went to his head, another hit him on his fat belly.

'Perverted bastard!' Valerie screamed from above.

'Please, Val, love. Can't we talk about it?'

'Fuck off, pervert!'

A pair of trousers were thrown out and he caught them. This was greeted by applause from the onlookers. Barry suddenly took notice of them but seemed unsure whether to join in the laughter or to concentrate on calming down his partner.

There was a crash of breaking plastic at his feet when a portable TV smashed to the ground.

'Val, please.'

'We're finished, you dirty bastard! Go on, tell everyone what you get up to when I'm not here.'

She disappeared inside, and there was a lull in objects jettisoned from the window. Barry attempted to make a pile of his belongings on the pavement.

He had stepped out this morning with nothing in mind but a stroll to the shop, buy a paper and some fags, then linger for a while where he hoped to see pretty girls standing at the bus stop. Valerie, however, had been awaiting her opportunity and remained in the house while Barry went out. As soon as the front door closed behind him, the first pair of trousers were despatched from the bedroom window.

'Share these with the neighbours, bastard!'

One after another, DVD cases were tossed in the air and rained down on Barry who raised his hands to protect his head. It was clear to see that they were adult movies.

The row ended abruptly when Valerie announced Barry's latest perverted activity to the crowd. She did this as the parents of Carrie Dobson were approaching.

'Go on, Barry, love, tell the Dobsons what you did to their daughter last week!'

Barry glanced to his right, spied Terry Dobson and started running. Dobson, tall and lean and easily in better condition than Barry didn't give chase. He and his wife, Mel, were more concerned with learning the details from Valerie of what Barry had done to their daughter. The onlookers laughed as Barry soon came to a standstill, bent double and struggling for breath. He hadn't made it to the end of the street. His immediate future was not looking good.

CHAPTER 84

Dinah

Dinah was having a rare evening at home alone, the television showing an episode of *Call the Midwife*. Marcus was round at Esther's preparing for the concert, and Sheena, as she was most nights, was at Nathan's. Dinah wasn't entirely happy about her daughter spending so much time in the company of a transgender. Her faith didn't lend itself to the approval of such a life choice. But Sheena was an adult now; she had to make her own way. In every other aspect of character, Dinah was lovingly proud of her daughter. Sheena had a powerful sense of what was right and wrong.

In the past few days, however, Dinah had wrestled with her conscience and prayed long hours in trying to marry her own sinful actions with God's teachings. She had lied to those two detectives when they called asking about Linus Jones and Dale Wycliffe. When it came to Linus, she had been deliberately vague. She hadn't lied, but she didn't provide as much information about the youth as she should have done. Linus was trouble, pure and simple. He had no redeeming qualities. He stole from his aunt and from his neighbours, he raced cars through the estate, dealt in drugs and harassed young girls like her Sheena. But Dinah couldn't admit to the detectives that she knew Linus well because she feared it would lead to questions about Dale Wycliffe. She'd lied blatantly when she denied knowing Dale, even though he had been a close associate of Linus Jones. She possessed a truth about Dale that only she would ever know. He had been the first man to share her bed since Gerry had abandoned her and the children. Dale had a maturity that was absent in his friend, Linus. He had sensed her longing, but he had behaved as a grown-up. He hadn't treated her as if she was a conquest. But for his lifestyle, Dale would have made a devoted life partner. After several months sleeping together, including a pregnancy scare, she had ended the relationship. The boy in him was still doing drugs and getting drunk with his mate, Linus.

She cried sorely the day she heard that Dale had been laid in the ground.

CHAPTER 85

Tara

The name of the M57 victim had been released to the media. Tara intended to use the information to begin a conversation on Elsa Remmel at choir practice. She believed that someone within the community choir knew the truth of how Elsa had met her death.

She dressed in modest clothes, having decided that she had done enough to advertise a sex worker lifestyle to those who were offended by it. This evening she wore jeans, trainers and T-shirt. She also discarded her wig. New growth of her own hair was now visible.

Seating arrangements were the same as for the previous practice, the positions set for the leisure centre concert. Amid the chatter and before Esther brought the choir to order, Tara blurted the news about Elsa Remmel.

'I hear they have identified that girl who was found on the M57.'

Hannah, Beth, Katrina, Valerie and Danni were all within earshot. None of them responded.

'I was relieved,' Tara continued. 'I was still thinking it was Mandy, and the bizzies just hadn't released her name, you know, until relatives had been informed.'

'We've already told you, Claire love,' said Katrina. 'Mandy just took off after she had a fight with Esther.'

'So, did anybody know this woman Elsa?' Tara continued, ignoring what Katrina had said.

'You'd do well to keep your mouth shut, little lady.' Tara looked up to see Raymond glaring down at her. With a downturned mouth he had never looked friendly.

'And why is that, Raymond?' she asked.

He ignored her question and went to his seat. Tara wasn't finished. She got to her feet and spoke loudly. 'Anyone here know anything about threatening letters sent to Beth and me?'

Esther's face turned pale, while others stared blankly at the slight woman asking the awkward question. There were no replies, as Tara scanned the room filled with community singers. She was not surprised when no information was offered.

'Just thought I would ask,' she added. 'It seems that Beth and I could be run off this estate because we have annoyed someone.' She felt a tug on her T-shirt as Beth tried to get her to sit. When Tara finally acquiesced, Katrina fired her a stern look.

'You silly girl,' she whispered.

'Well, if you don't ask,' said Tara.

Music and singing ensued for the remainder of the evening. It became quite intense as Esther insisted on perfection. They spent a lot of the session on their feet rehearsing how they would move as they sang. Esther was adamant that they would not present themselves as a rabble of incoherent movements. They were not a free-form gospel choir, she had told them. She had them swaying together on one song then stepping back and forth for another, arms in the air, fingers clicking, but all done in unison.

There was no time to mull over the incident with Raymond or the lack of response from the others to her questions. Tara was now certain that she had made enemies of the right people, enough to provoke further action from Treadwater's vigilantes.

CHAPTER 86

Beth

Esther was exhausted by the end of the practice. She felt that things had gone well, the harmonies were tight, the overall sound was great, and the movements weren't bad. She sensed, however, the ripple of unease around the room. Claire was intent on stirring things, continuing to ask questions about Mandy. And now she was talking about the woman who had died on the motorway. But Claire and Beth had also been threatened. Her choir was not the place for fighting. It had brought people together on the estate. She couldn't stand by and watch it being ripped apart by people like Claire. She would have a word with her before going home.

Beth was also determined to have a word with someone. Her target, though, was Stan Oldfield. Despite his age, he looked fit and strong, and he strutted about the place like a fucking general. She squeezed past several women still seated in the rows of chairs. Stan stood near the door waiting, presumably, for Hannah to join him. As Beth neared the old man, Esther stepped between them. Beth listened to her exchange pleasantries with Stan, then discuss how the evening had gone. She had no time to wait. Her temper was stoked. She would call the man out no matter who was there to see it.

'Why throw a brick at my window?' she asked.

'I don't know what you're on about, love,' Stan replied.

Esther stepped to the side, looking confused by what Beth had said.

'You fucking know exactly what I'm on about, Mr Oldfield. Your note said you knew who I was and what I had done.'

Esther attempted to intervene.

'Come on, folks, this is no time for fighting. We have a concert to prepare for. We are all friends here.'

Beth's eyes were fixed on the cold stare of the man, his expression smug as if he stood upon the moral high ground. Esther's words went unheeded.

'Well, what have I done?' Beth asked him.

'Please! Don't do this here, not tonight,' Esther pleaded. She gazed around, looking for support. The raised voices had caught the attention of others, including Tara.

'You're a murderer, that's what you are,' said Stan, unable to resist the challenge. 'You killed my brother and his wife. Robbed them of fifty quid to buy drugs.'

Gasps swept around the hall, eyes widened, and hands went to mouths in shock. Everyone in the room was now witness to the exchange.

'I didn't kill anyone,' said Beth. 'Bryn did the killing, not me. I did time for my part.'

'Why come here?' Stan asked. 'To rub my face in it? We don't want your kind living round here.'

'Stan, please,' Esther begged.

The man hadn't finished with the murderer who faced him.

'Jail time wasn't enough for the likes of you. If I had my way, you'd be strung up for what you did.'

'That's enough, Stan!' Katrina called. 'Leave her alone.'

'Nothing to do with you, freak. She started it.'

'Stan, please!' It was Hannah, ignoring the risk to herself by speaking out against her husband. 'Let's just go home.'

'Stay out of it, Hannah. I'll deal with you later.' He spoke again to Beth. 'You get out of this choir, out of Treadwater or–'

'Stan! Enough!'

Everyone turned to look. Dinah was on her feet, her face colouring with anger.

Stan met the gaze of the woman then suddenly grabbed his wife by the arm and walked out of the hall.

CHAPTER 87

Murray and Wilson

Murray stood by the bed looking at the pitiful excuse for youth slowly blink his way to consciousness. Justin's face had a collection of purple, black and yellow bruises that extended down his torso and both arms. His eyes were almost concealed behind swollen cheeks, and his head was dressed in a bandage. Murray had already asked his first question of Justin but after several seconds still had no reply. He tried again.

'Justin, how are you feeling, mate?'

'Fucked.'

'Well, I'm glad you're still with us. I'm DS Murray, Merseyside Police. Can you tell me what happened to you?'

Justin attempted to laugh, but it was drowned in a groan as he tried to move his arm.

'Who did this to you?'

'Doctor…'

'I don't think so, mate. Tell me what you can remember.'

'Hazzard. Deals in guns.'

It became a protracted interview, but eventually Murray obtained an address to check out. Little else that was said by Justin seemed to make any sense. The detective had been expecting information regarding Treadwater, something he could relay to DI Grogan. Instead, Boyle had rambled, and the only suggestion he made was that his injuries had nothing to do with the place where he lived.

Murray and Wilson drove to the address on Ince Road. As Wilson stopped the car outside the house, both men agreed that it seemed an unlikely place for Justin Boyle to have come across trouble.

'What was a tosser like Boyle doing up here?' Wilson commented. 'Who are we looking for?'

'All I have is the name Dr Hazzard. Don't know if it's male or female, young or old.'

The two detectives ambled along the sweeping drive beneath the trees.

'Nice-looking house, if you can afford it,' said Murray.

Wilson rang the doorbell and stepped back. Within a few seconds the door opened, and Murray and Wilson were greeted by an attractive woman in her forties with dark hair and tanned face.

'Dr Hazzard?' Murray asked with a smile.

'Yes, how can I help you?'

Murray introduced himself and Wilson then stated their business. When the conversation ended a minute later the detectives returned along the drive to their car.

'Just as I thought. Boyle was spinning a yarn. For a start, the doctor was a woman.'

'And she's been out of the country for the past month,' Wilson added. 'So, where does that leave us?'

'We can have another chat with Boyle when he's come around fully. So far, his story is complete drivel. How would a university lecturer in sociology become involved in arms dealing?'

CHAPTER 88

The choir

Carrie's parents weren't happy about what had happened to their daughter at the hands of Barry Sugden. They had not, however, contacted the police. Instead, as Sugden had attempted to flee, Carrie's father and several of his mates gave Barry something to remember them by. His means of transport from the estate was by ambulance to the Aintree Hospital. When he was found by the paramedics, lying in an alley next to the library, Barry was no longer in possession of his belongings that Valerie had thrown from her window.

Carrie was eager to get out of the house, to get to practice and to see Ian afterwards. She couldn't take much more of the questions drilled at her by Mum and Dad. Her mother knew that Carrie had a mystery boyfriend, but she didn't know it was a middle-aged divorced man and, she was certainly unaware that her daughter was pregnant. For the next few days, Carrie intended to focus on the concert and forget her worries over what to do about her baby.

Tonight was the last choir practice before the Saturday concert at the leisure centre. Before any final singing practice took place, the choir members were busy trying on specially printed T-shirts to be worn for the performance. The T-shirts came in a range of bright colours and were emblazoned with a motif of linking hands in a circle, symbolising Treadwater and its community spirit.

Many of the women approached Carrie to offer comfort and support after news had circulated of Barry Sugden's assault. It was too much for the teenager to bear, and several times she broke into tears. Danni gave her a big hug, and it was most appreciated by Carrie since Danni had been the one who saved her from a worse ordeal. Tara, already quite fond of Carrie, whispered words of comfort and suggested that she contact the police.

'Somebody should get that girl to the police,' she said pointedly to Beth and Katrina.

'Wouldn't do her much good,' said Katrina, while Beth smirked at the comment.

'You think it's better that Barry Sugden is dealt with by the people of the estate?' Tara asked.

'That won't happen either. Barry did a runner after Valerie threw him out. Didn't quite make it, though. He's in Aintree Hospital.'

At that point, Tara, Katrina and Beth witnessed Valerie's arrival. She made directly for Carrie, gave her a hug and spoke quietly to her before hugging again. Tara noticed Ian Bankhead whisper in Carrie's ear. The teenager smiled and gazed into his eyes. The two of them hugged, and Bankhead brushed a kiss on her cheek as they broke contact. Tara thought it looked rather more than an offer of sympathy from the man. It was something else for her to ponder, although she couldn't see much relevance to the cases of murder she was investigating. Following an afternoon phone call from Superintendent Tweedy, it was likely that she would be pulled off the estate after the concert had taken place.

When practice had finished there was excitement among the choristers in anticipation of the performance on Saturday. Tara stood by the door as people departed. Katrina was chatting with Beth, Dinah to Valerie and, for the second time in the evening, Carrie was standing close to Ian Bankhead.

The Glovers went by without a word, despite Tara smiling at Mary. Raymond stared right through her as if she weren't there. Stan and Hannah Oldfield left with their heads down.

'Good night, Hannah,' Tara called.

The old woman did not reply.

Sheena had joined the conversation with Valerie and her mother. There didn't look to be much cheer between them.

Suddenly, Carrie hurried by, sobbing heavily.

'Carrie?' Tara called after her.

'Leave her,' said Bankhead following behind the girl. 'She's all right.'

'Doesn't look all right to me,' Tara replied. 'What happened?'

'None of your business.' Bankhead barged past and hurried after Carrie.

Tara stepped outside and watched as Bankhead caught up with the teenager. Carrie's head was bowed as her crying continued. Ian seemed aware of people staring and persuaded Carrie to go for a walk.

'Carrie, you know I don't want this, but we have to. If it comes out that I'm the father, I will go to jail. I'll be a sex offender.'

'I don't have to tell anyone who the father is.'

'But people already know about us. They're going to know it's me.'

'Who knows? I haven't told anybody.'

'Doesn't matter how they know, they just do.'

'Well, fuck them! We can still run away,' said Carrie.

'No, we can't! The police would soon be after us – you're still underage. I'd be charged with abduction.'

Carrie wiped tears away with her sleeve.

'You're just saying that. You don't want to run away; you don't want to keep our baby, and now I think you don't want me anymore.'

'That's not true, Carrie. I love you. But if we keep the baby our lives will be ruined.' He attempted to put his arms around her, oblivious to those watching. She tore away from his grasp and hurried along the street. 'Carrie, please! Come back.'

She stopped, turned around and cried out.

'I'm keeping it, Ian. I'm going home right now to tell my mum.'

Ian bolted towards her.

'No, Carrie, you can't. Carrie!'

She tried to run, but Ian soon caught up with her and grabbed her from behind. She screamed. He put his hand over her mouth. She tried to wrestle free, but he was too strong and gripped her hair.

'No, you fucking won't,' he whispered harshly. 'I'll fucking kill you first.' He pulled her close and peered into her eyes. 'You're just a stupid kid. You're going to do as I say, Carrie, or we'll both end up in trouble. Now go home and keep your mouth shut. I'll make the appointment for you to get rid of it, understand?'

Her eyes filled with tears, but she couldn't summon any further resistance.

'Do you fucking understand me?' He grabbed her by the throat and squeezed. 'I'm sorry to hurt you. I still love you, but you can't do this, Carrie.'

'Let me go, Ian.'

Finally, he released her, and she hobbled away sobbing. Ian watched her go. He didn't trust her. He realised that he would have to act fast.

CHAPTER 89

The committee

'Ian is absent this evening,' said the chairperson, 'and I did not receive an apology. Has anyone heard from him?' The others in the room whispered and mumbled among themselves, but there was only one reply.

'I'm sure most of us saw them last night,' said the secretary. 'Ian and Carrie were having words outside the community centre.'

The chairperson repeated the question. 'Has anyone got any information on why Ian is absent this evening?'

'I heard a rumour that Carrie is pregnant,' a member blurted. 'Ian probably has enough to deal with.'

'OK,' said the chairperson. 'We'll leave the matter for now.'

'It means we are one short in the action group,' said another member.

'We'll just have to manage,' said the chairperson.

Tea and biscuits were served to all, and for a time the chat was light-hearted with everyone looking forward to the choir's performance on the coming Saturday evening. The chairperson was intent, however, on completing the serious business of their committee.

'From what occurred during practice last night, I am convinced that Claire Brady means trouble for us. She seems determined to ignore our warnings.'

'Her friend, Beth, is just as bad,' said a member. 'She's a convicted murderer, for goodness' sake!'

'Remember,' said the chairperson, 'we're not concerned with what someone has done in the past, especially if they have paid for their crime. Our objective is always to protect the good people on our estate. If someone threatens our safety or disrupts our settled way of life, then we act to put things right. Beth, as far as I can tell, has done nothing wrong. Stan Oldfield is out of order in making threats. Don't forget, he is under our surveillance for his own wrongdoing.'

No one challenged the chairperson's view of the matter.

'But we get rid of Claire Brady?' a member asked.

'Yes, I believe we should move to stage three,' the chairperson replied. 'It worked for her friend, Mandy, hopefully it will be the same for Brady. I think, though, we should postpone the action until after the concert.'

For one member of the Treadwater Residents' Committee, the expulsion of Claire Brady from the estate couldn't come soon enough. For another, Claire Brady's exit from Treadwater could only bring more trouble.

CHAPTER 90

The choir

Tara was awake early, out of bed and flitting from one task to another around the flat. She felt on edge but wasn't sure what had her feeling this way. The concert was this evening, perhaps she had a tingling of nerves about singing in front of a large audience. She was aware also that a threat still hung over her from a group of people on the estate. So far, she had only a couple of suspects in mind, but she was short on evidence to make any arrests. If she could not gather the proof, then Tweedy was going to pull her off the undercover role and bring her back to St Anne

Street. The only potential for success, she felt, was for the group to take further action against her or Beth. Then maybe they could be caught red-handed. That option, of course, was dangerous, and she now realised that's what was making her nervous.

* * *

Beth was chain-smoking from an early start. Ensconced in her sofa, a mug of tea, her roll-up tobacco and ciggy papers resting on the arm, she watched TV but paying little attention to the cookery show. She hadn't dressed and hadn't decided if she would even bother. How could she have allowed herself to become a member of a friggin' choir? All right, she could sing a bit, but she looked terrible, she had zero confidence, whilst all she could think about was Stan Oldfield seeking revenge for what Bryn did to his brother and sister-in-law. She could be forced off the estate and would have to start over again somewhere else. Perhaps it was best if she didn't turn up for the concert. No one would really miss her.

* * *

Esther hadn't been to bed. She sat up late making medals for each member of the choir, attaching silk ribbons to the gold-plated discs she had bought online. They were intended as a small token of thanks and to commemorate everyone's participation in the event. She got her head down on the sofa at three in the morning only to rise at seven to play through all the music for the concert. She wanted to be sure she had the arrangements perfect. By two in the afternoon, she would be at the leisure centre, preparing for the choir's arrival at four. Then it would be a final rehearsal followed by a buffet tea. She and Mary had prepared the food for her singers. Today, she prayed, would be memorable for all concerned.

* * *

Katrina had saved some money, enough for a makeover, a facial and nails. It was still a dream to be able to have her hair done too but, until that day came, she had to make do with a classy wig. She met up with Sheena at the bus stop, and both girls giggled as they toyed with ideas for make-up, shoes and what they might wear beneath Esther's ghastly T-shirts. It was going to be difficult staying sober before the concert. Both girls were already so hyped about the day ahead.

* * *

Danni had invited John Wilson to the show. It meant that she had to find another babysitter since Barry had scarpered. Hopefully, he was in agony on his hospital bed. To her delight, John suggested that he could bring Bradley and Mikaela to hear their mum sing. She could hardly believe she'd found such a man. She knew already that she was in love with the policeman that she'd once fancied as a kid on the estate. The future was looking good for Bradley, Mikaela and her.

* * *

As she began each day, Dinah was on her knees in prayer. Saturday was no different. In the silence of her bedroom, she praised God, gave thanks for all his blessings given to her and asked for continued guidance in all that she said and did. In particular, she prayed for everyone taking part in the concert, for Esther, Marcus, Sheena and all who lived on Treadwater. She worried that there were tough times ahead, and she asked for God's forgiveness for anything she had done wrong.

* * *

Mary prepared a hearty fried breakfast for Raymond. It was going to be a long day, so it was best to start on a full stomach. Still in bed, Raymond could smell the bacon and sausages frying. His wife knew how to get him going.

They'd had a new lease of life singing in the choir. Something so simple had brightened their outlook as they faced retirement and old age. Tonight, people would see Treadwater at its absolute best.

* * *

Carrie slipped quietly downstairs in her pyjamas. She hoped to catch her mother alone. It had been a sleepless night for her, and she guessed for her mum also. No mother wants to hear that her daughter is pregnant at fifteen, but she was Carrie's only hope of comfort and advice. Her mum would know what to do. She would always want what was best for her daughter and her three brothers. This morning, Carrie wondered if her dad had been told the news. As she pushed open the door to the living room, she soon found out. Mum and dad had been talking quietly. Carrie couldn't help bursting into tears. She'd hurt them, but now she needed them more than anything. She was always closest to her dad, always his little girl, but he frowned his displeasure at the news. She realised he was disappointed in her. Carrie had only one thing to say as she sobbed.

'I want to keep it, Dad. Please don't make me have an abortion.'

'No one will ever do that, pet,' he said. 'We'll help you through this.'

'Course we will,' said her mum. 'We're proud of you for being so brave. You don't have to tell us right now, if you don't want to, but it would be best to know who the father is.'

* * *

Ian stuffed several of his shirts into a holdall. His head throbbed from the gin he'd drunk right through the night. That little cow was going to sink him. As soon as she'd told her parents, he was done for. Half the estate would come after him. Barry Sugden got off lightly with a good

was certain there was no one who cared about him. His mother was long dead from drink, and his father, as far as he knew, was still doing time somewhere. He had an older sister living in Warrington. She was married, but that was all he knew of a family that had never really been one.

As he walked into Trent Lane, nearing home, he had a sudden recollection of a man's body being hauled from a manhole. Then his mind focused on those fucking letters telling him to stop his anti-social behaviour or leave the estate. Didn't these assholes realise that if he could leave Treadwater he would be gone in a flash? Who would ever want to live here if they didn't have to? Three of the wonderful residents approached him as he neared the entrance to his block. It was that faggot Nathan and two of his new friends. He lowered his head. He had nothing to say to the likes of them. But someone he hardly knew was first to speak.

'Hi, Justin! I'm glad to see you're OK,' said Tara. 'I heard you've had a rough time.'

'Fuck off. None of your business.'

Katrina was startled by Claire's greeting for the guy who had caused nothing but trouble on the estate. In a way, Claire got what she deserved from the little shit.

'Nothing ever changes eh, Justin?' said Katrina. She received a finger salute for her trouble. 'C'mon, girls, let's get on.'

Wearily, Justin climbed the concrete steps to his flat, still unsure of how he would get in. Then he saw the note taped to the frosted glass of the door.

'Key available from St Anne Street station, Merseyside Police.'

He noticed the splintered wood around the lock where the door had been forced open. And where was Buster? The door was secured with a metal plate and padlock. He stood helpless for what seemed like hours, staring vacantly at the door with its motley collection of rude signage. He felt incapable of deciding, incapable of even recognising his problem. Cold, wet and hungry, he had no one to care for him.

The door behind him on the landing opened, the sound of children's laughter swarmed through the silent void. He turned to face Danni, looking wonderful and standing beside one of those bizzies who'd asked him too many questions in the hospital.

'Hello, Mr Boyle,' said Wilson. 'I heard you'd discharged yourself from hospital. I thought you'd be needing this.' He tossed a key at Justin. Too much to expect him to catch it, the key bounced on the concrete floor.

'Concert's tonight, Justin,' said Danni. 'Are you coming along?'

Justin grimaced as he stooped to pick up the key. After fumbling for a while, he finally undid the lock, pushed the door open and stepped inside. He closed it behind him without a word.

'Takes all sorts, I suppose,' said Wilson, raising young Mikaela high in the air so that she screamed in delight.

A strange feeling took hold of Danni as they made their way downstairs and outside. What was going to happen now that Justin was back?

CHAPTER 93

The choir

Esther did a roll call. She didn't imagine that any member was going to miss their big night, but it was her way, her routine. She noticed straight away that someone was indeed absent.

'Where's Stan?'

The others looked around as if the old man would be hiding amongst them. All eyes eventually landed on the slight figure of Hannah.

'Em, sorry, Esther, but Stan isn't coming.'

'What's wrong, Hannah?'

'An upset stomach; he's lying down.'

Katrina and Valerie placed their arms around Hannah. She tried her best to smile, but her entire body was throbbing with adrenaline. No anti-depressant had ever made her feel as good as this.

'Right,' Esther announced, 'the basses will just have to manage without Stan. Let's have a quick warm up before tea then afterwards we'll go through to the stage for a sound check.'

The room bustled with activity. T-shirts were donned over clothing. There was laughter, giggles and Marcus playing the piano.

Esther went around greeting each person. She was impressed by Katrina's appearance.

'Wow! Katrina, love, you've really made an effort. You look great.'

'Aw, thank you so much, Esther. You're not so bad yourself.'

Katrina wore a figure-hugging, mid-length, black dress and enormous platform heels with sequins. Her face was exquisitely painted, an appearance any celebrity would be proud of. Esther wore a flared gold dress with a black chiffon wrap. She had also undergone a professional makeover and wore her hair in a bun. Somehow, Tara thought, this woman was not intending to wear one of her own T-shirts, not over that dress.

* * *

Tara took a few moments to sit at the side of the room and observe. She was convinced that several of the Treadwater vigilantes had to be present. Such an innocent-looking gathering and yet there was evil swirling beneath the surface of this joyous occasion. Why couldn't people behave like this all the time? A vibrant community, one that was not underwritten by warped street justice. She watched Esther, a big smile, looking elegant, pacing among her flock. Was she also the leader of this justice league? Were all these murders committed simply to protect her community choir? And if Esther were not ruling this estate, who else within the choir could do so? It was easy to assume that Raymond was involved, considering he'd been the first person to attempt to silence her. He'd been the one to issue threats. Perhaps, though, it was the quieter ones, those maintaining a discrete presence on the estate, who were responsible for executing justice. The community choir was a wonderful front for their horrific activities.

At one point, Sheena sat beside Tara to drink some tea. She also looked stunning in a pencil skirt of black leather, high heels and satin blouse.

'Looking forward to getting started?' Tara asked.

'Can't wait. You can feel everyone getting hyped.'

'It'll be hard to go back to the day job.'

Sheena looked puzzled by the remark.

'What I mean is,' Tara explained, 'wouldn't it be great if this was our job, our life?'

'Yes, I suppose so.'

Sheena was a bit too sombre, Tara thought, for such a young and pretty girl.

Soon the choir paraded into the packed sports hall of the leisure centre to cheers, applause and whistles. Each member took their place on a tiered platform, and under Esther's direction, they began to sing *Good Day Sunshine*.

There followed a programme of sixteen songs, but in a flash, it seemed, the night was over. It ended with raucous cheering, a standing ovation, and an encore of *You'll Never Walk Alone* that piqued the emotions of everyone. Tara felt her tears spilling, the passion had swept the hall. There was true community spirit, such was the power of singing.

Surely, no one could ever wish to spoil this. Flowers were presented to Esther, and she said a few brief words of thanks and praise for her family, the choir.

Endorphins were not in short supply as they filed off the stage. Hugs, kisses and tears of joy, it was their own accomplishment. Several members, however, already had their minds set on other matters.

* * *

Carrie had avoided Ian for the whole evening. She knew now that he was an entirely selfish man. Her mum had said so when Carrie had finally given him up, said his name, his age and his intentions. Tonight, Carrie knew that Ian Bankhead would face danger like he'd never done before.

* * *

Danni hugged and kissed Bradley and Mikaela. They were so excited to have seen their mummy on stage. Then she hugged the new love in her life, John Wilson. In the back of her mind, she too, had other things to worry about.

* * *

Esther drove home alone, went inside, kicked off the shoes that had nipped her toes all evening and poured herself a generous helping of gin and tonic. She slumped into her armchair, her dress spilling over the sides. She felt proud of her triumph, but emptiness had quickly swirled around her. The concert was over, and yet every flat note, poor timing and off-pitch rattled in her head. That was all she had left. Oh, she would so dearly love to be thinking of the next project but, somehow, she knew there would be no more. There was no future.

* * *

Hannah pushed her front door open and stepped into the dark hall. Carefully, she eased her way past his body. Stan was almost certainly dead, she presumed, since he hadn't moved, the knife in his stomach where she had left it. Tomorrow, she would think of how to get Stan out of her life completely.

CHAPTER 94

Ian

His thoughts were of Spain and Benidorm. He had mates there. They could put him up until he found a job and a place of his own. Ian was clever enough to know that he mustn't leave a trail. If the police weren't coming after him, he thought that Carrie's family certainly would. He'd heard what they had done to Barry Sugden, broken his arm, nose, several ribs and his jewels were probably out of action for life. There was the Residents' Committee also. Of course, he realised that if he left Treadwater they would not pursue him. All they cared about was the estate. Besides, he was a member, an important part of how they operated. They wouldn't touch him.

He couldn't take his car to Spain, not all the way. His plan was to drive to Manchester, leave it somewhere, take a train to London or Birmingham, then a ferry to France. From there he would make his way to Benidorm. He was reconsidering this plan when he chanced a look from his window. It was only a quarter to six. He didn't expect anyone to be stirring at this hour of the morning. It was dark, and it had rained sometime during the night. Someone was out there, however, waiting and watching. He couldn't see them, but he felt their presence, or were his nerves getting the better of him? He was packed and ready to go, so why was he hesitating?

He really wanted to see Carrie one last time, to hold her close, smell her hair and tell her that someday they could be together permanently. He'd written a letter for her, explaining everything, apologising for leaving her and promising that when she was of age, she could come to him. But still, he wanted to say goodbye.

He raced from the house, a bag in each hand. Quickly, he dumped them in the boot of the car and scurried to the driver's side. He saw the figure, forty yards away, leaning against a lamp post. In the darkness, he failed to recognise him, but he wasn't hanging around to have a chat. He started the car and rushed from Severn Way, driving around the perimeter of the playing fields, but instead of taking the exit from the estate he drove to the woodlands area, to Broad Oak Lane where Carrie lived.

The house was in darkness. Somehow, he'd hoped to see a light on in her room, but it wasn't to be. He ran to the front door and slipped his letter through the letter box. Back in his car, he couldn't resist composing a text, hoping it might wake her and they could share a goodbye. His nerve broke, however, and after waiting five minutes for a response, or for the light to come on in her room, he panicked and drove away.

Speed bumps slowed him down as he made for the exit to the estate. He kept looking at his phone for Carrie's reply. He didn't look ahead. Five figures and a van stood in the road blocking his way.

CHAPTER 95

Tara

Tara sat drinking tea, one of her pretend clients sat opposite her. He wasn't one for great conversation. They smiled, both feeling uncomfortable trying to pass the time. The whole idea seemed farcical now. There had been no further action by the vigilantes. She had been certain that something would happen directly after the concert. It was Monday afternoon, and the entire estate was as quiet as it had ever appeared on the surface. She believed also that Tweedy would call a halt to the operation when she spoke with him this evening.

As soon as her 'client' had departed, Tara spent the next hour on the phone with Murray. She hoped for some developments in the case.

'Not much to report, ma'am,' said Murray. She could guess that he was sitting at his desk, feet up, a sandwich or chocolate bar and a coffee the focus of his attention. 'The family of Elsa Remmel have formally claimed her body. They couldn't tell us much except that she came to England to join her boyfriend, Olev Eesmaa. She flew into Manchester, and we know that's where Eesmaa had stayed for most of his time. We still don't know how he came to be in Treadwater, but Elsa's parents said that their daughter had travelled to Liverpool in search of him. They had not heard of the Treadwater Estate.'

'No one that I spoke to admits knowing Elsa,' said Tara. 'But that's no great surprise. I saw Justin Boyle on Saturday. Did you get anything from him?'

'Not a thing. Refused to talk. Initially, he mentioned a Dr Hazzard. Wilson and I checked her out. She's a lecturer and had never heard of Justin Boyle.'

'Did Boyle say how Hazzard was involved?'

'He spouted something about guns, but it didn't make any sense. I don't think Boyle is relevant to the main inquiry. And there's been no progress on the identities of the other two bodies found on the playing fields. That's about it, ma'am. How did your concert go? Sorry I couldn't make it; I had a hot date. Would have loved to hear you sing.'

'I'm sure you don't mean it, Alan. The show went very well, but I was hoping that these vigilantes would have revealed themselves in some way or other. Everything has gone eerily quiet. Has Tweedy said anything more about calling this off?'

'Not to me. Truth is, we don't have anything else on this case that we consider to be a decent lead.'

'What about John, has he mentioned anything he's gleaned from Danni Pearce?'

'Nothing relevant, although he was telling me about some perv who was kicked off the estate after he'd taken a beating.'

'Strange that it didn't have the same MO as other so-called evictions.'

There was a knock at her door, so she ended the call to Murray. It was Beth.

'We're invited to Katrina's for a party to celebrate the show.'

'When?' Tara asked.

'Tonight.'

'I'll have to get some booze; can I get you anything?'

'Sure, but I'll have to owe you.'

'No problem, I'll see you later.'

Tara viewed the party as another opportunity to rouse the secret executioners. Surely someone within the choir had a connection to those who made decisions about who should live or die.

Shortly after eight, she called for Beth and the pair of them carried beer and a bottle of vodka round to Katrina's flat. The place was bursting with people, all of them choristers. Tara was a little surprised to see the older members at the centre of the revelry. Mary, Raymond and Hannah were among them, although Stan was missing.

'Hello, my two darlings,' Katrina called out, throwing her arms around Tara and then Beth. Katrina was certainly dressed for a party. She had glam all over, a sparkly dress and shiny heels, although she hadn't bothered with a wig. By now, everyone was used to her foibles, even the older men merely smirked at her antics.

Beth and Tara began drinking the cans of beer and were soon parted and chatting to the others. Tara, initially, looked around for someone of interest to engage. She noticed that Danni had not brought John Wilson along.

'Hi, Danni,' said Tara. 'Who's looking after the kids tonight?'

Danni glared. She did not like Claire Brady.

'A friend,' was all that she replied, then drank from her glass of vodka.

'Maybe someday soon they'll be singing in the choir?'

'Maybe.'

Fortunately, Esther joined the pair and had overheard Tara's remark about Danni's kids.

'A junior choir would be wonderful,' she said. 'It would be nice to get them at such an early age. We could have them for life.'

'You'd have your work cut out for you,' said Danni. 'My two are a handful.'

'Oh, I couldn't manage it on my own. I would need help for sure. Claire, I imagine you'd be great with kids.'

'Me?'

Danni frowned at the suggestion.

'I don't know, Esther. Never worked with kids before,' Tara replied.

Danni sneered at Tara's response.

'What's the matter, Danni?' Esther asked. 'Don't you think Claire would be good with children?'

'No, I don't.' Tara waited for the reason. 'She's a…'

'I'm a what, Danni?'

'You're on the friggin' game, aren't you?'

Esther's mouth dropped open.

'Danni!'

'Well, she is, Esther. Ask her yourself.'

Esther looked awkward with the situation. Tara decided to spare the woman's discomfort.

'She's right, Esther. Have to earn a living somehow.'

Esther turned away abruptly in search of more appealing conversation.

'Thanks for that, Danni,' Tara said sarcastically.

'No problem, love, you fucking deserve it.' Danni got to her feet. 'I need another drink.'

Tara was left alone until Katrina approached and offered her a glass filled with either gin or vodka. At that moment, Tara didn't care. She was going to need alcohol to get through the evening.

The dance music was replaced by a recording of the choir's performance at the leisure centre. Everyone settled down to listen. There were cheers and shouted comments as each solo was played. Tara drank her gin mixed with lemonade. It went down easily. She listened with the others as Hannah claimed a seat next to her.

'Did Stan let you out on your own tonight?' Tara asked.

'Oh yes. He's still a bit poorly.'

'I hope he gets well soon.'

Hannah merely nodded and continued to listen to the music. People were singing along to the songs they had performed and knew well. Tara sipped her gin. Already, she could feel its effects taking hold. She didn't think that she had been drinking so fast. By the time the music was paused for Esther to address her choir and to again express thanks for all their hard work, Tara was fast asleep on the sofa, her head resting on Hannah's shoulder.

CHAPTER 96

Hannah

Stan had never approved of her drinking and consequently Hannah had little opportunity to do so. Tonight, though, Stan wasn't here. Stan would never be with her again. The wonder of it all was that she had yet to grasp how much freedom she had attained. Katrina made sure that Hannah's glass was filled with whatever concoction was circulating in the flat. Hannah didn't mind what she was drinking. She enjoyed the onset of a happy drunkenness. Claire had already fallen asleep from whatever she'd been drinking. Eventually, Hannah managed to free herself from the body slumped beside her, and she moved to a seat next to her friend, Mary. Her husband Raymond was dancing with Valerie in the middle of the room, although Valerie, her arms draped around his shoulders, was struggling to stay upright.

Later, the music changed to seventies hits of Mud, The Sweet, Donna Summer and the Bee Gees. Katrina and Sheena danced alongside Valerie and Raymond, while Beth swayed next to Marcus. Dinah observed it all from the kitchen. She didn't drink and did not approve of people losing control under its influence.

Perhaps the most astonishing sight at this party was the lack of reaction to Carrie sitting close to Josh Forsyth, a teenage member of the choir, the pair kissing and hugging. No one seemed to mind. Carrie had moved on quickly from Ian Bankhead. An early morning encounter with the members of Carrie's family, and Bankhead had failed to escape. His day was spent at A&E in the Royal Hospital. Two broken arms, a broken leg and jaw, he would be there for a while.

'How's Stan doing?' Mary asked as she rolled her shoulders in time to *Rock Me Baby* by George McCrae.

Hannah grinned widely.

'He's dead, Mary,' she said as if it were a hilarious punchline.

Mary hadn't heard properly. She smiled politely.

'So, he didn't fancy coming to the party then?' Mary continued.

'No, Mary. He's dead. I killed him.'

'You what?'

'I killed him, Mary. Stabbed him with the bread knife. He was trying to stop me from going to the concert on Saturday.' Hannah calmly sipped her drink.

Suddenly, Mary grasped what Hannah had been saying. She sat upright and wondered for a second whether Hannah was simply drunk.

'Say that again, Hannah.'

'Stan's dead. I killed him.'

'Are you sure? Where is he?'

'He's lying in the hall. I can't figure out what to do with him.'

Mary tried to beckon Raymond, but his hands were all over a writhing Valerie. She gazed about the room, desperately needing to summon help. She was sure there was something wrong with Hannah. She wasn't talking sense. Maybe she'd had a stroke, or it was the drink. Mary didn't understand.

Eventually, Katrina noticed that something was up with the two older women seated in her armchairs. Mary's face looked shocked. Katrina came over.

'All right, ladies? Need another drink?'

Hannah smiled and handed her glass to Katrina. Mary followed her to the kitchen. There she explained to Katrina and Dinah what Hannah had just told her.

'She's drunk!' Katrina laughed.

'I don't know. She's not that drunk. Go ask her,' said Mary.

Katrina took a glass refilled with gin and bitter lemon out to Hannah and sat down beside her.

'Hannah, love, are you all right?'

'Oh yes, dear. It's a lovely party. I'm really enjoying myself.'

'Why is Stan not here?'

'He's dead, love. Didn't Mary tell you? I killed the bastard. I really love this song. Knock three times on the ceiling if you want me,' she sang.

Katrina rubbed her hand on Hannah's thigh.

'OK, Hannah, love. I'll be back in a sec.'

'What the hell do we do?' she asked Mary and Dinah in the kitchen.

'I think we'd better go round there,' said Dinah.

CHAPTER 97

Mary

Mary felt deceived. She was frightened too. It was horrifying to have been married to someone for forty years and only now to discover what he got up to in secret. Mary had stumbled into Raymond's hidden life.

She had accompanied Dinah and Katrina to Hannah's house on Conwy Drive, a cul-de-sac that sat directly opposite Katrina's. Hannah quite happily handed her key to Mary and told her that she was going to stay at the party and enjoy the music.

Dinah pushed the front door open until it hit something solid. She looked apprehensively at the other women.

'Put a light on,' said Katrina.

Mary held back. If this story was true, she had no desire to see the body of a dead man.

Dinah stepped into the hall, flicked a switch near the entrance to the living room, then turned around.

'Oh my God!'

Katrina barged in to see the stiffened body of Stan Oldfield lying on a blood-soaked carpet. Hannah had left her husband in the spot where she'd killed him.

'Check that he's dead,' said Katrina.

'He's stiff and cold,' said Dinah leaning over the body. 'I'd say he's been dead for a while.'

'At least since Saturday,' Katrina suggested, 'or he would have been at the concert.'

'Is he dead?' Mary called from outside.

'Sssh! Yes, he's dead, love,' said Katrina. 'Keep your voice down. No need to tell the whole world.'

Dinah switched off the hall light and ushered Katrina from the house, closing the door behind them.

'What are we going to do?' Mary asked. 'We can't let Hannah go back in there.'

'Doesn't seem to have bothered her so far,' said Katrina.

'Can she stay with you, Mary?' Dinah asked.

'Yes, of course.'

'Good. Katrina, can you get Raymond to deal with the body?' Dinah said.

'You're not going to call the police?' Mary asked. Confusion was quickly taking hold of her. Why had Dinah mentioned Raymond?

Dinah and Katrina placed Mary between them and slowly walked away from the house. Dinah spoke quietly.

'No, Mary. No police. Hannah is our friend. We don't want her to get in trouble and be taken away from us. Stan was a hateful man. He abused Hannah for years. We must protect her now. We're all she's got.'

'But why are you getting Raymond to come round?' Mary asked.

'He knows what to do, Mary,' Dinah said.

'How does he know what to do? What are you talking about?'

'Please, Mary, for now you have to trust us. If you want to help Hannah, you must do exactly as we say.'

CHAPTER 98

Tara

All before her was blurred and fuzzy. It was daylight, but she couldn't be certain, not when her eyes were behaving so strangely. She felt stiff, and her breathing was laboured. She was sucking at the air, and the sound she made echoed in her ears. Suck then puff, like she was blowing into a bag.

Tara was aware of her lying down but not in a bed. It felt weirdly comfortable, but she couldn't move her arms. And her legs were stuck together. She tried to bend them at the knees, but the rest of her body stiffened further with the attempt. Her head wouldn't do what she wanted it to do either. Then she realised what had happened to her. She was wrapped. Plastic film enveloped her entire body. Thankfully, she could still breathe. That was all. She couldn't see clearly. She could scarcely move, and certainly could not stand. And there was silence except for the noise of her breathing. She realised now that the blurred light was merely the blue and grey sky above her.

Suddenly, she panicked. She was lying on a road, just like Elsa Remmel. Soon a car, a van or a truck would cut her to pieces. She rocked her body to and fro, gaining sufficient momentum to roll onto her left side. Her view confirmed little but enough to know that she was not lying on a motorway. There was slight relief, but still there was the mystery of where she could be. Would someone come for her? How long had she been lying here? How much longer before someone found her? Tara prayed.

She felt raindrops bouncing on her plastic shroud. A while later, she felt the sun warming her. Her notion of time was terribly awry. She knew at least a day had elapsed because darkness had come and gone once. Her throat was parched. She wouldn't survive for long without water. If she was in a remote place, she might never be found. Her thoughts were like a river in flood, rushing by, swirling one with another, tumbling backwards then fading to oblivion. She strived to remember what had happened to her. Who had done this to her, and who had left her here to die?

In the stillness, she managed some sleep. She guessed at her location, wondering how far she was from home. The plastic film did not prevent tears seeping from her eyes. They say that in the moments before death your entire life passes before you, so she tried to suppress her memories. She wasn't ready to die.

She felt something touch her. It was a shock having felt nothing for such a long time. Another touch – like a kick. She heard a sound other than her breathing. A snort. Something nudged her. Fear and relief faced each other in her mind. Was this freedom, her rescue, or her demise? Soon her ears were filled with more sounds: snorts, grunts and moos! Cows, she was in a field with cows. They were inquisitive but passive animals. For what seemed like hours she was visited by snouts, nudged, licked and bitten several times.

Much later, there arose the sound of an engine and it was drawing closer. She felt the thuds of the cows moving faster on the earth as they hurried somewhere. Then the engine sound changed. The vehicle had stopped but the engine was idling. She tried to shout, and a noise certainly came out of her mouth. She imagined she sounded like one of the cows. Then she heard a glorious human voice.

'What the blazes!'

'Help me! Please help me!'

'Oh my God!'

There were hands on her now, pulling and grappling at the plastic film. Tara cried with joy and panic.

'Hold on, I'll get you out.' It was the voice of a woman.

The woman produced a penknife from the pocket of her fleece jacket. Carefully, she sliced at the plastic film, firstly at the side of Tara's head and then down the front of her torso. Soon, she exposed a young woman's face fraught with panic and tears.

'You're all right, love. You're all right. What the hell happened to you?'

Once her arms were free, Tara hugged her rescuer and sobbed into her shoulder.

'I need some water,' she said.

CHAPTER 99

Tara

Hospital was an inconvenience Tara could do without. Yes, she needed to be checked over. She was dehydrated but lying in a bed attached to a drip was a waste of valuable time. Her parents had come to visit, unaware of the details of her ordeal. Then Kate dropped by, and she was more able to cope with hearing the terrifying story. There had been so many incidents involving Tara over the years, and even Kate had first-hand experience of some of them.

Eventually, with her well-wishers gone, Tara was able to discuss her ordeal with her team.

'I don't know,' was her answer to many of Tweedy and Murray's questions. She didn't know how she ended up in a field somewhere east of Southport. She didn't know where her abductors had wrapped her in plastic film. She didn't know who had carried out the deed. She didn't know anything from the time she'd been drinking at the party in Treadwater.

'Who else was at this party?' Murray asked her.

Tara sat upright in bed, covered by a sheet and blanket. Murray, she thought, was slowly acquiring the same old man look of concern displayed by Tweedy.

'Only members of the choir. We were celebrating the success of the concert.'

'What were you drinking?' Murray continued.

'I can't remember exactly. I started off with a can of lager that I had brought with me. Then it was generous measures of gin and vodka. I don't remember how many.'

'Do you recall leaving the party?' Tweedy asked.

Tara thought for a second. Her mind kept jumping forward to her time in the field and her rescue.

'I can't remember anything until I woke up in the field, sir.'

'Where was the party?' Murray asked.

'Katrina's flat. She's the transgender woman I met when I first came to the estate.'

'We'll get someone to look over the place and to have a word with Katrina.'

'No, Alan, don't do that. I want to go back there undercover. I must see this through now. If I was drugged at the party, it proves that members of the choir are involved.'

'You should be taking some time off to recover, Tara,' said Tweedy.

'Thank you, sir, but I've come too far with this to let it go. Somebody at that party spiked my drink and I passed out. I'll try to figure out who gave me the drink and hopefully it will lead me to this group of vigilantes.'

When her colleagues had departed, Tara was left with her thoughts once again. If only she could remember who gave her that last drink.

CHAPTER 100

Tara

Tara made a deliberate effort to be seen walking back into the Treadwater Estate. Stepping off the bus outside the library, wearing a short skirt, heels and a red leather jacket, she immediately spotted Esther carrying an armful of books.

'Hi, Esther, have you recovered from the party on Monday?'

'Oh yes, it was great. What about you, Claire? How's the head? It all seemed too much for you.'

Tara drew closer to the choir mistress. Esther looked immaculate in a short-length woollen coat and dark trousers. Her hair rested on the collar of her coat and her smile also rested easily. Tara found it hard to believe that Esther could be mixed up in such horrifying activities. But she was a suspect like every other member of the choir.

'I had a bit too much to drink,' Tara said.

'Well, it's good to see you looking so well this morning. Don't forget, we have a practice this evening. See you later.'

Esther proceeded to the library, and Tara, having forgotten all about choir practices, now realised she had a great opportunity to parade herself in front of those who had dumped her in a field.

Her walk to Deeside Crescent did not afford any further meetings, but she noticed one or two curtains move as she strolled by. When she reached her building, she found Beth outside leaning against a wall and smoking a fag.

'Hiya, Beth, did you miss me?'

Beth discarded her cigarette and stood upright.

'Where the hell have you been? I've looked everywhere.'

To Tara's surprise and delight, Beth threw her arms around her. It was progress.

'Put the kettle on,' said Tara, 'and I'll tell you all about it.'

Five minutes later, they were seated in Beth's flat, both cradling mugs of strong tea.

'Somebody spiked my drink, Beth. At the party.'

'I thought you'd just knocked it back too quickly. But I don't remember much either. I was pissed by the end of the night.'

'Did we walk home?' Tara asked.

'You don't remember?'

'Not a thing after passing out.'

'Shit, Claire, you must have been totally fucking wasted. It was five o'clock in the morning before I staggered home. Katrina suggested leaving you to sleep it off on the couch. I didn't argue, but then I couldn't find you later that day or the next one. What the hell happened to you?'

'All I know is that I woke up in a field with cows. I was wrapped in plastic and couldn't move. Luckily, I was able to breathe. I was lying there until yesterday afternoon.'

'Somebody from the estate did that to you?'

'Someone from the choir, Beth. Someone who was at the party. Spiking my drink was just the start of things.'

'But why come back here, Claire? They might do worse next time.'

'I know that, but they don't frighten me. I'm going to get the bastards who did this. I reckon that's what happened to my friend Mandy, only she didn't survive. She's probably lying dead in a field somewhere.'

'Shit, Claire, you need to be careful. But why didn't they take me as well? We both got those damned letters.'

'I don't know, but we need to find these people before they try it again. Can you remember who was still at Katrina's when you left?'

Beth shook her head, then reached for her tobacco and roll-up papers.

'I'm not sure about that. Katrina, obviously, and maybe Sheena and Marcus.'

'Any idea who might have spiked my drink?'

Beth scoffed at the question.

'Fuck's sake, Claire, we were all getting hammered. Even poor Hannah was knocking it back.'

'I can remember sitting next to her for a while.'

'You fell asleep with your head on her shoulder. The poor woman could hardly move. Katrina had to rescue the glass from your hand.'

'Katrina? That's it! She took my drink away knowing it had been spiked.'

'Don't be daft, Claire. Katrina wouldn't be mixed up with those fucking loonies. They hate her, and she hates them. That fucking Dinah woman, Stan and Raymond all look down their noses at Katrina.'

CHAPTER 101

Tara

If members of the choir had been startled by Claire's first appearance at practice, several were dumbfounded when she strutted into the hall on Beth's arm. Tara saw the shock register on Katrina's face. She thought it strange that Katrina had made her way to practice alone, without calling for Beth.

Before she had even taken her seat, Tara noted the facial expressions from several others and realised that these were the people who at least knew of her ordeal. She was certain that some of them had been responsible for her being dumped in a field.

When she sat down Katrina placed a hand on her thigh.

'Where the hell have you been, Claire love?'

Tara smiled, but it quickly changed to a sneer. She had no trust in any person in the room.

'Had a few rough nights, that's all.'

'Glad you're back with us,' said Katrina. 'I was worried about you when you passed out at my place.'

'Were you really?'

Before Katrina could respond, Esther called the members to order and launched into another speech of thanks.

'We can do great things if we support each other,' she said. 'Our next venture is to perform at one of the big music festivals, so we have to practice, practice, practice.'

Everyone applauded. Tara mused that if she uncovered the truth about this estate, several members may not be around for the next big performance.

When they began to sing a song they knew well, *I Say a Little Prayer*, Tara noticed that Mary wasn't joining in. She sat next to Valerie, where the rows of seats swept in an arc around the room. Her head was down until Valerie nudged her, and she finally joined in the singing.

Tara hoped she'd done enough to show the relevant people that she was up for a fight. She realised that she must take extra care going about the estate. It was hard not to be frightened, but provoking these people was the reason she was still here.

CHAPTER 102

The committee

It was intended to be a short meeting. They had only one decision to make. Claire Brady had defied them. She had ignored their written warnings. They had expelled her from the estate. For most of the people who crossed them, it was sufficient warning not to return.

'Why the hell didn't she clear off like her friend Mandy? She got the message and hasn't come back.' Raymond spoke quietly but forcefully. No one disagreed with him.

'What happens now?' Katrina, the secretary, asked. This evening Katrina was not her usual bubbly self. Even at committee meetings she had always brought some cheer along. Tonight, though, she was worried. She'd asked the question knowing full well what the answer would be.

'Claire's a nice girl,' she said. 'I know she's on the game, but I don't think she deserves to die for it.'

'Then she shouldn't have ignored our warnings,' said Raymond. 'She got up my nose right from the start, asking too many questions.'

'Maybe a last warning,' Katrina suggested. 'I could talk to her, get her to stop the sex work on the estate.'

'No!' Raymond blurted. 'We can't expose ourselves like that.'

'Didn't seem to bother you when you were ogling her,' Katrina chided. 'Why can't we issue another final warning? Claire could easily become one of us, you know. I think she is that kind of girl. She's strong-willed.'

The others looked doubtful, but Dinah was more certain.

'No further warnings,' said Dinah. 'Are we all agreed?'

All heads nodded in accord except for Katrina's.

'Raymond, will you please organise your team to carry out the sentence. Claire Brady to be executed by the usual means.'

Katrina couldn't hold back her tears.

'I thought any decision had to be unanimous,' she said. 'I don't agree with this.'

'Needs must, Katrina,' said Dinah, looking grave.

Katrina knew better than to run against the committee, and she knew better than to ever cross the chairperson, Dinah Sandford.

CHAPTER 103

Danni and Wilson

She jumped at the sound of knocking on her door. Mikaela rose from playing with dolls on the floor and rushed after her mother. The child smiled with delight when John came in. Straight away, he swung her into the air.

'Hiya, Mikky, what you up to?'

'Playing with my dolls.' She thrust a naked Cindy into his face.

'Off you go and play, I'll see you in a minute.' He lowered her to the floor, and she trotted off. 'Now, missus, how are you?' He engulfed Danni with his broad frame. She kissed him, feeling instantly aroused.

'I'm good,' she whispered, kissing him again.

Danni was good. She'd stopped her daytime drinking and hardly felt the need for her pills. Enthusiasm to clean the flat, play with her children and to spruce up her own appearance had come from having John Wilson in her life. Already, she was deeply in love.

She had a meal prepared, the first proper sit-down dinner she'd made in years. John scoffed it, enjoying every mouthful of a beef casserole with tiny roast potatoes and peas. Danni was thrilled as she watched him eat. Nervously, though, she ran her hand through her hair, the pink colour fading, her natural dirty fair becoming prominent. She had trouble believing this was happening to her and the kids. Bradley and Mikaela had taken to John instantly, and he was super with them. She worried that something might spoil it.

John played on the floor with Bradley and his trucks, and with Mikaela and her dolls. It was surreal, a burly copper playing with Ken and Barbie. Fortunately, both kids crashed out earlier than usual, leaving Danni and her man to enjoy an evening in front of the telly and then to bed. After they'd made love, they lay in the darkened room talking quietly to each other. For Danni, it was heavenly fun, giggling over something John had done when he was fourteen that ended with him waist deep in mud on the building site that was now the primary school. As one subject was exhausted, they moved on to another, neither one wishing to fall asleep.

'How's your mum doing without that guy she threw out?'

'Putting on a brave face,' said Danni. 'I think she misses the company, but not the slob that was Barry.'

'Where did he go?'

'Who cares? He got a hiding from…' Danni hesitated, suddenly aware that her lover was also a bizzie. She had to get used to that. Wilson sensed her unease.

'Don't worry, Danni, I'm not going to arrest anyone. Barry got what he deserved.'

'I know. I think it's great that you're a bizzie. You should be proud of it, coming from Treadwater. I was going to say that Barry got a hiding from Carrie's dad and his mates when he found out that Barry had assaulted his daughter.'

'Oh.'

'What do you mean, oh?'

'I thought you were going to say it was the vigilantes on the estate that did for Barry.'

'Vigilantes?'

'Yeah, the people responsible for the bodies dug up on the football pitch and the guy fished out of the sewer outside of your flat.'

'You don't believe that nonsense, do you?'

'Someone killed those people, Danni.'

Danni sat upright.

'I know, but you grew up here, John. Surely you don't think that ordinary folk can murder people?'

John gently stroked her back and she cooed.

'That's what we're trying to find out. Believe me, Merseyside Police aren't going to let this go. We're keeping a careful watch on the estate. We'll soon find the culprits.'

Danni lay down and John kissed her. Soon they were making love again. When it was over, and John had succumbed to sleep, Danni lay awake thinking how her idyllic evening had been sullied by the thought that they were being watched. She would have to warn the others.

CHAPTER 104

Danni and Wilson

Danni started the new day feeling that everything had changed. John left early for work, leaving her with a loving kiss and a promise to see her again soon. She hoped it was true, that all would be well when he next shared her bed.

She made breakfast for Bradley and Mikaela, then delivered them to nursery school.

It was an established rule that members of the committee would never communicate information by phone that might incriminate any of them. All she could do was either summon them to her home or go to theirs. Danni felt that there was something potentially dangerous that everyone needed to know.

Raymond was waiting by her door when she arrived home from the nursery.

'Has it got something to do with him?' Raymond nodded towards the door of Justin Boyle's flat.

Danni was still climbing the stairs but stopped halfway when she saw Raymond.

'No, it's the bizzies,' she said.

'Bizzies?'

'They're watching the estate, on the lookout for vigilantes.'

Raymond laughed.

'Is that all?' he said. 'Don't mean anything. We're always careful, you know that, Danni. Of course, if you have more to tell since you're sleeping with a copper…'

Wilson stopped his car outside the flat he'd left only an hour earlier. If he'd known what his first task of the day was going to be, he could have saved himself a journey to St Anne Street station. The matter of the vicious attack on Justin Boyle had not been closed. He'd been sent by Tweedy to conduct another interview with the victim. He stepped into the entrance hall and saw Danni standing on the stairs, talking to someone on the landing above.

'That's got nothing to do with it,' Danni said. 'John doesn't know anything, and besides, he's really one of us. He grew up on Treadwater.'

Wilson stopped on hearing his name.

'But there is something,' said Danni. 'I can't be sure. It's just a gut feeling.'

'About what?' Raymond asked.

'We need to get everyone together. I'll tell you then.'

Wilson had heard enough. His shock was mixed with the disappointment of learning that the new love in his life was possibly involved in murder. Silently, he stepped back outside and returned to his car. Immediately, he phoned Murray. When he'd related the story, he retraced his steps to the building and met Raymond Glover coming out. The two men nodded as they passed. Rather than confront Danni with what he'd just learned, he knocked on Justin's door in the hope of getting an interview. He had yet to decide exactly how to deal with the woman who had just become his ex-girlfriend.

CHAPTER 105

The committee

'Let's just settle down,' Dinah warned. 'There's no need to panic. Let's hear from Danni.'

Seated with the entire committee, except Ian Bankhead, around the coffee table in Dinah's living room, Danni expanded on the information she'd given to Raymond earlier in the day.

'Claire Brady. I don't like her,' she began.

'None of us do, that's why we're getting rid of her,' said Raymond.

'It's not just that,' said Danni. 'Ever since I clapped eyes on the bitch in the park, she seemed familiar. I was never certain, her shaved head put me right off, but I think she's a bizzie. I think she's the copper who came asking questions round here after they found Eesmaa in the drain.'

'Shit! How sure are you, Danni?' Sheena asked.

'Fairly sure, since John told me about the police keeping a watch on the estate.'

Of all the members, Katrina's reaction was the greatest display of shock. Her hand went to her open mouth.

'Oh my God! Oh my God! A fucking bizzie!' she cried. 'What are we going to do?' She grappled for a tissue in her bag and used it to wipe her eyes.

Dinah glared with disgust at the big woos sat in her home. Katrina – or Nathan, to give him his proper name – was an inconvenience on her committee, and she didn't know how much longer she could tolerate him.

'OK, calm down,' said Dinah. 'Nothing has changed. The police still have no evidence about us.'

'Except that we have already threatened this Brady woman, abducted her and dumped her in a field,' said Danni, her courage also wavering.

'And by tomorrow we'll be rid of her for good,' said Raymond.

'You're not going ahead with it, surely?' Katrina piped up.

'All the more reason to carry out the sentence,' said Raymond.

'But we were getting rid of her because we thought she was a prossy! Now we know she's a bizzie, we can't do her in.' Katrina was using her tissues, sniffing tears.

Dinah examined each member trying to gauge opinion from their expressions. They had an important decision to make. It could save them, or it could sink every one of them.

CHAPTER 106

Wilson

His concentration had gone to the wall. Nothing at St Anne Street held his attention, except for events on the Treadwater Estate. His discovery about Danni had stunned him. He conjured reasons for having heard things incorrectly. Maybe Danni knew of the vigilante group but wasn't involved. But she had mentioned something about getting the rest of them together. She must have meant the vigilantes.

He passed on the invitation to go for a pint after work with Murray and some of the others in the squad. Instead, he drove to Treadwater. He hadn't planned on calling with her this evening but, somehow, he had to get to the truth about Danni Pearce.

'All quiet? Where are the kids?' he asked.

'Staying at mum's tonight,' Danni replied. 'I thought she could do with some company, take her mind off Barry Sugden.'

John could tell already that Danni was uneasy. It was in her kiss, or rather the lack of passion in her greeting.

‘What brings you here?’ she asked. ‘I thought you had to work late this evening.’ She sprawled on the sofa, a glass of vodka in her hand, while he made do with the armchair.

‘Had enough work for one day. I wanted to ask you something.’

‘OK? Sounds ominous.’

‘Do you fancy us going on holiday together? You and the kids, I mean. I’m sure you all could do with a break.’

Danni broke into tears. Wilson had proffered his excuse for calling, but already he was sorry for deliberately leading her on and raising her hopes. Whatever she might have done, she did not deserve the deception. She came and sat on his lap. This time her kiss was brimming with true affection.

‘I’d love to go with you. Thank you. When?’

‘Soon as I can arrange some leave. That’s not likely until we get this case cleared up.’

‘What case?’

‘Treadwater. We still have to solve six murders linked to this estate.’

He felt her stiffen in his arms. She pushed herself off him and fetched a tissue. Wilson eyed her carefully. Something was up; he was sure of that.

‘Are you staying the night?’ she asked. ‘Or have you called just to invite me on holiday?’

‘I can stay if you like. But maybe you have other plans?’

‘I have to go out later – to a friend’s, that’s all.’ She returned to his lap. ‘So where are you taking me on holiday?’

‘How does Greece or Turkey sound?’

‘Great.’

She took him by the hand and led him to her bedroom. He tried to suppress the guilt he was feeling. He knew that he was soon to break her heart; his own was already broken.

CHAPTER 107

Tara

Beth finally received a benefit payment. She wasted no time in spending most of it on some good crack. Late in the night, she lay on the sofa, her mind in a faraway place. She was oblivious to the rumpus from the flat above.

Two strikes from a sledgehammer and the door flew open. Tara jumped awake. Instantly, she reached for her phone. The bedroom door was thrust open. Two hooded figures rushed in. The phone was kicked from her hand, and it clattered against the wall.

'Get up, now!' one of them shouted.

Tara tried to resist the hands grappling for her. She slapped at them and cowered against the headboard of her bed. She kicked. Screamed.

'Get off me!'

A strong hand gripped her neck. Something was forced into her mouth. It felt like paper towel. She tried to spit it out, but the hand kept pushing more in until her eyes bulged, and she struggled for breath. Her head was forced downwards to the mattress. Someone grabbed her wrists and wrenched them behind her back. Her cries were muffled. Her wrists were secured with cable ties and with her feet kicking outwards, she was dragged from the bed.

She'd counted two assailants, but in her living room there were at least two more, one standing near the hallway and another by the window. Tara struggled to break free. Somehow, she'd believed she would have time to alert Murray but that was folly. She was on her own.

The figure standing by the window approached her. A hood was produced and pulled over her head. Tara had a strange sensation. Perfume. The figure before her was female. Barefoot and in pyjamas, Tara was hustled and finally dragged down the stairs, past Beth's flat and into the street. Everything was accomplished with little disturbance of the night's silence. Even if someone on the street was witness to this abduction, they were never likely to tell.

Tara heard the rattle of a van door being opened. She was lifted inside. Hands pushed down on her shoulders until she dropped to the floor. The door was gently pressed closed, the engine started up and Tara toppled sideways as they moved off.

CHAPTER 108

Danni

Danni checked the time on her phone. It was approaching midnight. She needed to go now. John lay asleep beside her, his arm draped across her shoulder, her back nestled into his chest. Gently, she slid his arm away and eased herself from the bed. As she gathered her clothes from the floor, intending to dress once she'd left the bedroom, John spoke.

'What's up?'

'Nothing. You go back to sleep.'

'What time is it?'

'Midnight,' she whispered without any need to do so.

'Where are you going?' He switched on the bedside lamp then rubbed his eyes.

'I forgot about calling with my friend.'

'But it's late, Danni. Surely you're not going at this time of night?'

'She will still be up, doesn't go to bed till really late. You go back to sleep. I'll see you later.'

He was out of bed in a flash and took her by the arms.

'What are you up to, Danni?'

'What?' She tried to brush him away, but he wasn't for moving. 'I'm calling with a mate, that's all. She's going through a hard time. I just want to be there for her.'

'You're lying to me, Danni. I want the truth.'

'Fuck off me, John. I don't have to tell you anything. Leave me alone. I have to go.'

Wilson did not relent. He could easily hold her still. Her struggles were feeble. Unable to break free, she spat in his face. He thrust her onto the bed and pinned her down.

'Tell me the truth, Danni, are you one of these vigilantes?' He pressed his weight into her body.

'I don't know what you're talking about. Let me go!'

'Or what, Danni? You'll have your mates sort me out? I fucking love you, but you're up to something. I know it. I heard you today talking to Raymond Glover.'

Her eyes watered as they searched his. More than anything, she wanted to tell him that she loved him, but it was too late. Already, he knew too much. She felt helpless beneath him, his eyes waiting for an answer.

'Come on, Danni, love. Six people are dead. Please tell me you're not involved.'

She couldn't. She loved him. She couldn't lie to him anymore. But her voice was lost in her crying.

'Danni, please! My friend's life is in danger. You know her as Claire Brady, but she's really DI Grogan. I can't let anything happen to her. Tell me who they are.'

Danni was incapable of answering. Her sobs came heavily, her life, her wonderful new life with John Wilson had lasted only a few days. She was finished. Her thoughts went to her kids. What would happen to them? She closed her eyes, but it didn't take the trouble away. John still had her pinned to the bed. When she opened her eyes again, John was also crying.

'Danni, six people have been murdered. Don't let there be any more deaths.'

'I can't.'

'Why, Danni? Don't you care about me, about us?'

'It's too late.'

'What do you mean?'

She refused to answer. Wilson pushed her into the bed, his full weight astride her.

'What do you mean, Danni?'

'They're taking Claire tonight.'

'And?'

'That's it. She'll be killed, and you won't fucking ever know who did it. Now get the fuck off me, cop!'

'Where, Danni? You have to tell me.'

CHAPTER 109

Tara

They drove for less than two minutes. The van door opened, and Tara was hauled out. She refused to walk, but her body was so slight, one of the men gathered her in his arms and carried her. She heard a metal door close behind her as she was set down again, her feet resting on cold concrete. There were no voices, but she caught another whiff of ladies' perfume. She presumed that she had been in this place previously when they'd wrapped her in plastic and then dumped her in a field. This time, she realised, breathing holes would not be applied. She shivered from cold and from the fear of how close she was to death. No one knew she was here.

Suddenly, a hand grasped the hood and pulled it off. She squinted from the brightness of a single strip fluorescent tube above her head. The room appeared to be a lock-up garage. Now she stood face to face with her executioners. Raymond Glover was of no surprise. Billy, the caretaker of the community centre, was not a man she knew well. They stood guard either side of her. Some of the others proved a shock and the rest were merely confirmation of her suspicions. Dinah and daughter, Sheena, stood opposite her, both looking stern and unrepentant. Tara felt the pain of disappointment, but it was no surprise that Katrina stood next to them. She didn't look her best, wigless, devoid of make-up, and wearing dark jeans and trainers. Her gaze was set downwards, refusing the eye contact that Tara craved from those about to end her life. The undoubted leader of this residents' select was Dinah Sandford.

In the few seconds before anyone spoke, Tara took in the rest of her surroundings. Glancing behind, she spied the apparatus used to wrap a human body in plastic film. It was a blue metal frame about five feet high set on castors, holding a large roll of film loaded and ready. To her right, a sample of the group's work lay on the concrete floor. Human remains mummified in polythene, but Tara had no idea of the victim. She prayed that it wasn't Beth.

Dinah spoke at last.

'Where is Danni?'

No one replied as Tara reeled from hearing the name. She thought immediately of John Wilson. His relationship with Danni was not going to last for long. 'You know we can't do this without her,' Dinah said, angrily. 'Everyone must be present.'

'There are enough of us here, Dinah,' said Raymond. 'Danni has witnessed enough killings to remain implicated. Let's get on with it.'

'I don't like it, Raymond,' said Dinah. 'She should be here, especially after what she told us today.'

Tara was grateful for any delay. The longer they debated, the more chance perhaps that someone would come to her rescue, or that these people would call it off. She managed to expel the paper from her mouth.

'We need to get on with it,' said Billy. 'She knows who we are now. She has to die.'

'And she's a bizzie,' said Sheena.

Of all those present, Tara was most shocked to see her. Sheena was still only a teenager.

'I'm DI Grogan, Merseyside Police. It's time to stop this madness. Don't make it any worse for yourselves by killing a police officer.'

'Shut up, bitch!' Katrina sparked into anger. 'Your lot helped create us. You're so fucking useless at protecting ordinary people – that's why we do this. Every one of us has a good reason for being here.'

'Enough, Nathan!' Dinah snapped.

'My name is Katrina. Shame on you too, Dinah.'

This was her only hope – that they would turn against each other.

'Just be quiet, please,' said Dinah.

'Come on, let's get it over with,' said Raymond. He went to the wrapping device and wheeled it forward.

'Hold on, Raymond. You know we have a statement to make,' said Dinah.

The man rolled his eyes.

'Claire Brady, or as you are now known to us as DI Grogan, you have been found guilty of activities that threaten the safe and peaceful living of the residents of this estate. You have received two written warnings to desist from your behaviour and a final warning when you were deported from Treadwater. Having defied all attempts to evict you from this place, your final sentence is death. OK, Raymond, proceed.'

'Hold on a minute,' Tara blurted. 'Don't I get to say anything?'

'No. You've had your chance,' said Billy.

'You warned me because you thought I was a prostitute. I'm a police officer, my cover was to pretend to be a sex worker to find the killers of six people on Treadwater. Six people that I now realise were put to death by you.'

'Stop talking,' said Raymond. 'You've just condemned yourself a second time.'

Billy stepped behind her and she felt the ties on her wrists being cut. This was her chance to run. She bolted forward but crashed into the line of people, knocking Dinah to the floor. Katrina grappled for her arms, and finally, Sheena caught her by the waist.

'Don't be daft, love, you can't fight us all,' said Raymond as Tara was hauled to the centre of the garage.

She now stood directly below a metal ring that was fixed to a roof beam. Sheena secured her hands in front of her with a cable tie. Raymond stood on a plastic step. He took hold of Tara's arms and forced them upwards as she fought and screamed.

'Tape her fucking gob!' Raymond shouted. 'For fuck's sake, she'll waken the whole estate.'

Sheena grabbed a roll of duct tape from a bench and rushed forward.

'Please, Sheena,' Tara pleaded. 'Don't do this.'

Through her tears she saw the cold eyes of the teenager. Tara realised she was finished. Sheena wrapped tape around her mouth and head. Using another cable tie, Raymond attached her bound hands to the metal ring. Only her toes were touching the ground. Her body swivelled from side to side and the pain grew in her stretched body. She heard the wrapping frame being wheeled into position. Billy gripped an edge of the plastic film and pulled it forward until it touched her body. Then Raymond began to wheel the frame around her, circling her body as Billy ensured that the film was slowly enveloping her.

She felt the constriction as more of the plastic covered her, from her feet to beneath her shoulders. Soon it became unbearably tight. She called for mercy. The other committee members looked on, showing no emotion.

Raymond stepped forward and released her hands from the ring in the ceiling. The ties at her wrists were cut, while Billy held her body upright. Then her hands were placed at her sides and Raymond resumed the circling with the wrapping machine. Several rotations later, her arms were tightly bound to her body. Only Tara's head remained free. Billy cut a three-metre strip of film from the roll and Sheena stepped forward to assist Raymond in holding Tara upright. The others looked on silently. They'd seen it all before. Tara Grogan was no different from any of the others. Tara gasped a final breath. Billy stretched the film across her face and behind her head.

CHAPTER 110

Tara

There was a gentle tap on the garage door. Everyone stopped. The members looked behind them.

'It's probably Danni,' said Dinah. 'Let her in.'

Sheena raised the roll-up door to see Danni, looking frightened in the darkness.

'I'm so sorry,' Danni said.

Raymond circled Tara once again, the plastic film gradually suffocating the police officer. But Danni was not apologising for turning up late.

Suddenly, uniformed officers rushed inside, pulling the committee members to the ground. Billy attempted to run, but Wilson caught him with a punch into his midriff and he dropped to his knees. Murray, following behind the uniforms, spotted the body writhing on the floor.

'Tara!'

Quickly, he tore at the plastic with his bare hands. But it was firm and tight. One layer came away only to reveal another. Finally, he poked his finger through and found her mouth. There was a sudden gasp for breath. He tore at the film until he revealed the tortured face of his boss. For her to be conscious and breathing was all he'd hoped for.

CHAPTER 111

Interviewing officers: DI Tara Grogan and DS Alan Murray

A day later, at Tara's insistence that she was well enough to return to duty, she and Murray had reserved several interview rooms at St Anne Street station. In addition to the files for each victim of the Treadwater vigilante group, a file was initiated for each suspected member.

Marcus Sandford entered interview room one, accompanied by a duty solicitor. He wore a T-shirt and baggy jeans, his face looked tired and pale. His eyes darted nervously from Tara to Murray and then to his brief. Following the formalities of how the interview would be conducted, Murray was first to speak.

'Tell us about your involvement in the killings, Marcus?'

The youth could hardly wait to answer. He was highly agitated by the suggestion that he was involved.

'I had no idea about mum and Sheena, you must believe me. They never said anything, honest. They've messed everything up.' Tears followed his outburst.

* * *

Their next interviewee was Billy McGuinness, the only suspect who was not a member of the community choir. Tara didn't think much of his attempts to proclaim his innocence.

'I'm just the caretaker at the community centre. I was just helping out, like. I didn't know that people were getting killed.'

'Our information,' said Tara, 'is that you helped with the heavy lifting.'

'No way.'

'You were a dab hand with that wrapping machine, weren't you, Billy? I speak from personal experience.'

* * *

Interview room two held Raymond Glover. Tara steeled herself for the encounter. On this occasion the man was no threat, but Tara knew she must hold her temper.

'How many victims, Raymond?' Tara asked. Glover sat upright, fearless. He was already resigned to spending the rest of his life in prison.

'The four buried on the playing fields caused us a lot of heartache. Selling drugs to the kids on the estate. We did them all the same night. It was easy. They were all off their heads in a squat. Never knew what hit them.'

'Names?'

'Linus Jones, Dale Wycliffe, Simon Maloney and Pete Samuels. Dealers, joyriders, thieves, and rapists. No regrets; would do it again.'

'The others?'

'A bloke called Eesmaa, but you already know that. We got spooked by a police patrol car on the estate. That's why he got put down a drain in a hurry. As for the girl, she was an accident. She wasn't supposed to die. She came around asking questions about Eesmaa. We only intended to get rid of her, same as you DI Grogan, but she fell out of the van on the motorway. Young Sheena was driving. She panicked and left her.'

'Anymore?'

'Two.'

'Where are they?'

'Buried on the building site next to the estate.'

'Names?'

'A couple of squatters who refused to leave the estate.'

'Names?'

Raymond shrugged a don't know.

'And what about Mandy Wright?'

Another shrug was accompanied by a conceited smile.

'We didn't kill her, so your guess is as good as mine, Inspector.'

* * *

When they re-entered interview room one, in the late afternoon, they found Sheena Sandford resting her head and arms on the table in front of her. She sat up when Tara greeted her. The teenager looked exhausted, her hair unbrushed and her eyes puffy from frequent bouts of crying. Of all the participants in the vigilante group, Tara was most surprised by Sheena. She had also reserved her sympathy for this girl.

'How did your group start?' Tara asked.

'Mum and Raymond, I suppose. They had good reason to clear the scum off our estate. Both had suffered because of drug dealers and rapists. Raymond Glover's son died after getting hooked on heroin at uni. A bad batch of gear was in circulation. Two others died at the same time. Nobody was ever caught. Raymond was adamant that all drug dealers would be removed from Treadwater. Dale Wycliffe raped me. Bizzies did nothing about it. Your lot said it was my word against his.'

'What happened?'

'He had an affair with our mum. When she ended it, he came after me. As he was raping me, he told me that he was just getting back at mum.'

* * *

Tara found herself unable to initiate the questioning of Katrina. Despite the fact that she was an undercover officer, early on she had come to regard Katrina as a friend.

'So, where do you stand on dishing out street justice?' Murray asked. Katrina wore a grey sweatshirt and leggings. She needed a shave.

'I joined my friends because I know what it's like to suffer abuse. Look at me, for fuck's sake. Since I was fourteen, I couldn't cross the road without some homophobic prick calling me shemale or fifty-fifty. Even Dinah only puts up with me because I'm her daughter's best friend. I suppose that's because Dinah is a born-again Christian. She has a forgiving heart. The sooner we get shot of all the arseholes in this world the better for those of us who just want to be left alone.'

* * *

Dinah Sandford had been detained into the evening before being interviewed. She gave the impression of having prepared her answers. There was no sign of fear or regret in her responses. She behaved as she had done when chairing the meetings of the committee.

'The body of Stan Oldfield was recovered from the lock-up. What had an old man, an army veteran, done to attract the wrath of your group?' Tara asked.

'He had abused his wife Hannah for years. You should have seen that much for yourself, DI Grogan.'

'Seems he died from stab wounds. That's not your usual *modus operandi*?'

'Needs must on occasion. He was difficult to subdue when we took him.'

'Why use the choir as a cover for your actions?'

'Unintentional. All of us happened to join the choir around the same time that Raymond first suggested the committee.'

'Committee?'

'Yes, we operated by committee. All decisions had to be unanimous. Without that we took no action. All members had to witness executions, so that all of us were implicated. We hoped to prevent any member from ever having a change of heart.'

'Very noble of you,' said Tara. 'I will need a full list of your members.'

* * *

'Your actions saved my life, Danni,' said Tara. 'Thank you for that.'

'What'll happen to my kids?' said Danni, ignoring Tara's offer of thanks.

'I can't say. Social services will carry out a full assessment of the situation.'

'Social services – the bloody reason I joined the damn committee in the first place. Whole estate bursting with dope addicts and all the social do is give them counselling and free fucking hits of methadone. Useless bunch of tossers. Can I see John?'

'Not now.'

* * *

'We want to know about your involvement with the residents' committee,' said Tara.

'I thought it was a great idea at first,' Esther said, tearfully. 'A committee to look after things like fundraising and social activities on the estate. Dinah said she was happy to take it on, that there was no need for me to be involved. I had enough to think about with the actual choir, the music and practices. I trusted Dinah. She's been a good friend to me. For instance, when I was concerned for young Carrie, who was having a relationship with a much older man, Dinah sorted everything. Like I say, I trusted her completely. But I felt something was going on. I was never entirely certain who the other members of the committee were, but there were a lot of whispered conversations in quiet corners. Mary, Hannah and Dinah couldn't be involved in such evil acts. I suppose I lost control of things. I built my choir, Claire– I'm sorry, DI Grogan, to benefit the community. I didn't mean for this to happen. It's terrible. I'll never forgive myself.'

* * *

'I hear you're about to become a father. Carrie's parents told us,' said Murray.

Bankhead lay on a bed in Aintree Hospital, both arms and his right leg in plaster. His jaw was also wired, so his speech was difficult to make out.

'Don't know what you're on about,' he said.

'Carrie's parents also allege that you have been having sexual relations with her daughter while she was underage. That makes you a rapist and paedophile.'

'Any truth in the rumour that you were also involved with this group of vigilantes on Treadwater?'

'No comment.'

CHAPTER 112

Treadwater

Justin had no cash to buy any gear. Instead, he nicked four cans of lager from a shop in Bootle and ran for a bus. The bastards at the dog rescue centre wouldn't give him his dog back. They told him that he wasn't fit to look after a pet.

Later, he had a check-up at the hospital, to make sure his head wound had healed properly. He couldn't be arsed with that. Besides, the bizzies were still looking to ask him more questions about the hiding he got. They think it had something to do with the residents' committee. Fuck's sake, he knew better than to cross them.

The big cop, DS Murray had told him that his story about a Dr Hazzard hadn't checked out. According to Murray, this Dr Hazzard was a woman, some kind of lecturer at Liverpool University. Well, it weren't no fucking woman who picked him up at Crosby and, along with two other blokes, near kicked the life out of him and left him for dead. Typical bizzies. Fucking useless at catching the real crooks.

* * *

Beth smoked another roll-up. She missed the company of Katrina and even that Claire, who turned out to be a fucking bizzie. But she did like her. She seemed to understand her and didn't judge, despite her history as an accessory to murder. First time in her life she had anyone resembling a friend and now both were gone. She didn't think she would bother with singing in the choir again. It was fun with Katrina.

* * *

Hannah held Mary's arm as they wandered across the playing fields towards the library. Both their husbands were out of their lives now and for hugely different reasons. Dinah had told Hannah she had nothing to fear. They had taken care of Stan. No one would ever know that she had ended his life. Mary and Hannah swore to look after each other. Hopefully, Esther would restart choir practices soon.

* * *

A cool wind swept across the open space next to the Treadwater Estate. A building site, abandoned due to planning issues, was reopened to allow a JCB to excavate the earth beneath which they hoped to uncover the final two victims of Treadwater's special committee. Tara stood next to John Wilson and Alan Murray as others took charge of the operation. Behind her, a small gathering of Treadwater residents stood on the other side of the wire fence. She didn't recognise any faces.

Suddenly, a halt was called to the digging. Two forensic officers had noticed something. By the end of the day the two bodies would be removed and taken away for examination. The process of identification would begin, but in this instance the police already had arrested the perpetrators.

* * *

Tara couldn't help wondering what had become of Mandy Wright.

She soaked in the bath, her radio playing low so she could hear the laughter of her god-daughter, Adele, playing with Kate in the living room. It was great to be home with the people she loved. Later they were going for ice cream by the Albert Dock. Soon, too, the recent past would be shelved in a memory already brimming with horrific experience.

If you enjoyed this book, please let others know by leaving a quick review on Amazon. Also, if you spot anything untoward in the paperback, get in touch. We strive for the best quality and appreciate reader feedback.

editor@thebookfolks.com

ALSO IN THIS SERIES

AN EARLY GRAVE (Book 1)

A tough young Detective Inspector encounters a reclusive man who claims he holds the secret to a murder case. But he also has a dangerous agenda. Will DI Tara Grogan take the bait?

All available on Kindle and in paperback.

THE DARING NIGHT (Book 2)

Liverpool is on high alert after a spate of poisonings, but DI Tara Grogan is side-lined from the investigation. Yet when she probes into the suicide of a company executive, she becomes sure she has a vital lead in the case. Going it alone, however, has very real risks.

Available on Kindle and in paperback.

LETHAL DOSE (Book 4)

Investigating the death of a journalist, DI Tara Grogan stumbles upon his connection to a number of missing women. Is it possible the victim was actually a serial killer? Tara closes in on the truth but can she evade a fatal jab?

LETHAL JUSTICE (Book 5)

When a body is found, cruelly crucified on a makeshift wooden structure, DI Tara Grogan suspects it is the work of a secretive religious cult. Focusing on this case and with her guard down, she becomes once again the target of a man with murder on his mind, among other things. Will the wheels of justice turn quick enough to save her from an awful fate?

LETHAL MINDS (Book 6)

Following a murder, a drugs feud in a notorious Liverpool estate is kicking off when a missing woman's body is found in the Irish sea. DI Tara Grogan has her attention divided, and someone with a grudge to bear has her in his sights.

OTHER TITLES OF INTEREST

When a respected member of the community is murdered, it is not the kind of knife crime London detectives DI Nash and DS Moretti are used to dealing with. Someone has an agenda and it is rotten to the core. But catching this killer will take all of their police skills and more.

Reporter Stacey Logan has little to worry about other than the town flower festival when a man is shot dead. When she believes the police have got the wrong man, she does some snooping of her own. But will her desire for a scoop lead her to a place where there is no refuge?

When a woman is found dead in Hastings, Sussex, the medical examiner feels a murder has taken place. Yet she feels the police are not doing enough because the victim is a prostitute. Dr Callie Hughes will conduct her own investigation, no matter the danger.

Printed in Great Britain
by Amazon